"What a journey *Divorced Girl Smili*... g
reasons. Pilossoph writes about the broken pieces of our self that need putting back together, the part of our self we keep hidden or unavailable, she writes truth, and writes the story with the strong, honest and humorous voice I have come to love and crave. She is the voice for divorced girls everywhere and for mothers, sisters, wives, friends and daughters."

–EMILY LEWIS, MRS. MOMMY BOOKNERD

"I laughed out loud, felt the pain and angst caused by divorce, and felt satisfaction. It was heartwarming to read about making new friends, rekindling old friendships, and accepting that things do happen for a reason."

–RHONDA BRITTINGHAM, CHICK LIT +

ISBN: 1490463763
ISBN 13: 9781490463766

Divorced Girl Smiling

A novel by

Jackie Pilossoph

This book is dedicated to the real life Cinnamon Girls:
Anne, Chris, Kris, Jill and Ruby

Divorced Girl Smiling

Chapter 1

The first time I admitted to myself that something was seriously wrong with my marriage I was in a high-end women's boutique trying on cocktail dresses for Paul's upcoming company Christmas party.

I couldn't stand going to my husband's work functions. It wasn't because of Paul's co-workers. Most of the people who worked there were really nice, and so were their spouses. It was Paul's bosses I dreaded.

The partners of his law firm, *Concerto, Fane and Manus*, or as I liked to call it, *Conceited, Fake and Manipulative,* never failed to make me cringe. Nonetheless, I was doing what a good, supportive wife of an attorney in a prominent Chicago law firm does: trying my best to look spectacular, so Paul would be proud to show up with me on his arm.

First, there was John Concerto, 68. John thought he was Hugh Hefner. In the thirteen years I'd known him, he somehow managed to put his hand on my butt at every single party. Yes, he was a nice looking older man with a lot of money, but why on earth would I want him touching any part of my body, let alone my butt? I'd always felt that if I was going to let a guy put his hands on me, I certainly wouldn't pick a guy like John. If I was going to have an affair, I'd do the cougar thing. Not that I had any desire to cheat. I didn't even enjoy having sex with my own husband, so why would I go out of my way to have sex with someone else?

Nonetheless, it was inevitable that after three or four martinis, John would whisper in my ear how much he wanted to take me to St. Lucia where his yacht was docked, while subtly placing his hand on my behind until I jumped away. I was shocked in every instance that not one single person noticed the groper, including Paul!

Apparently, John thought just because he was a successful litigator and the main partner of the multi-million dollar firm, he had the right to maul any girl, including the wife of a guy who worked for him. Honestly, if I had a dime for every time John Concerto's hand was on my ass, I'd be just as wealthy as him!

Then there was Michael Fane, 57. Michael wasn't attractive; in fact, I considered him to be more on the ugly side. But Michael knew how to talk. He was smooth. He could work a room like no one I'd ever seen. That's why he wins every case he tries. I'm serious.

At every party, I could be sure he would come up to me and ask me questions about my real estate business. Years earlier, when I was just starting out, he spoke to me condescendingly, implying that my job was just for fun, that it was cute, and something to occupy me while my hubby was working all day since we didn't have kids yet.

Over the years, though, my business had grown at an unbelievable rate. I'd taken advantage of the booming real estate market in the late nineties up until about 2007, and had set records for commission income that no one in my community had ever seen. So nowadays, when Michael and I talked about my business, I felt like he was still patronizing me, although, not to sound like an egomaniac, his enthusiastic remarks about how impressed he was were warranted. My business was successful. But whatever I talked about with Michael, whether it was my work, his work, my husband's work, the weather, or even why Chicago didn't get the bid to host the 2016 Olympics, one thing always remained. Michael was phony. Whatever came out of his mouth always seemed rehearsed. And staged. He wasn't a bad guy, he just wasn't genuine.

Paul's last partner/boss was Stuart Manus, 68, same age as John, but he seemed much older. Stuart was perhaps the smartest, most conniving of all the attorneys at the firm. And he had this obsession with the fact that Paul and I didn't have kids yet.

"So, when are you and Paul going to have some little Bensons?" he would ask at every party for the first few years Paul worked at the firm. It then got to be awkward when I turned 35, and Paul and I were still childless. "So, how's the booming real estate market? I hear you're doing quite well," he'd say to me, "That leaves no time for little ones, huh?"

"Right, Stuart," I'd respond, "No time for little ones." Then I'd excuse myself to the bathroom, tear up for a minute or so, and then rejoin the party and resume my role as the happy, perky wife of a prominent litigator. So, here I was, buying a dress to impress these three guys, all of whom I had zero respect for and absolutely no desire to spend time with.

As I looked at myself in the mirror, silently scrutinizing my one size too large figure in the seventh of eight black dresses I'd brought into the room, I heard a woman gigging. I froze. Next I heard some heavy breathing. More giggling. More breathing.

I put my hand over my open mouth, heavily suspecting that two people in a nearby dressing room were having sex. I knelt down and peeked under my door. My head was literally almost on the carpet when I got proof. Sure enough, I saw two sets of legs. The woman's were bare, the guy had on jeans. From what I could tell, he had her up against the wall.

I felt like I should be offended, but I wasn't at all. I was quite happy for them, giddy almost. And that's the exact moment when depression came crashing into me like a tsunami. I realized right then, I couldn't remember the last time Paul and I had sex. It was more than days ago, more than weeks ago, maybe even more than months ago. I seriously could not remember.

Was this normal for two people who had been married for twelve years? I wondered. I had always found my husband extremely attractive, and the sex with us had consistently been pretty good. Not out of the ballpark outstanding, like it had been with Brad Harrison, my boyfriend right before Paul. But good. Sex with Paul was normal, very unlike Brad Harrison, who would do things like push me up against walls, take my clothes off with his teeth, and lick *Cool Whip* off my stomach.

And then there was "the stranger game." Brad would basically ask me to meet him at a bar and tell me to pretend I didn't know him. Then, he'd start hitting on me and ask me to go home with him, continuing the game even after we were back at his place. It was creepy and sexy at the same time. I had to admit, Brad was fun and exciting and breathtaking at times, but he was a loose cannon, and at the time I didn't feel he was marriage material.

Brad was a musician who lived paycheck to paycheck, barhopping around Chicago with his guitar. He didn't have any interest in a long-term commitment, a family, or growing up anytime in the near future, so I decided to forego the awesome, award-winning sex and go for stable, ambitious and normal: a good-looking, polite law student named Paul Benson.

Now, hearing the heavy breathing, and seeing the legs of the dressing room sex fiends, I wondered for the first time in more than twelve years if I'd done the right thing, dumping Brad for Paul.

Hearing some gasping and some kissing noises, I quickly changed back into my clothes, gathered my things, including two dresses I decided to buy, and dashed out. I figured I would try both of them on again at home and then return one.

Just as the Katie Holmes look-a-like salesperson asked me how I was paying, out came the blissful couple, giggling and holding hands. They were glowing. It was actually kind of cute, and I wondered how long they'd been dating. Two weeks? Two months? I was sure they hadn't known each other very long, based on my own experiences. Sex and lust and all the good stuff like that always faded, with friendship, comfort and commitment taking their place. And that's what I had with Paul. So we weren't having sex. So what? We were beyond that. 'We have a deeper relationship,' I rationalized. We were a normal, married couple.

"Six ninety seven, eighty five," said the sales person. I gave her my credit card and then casually turned around to get a better glimpse at the sexual deviants, who were now standing behind me, waiting to be rung up. Close up, they looked around my age, 38. That surprised me. Would *I* have sex in a dressing room at this stage in my life? Probably not. In my Brad Harrison days? Maybe. But now, the thought seemed immature. Then again, it was surprisingly appealing.

"So, where are we going tonight?" she asked him.

"It's a surprise."

"You're so good to me," she gushed.

I wanted to butt in and say, "Just wait until you're three years in. It won't be so hot."

The guy gave her a huge grin and then said, "Well, *you've* been good to *me* for twelve years."

My jaw fell to the ground. No way. I looked at the girl's left hand and sure enough, on her ring finger sat a diamond ring and wedding band. They were married and/or together for twelve years and were acting like this?! I was dumbfounded.

"Thank you," said the salesperson, handing me the dresses on hangers.

"Sure," I said, sadly.

I walked away, but turned around one last time to look at the people of whom I was now completely insanely envious. They were paying for a sexy top she was buying. I put my head down, feeling sadder than I could ever remember. Not only had I just paid for two dresses for a party I didn't want to attend, I was paying the price for settling into a marriage that was in all honesty, lukewarm. As a matter of fact, I was paying for it every day.

Chapter 2

"I'm just going to say it, so don't get mad," said J.J., my twenty-seven year old assistant in response to my dressing room story, "You need to get laid, girlfriend."

I didn't say anything right away, opting to sip my Grande skim latte with extra foam instead.

J.J. added, "Badly."

Jessica Jordan McNealy, known to all as J.J., had been working for me for five years, ever since she'd graduated college. Her organizational skills were about the worst I'd ever seen, she was constantly late for meetings, and her standard response to most people was, "Relax, I got this covered. You worry too much."

She'd forget to enter appointments into the computer, she'd show up late for open houses (that *she* was hosting) and twice, she forgot important documents at closings, e.g. the closing statements.

"No biggie," she'd say, "I'll just shoot back to the office and get it. Be back in a flash. Relax!" I'd be so embarrassed at this point, I'd pretty much want to crawl into a hole, not to mention I'd be terrified that my business was going to go into the tank because of how irresponsible we looked.

So why did she remain employed by me? Because the good J.J. far outweighed her faults. People loved her. They gravitated toward her. She had this energy and excitement that made clients want to be around her. When it came to J.J., things always had a way of working themselves out. In fact, they'd end up great. She made people laugh, she made people feel good, and she put people on a high with her larger than life grin, her sparkling eyes and her infectious, happy demeanor.

Even during a tough economy and a bad real estate market, I held my assistant largely responsible for the growth in my business. Lots of times clients recommended me because of *her.* So, J.J. was priceless to me. Yes, she screwed up from time to time, a lot, in fact, but I overlooked it and so did my clients, because she made up for it in so many other ways.

"Relax! You worry too much," I'd tell myself whenever I had a fleeting thought of replacing her, which was almost never.

"Here's what I'm recommending," J.J. said, leaning over my desk and granting me an unwanted look down her shirt, "Go home tonight and attack Paul. When was the last time you did that?"

"None of your business!"

"Oh, yes, it *is* my business," she said, "I have to make sure you're happy, because when you're happy, you're more productive and you make more money and my bonus is bigger."

All I could do was smile and agree with her. She was so cute, so young, so spirited, and so untainted in love. J.J. was in love at the moment, madly in love, actually. Her boyfriend was Christian Maverick, an actor and comedian who was currently starring in a production at *Second City.* Christian was a local celebrity, and he and J.J. were always being photographed and talked about around town. Part of me knew J.J. really liked the limelight, but truly, I could tell it was more than that. She was extremely happy in her relationship.

"Listen, it seems like you love the guy," she said, "Right?"

"Yes, I do," I said, wanting to add, "I think..." but holding back because I didn't want to get into *that* discussion with J.J. or with anyone.

"Plus, he's gorgeous."

"Yes, Paul's good looking," I smiled.

"So give him what he needs. And what *you* desperately need. Trust me, sex is the easy part in relationships. It just takes a little effort. You'll see."

"I think you're right," I said, feeling hopeful for the first time in a long time, "I can fix this."

"Of course you can. You're hot, girl!"

"Thanks, J.J."

"Use *all* your goods, if you know what I mean."

I had no clue what she was talking about but I answered, "Right..." After all, she was right about the sex. I could easily fix my non-sexual marriage. Paul and I had history. We once had pretty decent sex. I think. Why had we stopped? Was work and everyday life too much for us, to the point where we couldn't find time for a basic biological need? No way. My sexless marriage could be salvaged. Maybe it would even flourish after a passionate evening together. I convinced myself that tonight would be the rebirth, rejuvenation, and rekindling of our union.

I ended up leaving the office early, stopping at *Victoria's Secret* and preparing my house for the ultimate romance filled evening.

When Paul walked in the door at 7:30, the house was dark, flickering candlelight providing the only light.

"Missy," I heard him shout, "What's going on? Is the power out? Where are you?"

"I'm upstairs," I called, "Come up here."

When my husband appeared in our bedroom doorway his jaw was on the ground. With candles burning on the nightstands, there I stood in a red lacy push-up bra, a matching thong, and a black see-through teddy. In each hand, I held a champagne glass.

"What's all this?" he asked with a nervous grin. He looked really cute.

"Do you like it?" I asked seductively, slowly walking toward him.

"Uh...sure..."

I handed him one of the glasses. My heart was pounding. I was feeling nervous, but in a good way.

"This is to you and me, and to doing something we haven't done in *way* too long."

Paul looked shocked. I wasn't surprised. After all, I'd never done anything like this with him. With Brad Harrison, maybe, but not with my own husband. And thinking about that, I felt a little bit guilty.

I put my champagne glass on the nightstand, got really close to Paul and gently pushed him into a seated position on the bed. "I love you, sweetie," I whispered, "I want to make you feel really, really good." Then I took a pillow off the bed and put it down on the carpet. I unbuttoned his pants and got down on my knees, onto the pillow.

"Wait," he said.

I looked up at him. "What is it? Are you okay?"

When Paul chugged his champagne, I knew something was really wrong. I stood up.

"Missy," he said sadly, "we have to talk. I don't know how to say this."

"You're scaring me."

His voice was shaking when he said, "I'm in love with someone else."

Chapter 3

My gut reaction to hearing my husband of twelve years tell me he'd been having a two year affair with Priscilla Sommerfield, a personal trainer at his gym, was to let out a scream.

Then, I shouted, "How could you do this to us?" and proceeded to punch and hit and kick him until he was able to grab my arms and hold me down on the bed. Tears were flowing and I was semi-hyperventilating while I called him a cheater, liar, pimp, asshole, fucker, scumbag, and disgusting pig, who needed sexual addiction therapy.

Still holding my arms down, Paul said, "I'm shocked that you're even upset. I didn't think you'd even care."

"Not care about my husband fucking someone else?" I shouted.

"When was the last time *you* fucked me?"

"Well, what do you think I was planning on doing tonight?" I fired back.

"It's too late, Missy. It's done. I love her."

An hour later, he was standing at the door with a suitcase in each hand, his head down, almost in shame. Just before he walked out, he turned to me. "You're a great girl," he said in a sad, condescending tone, "You deserve better than being married to someone you don't love."

Through tears, I asked, "Is that what you think? That I don't love you?"

Paul let out a bitter chuckle, "Come on, Missy…"

"Come on what? Is that what you think?"

"Do you even know how to love somebody?"

This statement was shocking. "What? Is that how you feel about me?"

"Yes," he said, putting his head down in sadness, "Let's talk in a few days."

"What is there to talk about?"

The next words I heard felt like a knife in my gut. "The divorce."

Now I knew Paul had been planning for quite some time to leave me. And while I was in shock and on the verge of more tears, I was now pissed. Anger like that of a hungry tiger was enveloping me, and I had a quick fantasy that tomorrow morning I'd hire a shark lawyer and take Paul for every cent he had. And believe me, he had it.

Priscilla Sommerfield. Who the hell was this bimbo stealing my husband? The only thing Paul told me about her was that she was a personal trainer at his gym, and thanks to a friend of a friend of J.J.'s who worked out there, I found out the next day, Priscilla had big, fake boobs, rumored to be the biggest in the northern suburbs of Chicago. Hearing that was like taking a bullet in the stomach.

The next couple weeks were worse than being in hell. Paul had moved into Priscilla's apartment. So, while they were playing house and celebrating the holidays, and while *she* was attending Paul's company Christmas party, getting *her* ass grabbed by John Concerto, I was retreating into a state of major depression. I seriously had tears in my eyes during every waking moment, and slept eleven hours a night. I skipped work a lot, ate a pint of Haagen-Dazs for breakfast and lunch every day, and drank a bottle of wine every night.

Shortly after Paul moved out, J.J. had called Gina, my much younger sister and my one and only sibling, a cupcake bakery owner in New York City, to tell her the news I didn't have the heart to. And since then, Gina had called every single day.

"Oh my God, Miss, are you okay?" said my beautiful, sweet sis, who I visited twice in the past decade, "Should I come out there and see you?"

"No, please don't. I'm a miserable blob who just wants to feel sorry for myself alone. No need to drag anyone else down with me."

"I hate him," she said. I could feel her anger about her soon-to-be ex-brother-in-law all the way from Manhattan.

"Yeah, I guess I do, too."

Gina called me every morning and almost every night, and during each conversation, she'd beg to come see me. I always told her no. I loved my sister dearly, but I knew she was busy with her business. Like me, she'd thrown herself into her work and had become a huge success, baking cupcakes for celebrities' kids birthday parties.

At 29 years old, Gina had baked for celebs that included Gwyneth Paltrow, Madonna, and Sandra Bullock, and had been a guest on *Good Morning America, Today,* and *Ellen.* She didn't need to take time off to come to Chicago to see her depressed, unable to leave the couch older sister. I truly didn't want the girl who idolized me to see me in the state I was in.

On the contrary, I let J.J. see me unravel. My assistant had basically been living with me, trying to get me out of my miserable slump. She was constantly giving me pep talks about what a great new life I had ahead of me, how I didn't want a man who was a cheater, anyhow, and how at 38 years old, I was about to become a cougar, and that it was going to be really fun.

Also to cheer me up, J.J. went through her iPhone address book naming single guys she thought I might like. She was also constantly making cracks about Priscilla's past porn career.

"You know something, J.J.," I said to her one night while taking big gulps of my third glass of Pinot Noir, tears forming in my eyes, "You're a really good friend. And I don't have many friends."

"You have Gina."

"Actually, did I say I don't have many friends? I meant to say, I don't have *any* friends. Besides you and Gina, I don't have one girlfriend."

"But you have the two of us."

"That doesn't count. Gina's my sister and you work for me."

"I'm still your friend."

"It's not the same thing. You have to be nice to me. I'm your boss."

"I take offense to that. I love you, Miss!"

Now I started to cry. "I know you do, thanks."

"What about your high school friends? A couple of them have called a bunch of times and they keep leaving messages at the office. They're going to think I'm not giving them to you."

"I know," I said through tears.

"If you want to have friends, you can start by calling them back."

"I should. It's just...it's a long story."

"I have time," she said, "Did something happen?"

"I don't want to talk about it right now. I'm depressed enough as it is."

"Okay, but you brought it up."

"I know," I smiled.

J.J. hugged me and then pulled away and said, "Miss, you have no idea how awesome you are. You're beautiful and you're smart. You're the total package. Guys are going to fall all over you and you'll forget all about Paul the prick."

"He asked me if I knew how to love somebody. Am I just a heartless bitch?" I asked, on the verge of tears once again.

"My theory is, you just didn't love *him.*"

"Can you believe I'm going to be a divorced girl?" I asked.

J.J. put her arm around me. "So what? Do you know how many divorced people there are out there? Besides, you're going to be a hot divorced girl."

That night, after she left, I did something significant. I went upstairs and into my bedroom. I stood in front of my dresser, specifically in front of my jewelry box. Then, I took my wedding rings off.

I stared at my bare left ring finger for a long time. Then, I put my wedding ring into the jewelry box. My engagement ring, however remained in my hand. I stared at it. Twelve years I wore this ring, this ring that was supposed to symbolize commitment, trust, and friendship. And passion, of course, something that for some reason died, or perhaps was never there.

I continued looking at the ring for so long, it was almost as if I was seeing it for the first time. A beautiful cushion cut diamond, the platinum band was skinny, its purpose to make the big diamond look even bigger. The diamond: a two and half carat, H color grade with VS2 clarity. How I remembered those details after all this time, I'll never know. Little diamonds framed the big diamond. Truly, the ring was exquisite.

This setting wasn't the original setting. When Paul got down on his knee and asked me to marry him, he presented the original center stone, but on a plain gold band. About three years into the marriage, I asked Paul if I could upgrade to the diamond setting. Since money had never really been an issue with us, and we didn't have kids yet, he didn't even bat an eyelash when I told him the price of putting the diamond on the cushion cut setting: thousands.

What I realized at this moment was, no matter which ring I would have been holding in my hand, the original, simple setting, or the fancier, more glitzy ring I wore for the last nine years, here it was in my hand for the last time, before I would put it into a jewelry box where it would stay. The lovely ring that looked as if it belonged to a fairytale princess now didn't really belong to anyone.

The last thought I had before I placed it into the box was something sort of funny. All these years I'd worn my ring. It had rarely been off my finger, yet somehow I'd failed to notice something pretty significant. I couldn't help but smile as I set the ring into the box.

The damn ring was BIG!

Chapter 4

Senior year of high school

I'm posing for a picture with three other girls. We all have our arms around each other. I'm hoping the photo turns out well because I plan to have it developed into an 8X10, so I can hang it on the wall of my dorm room at Northwestern University, where I'll be moving in about two weeks.

These are my very best friends, and the thought of all of us being apart at college is making me physically sick. I've spent the last four years doing everything with these girls. They are like sisters to me. I can't imagine ever meeting friends who mean half as much to me.

"Say cheese!" says Anna's mom.

We all say cheese and give our best grins. Anna's mom snaps a picture. "One more," she says, "Just to be sure." She snaps another one.

I have something for you guys," says Catherine, "Come sit down."

The four of us gather around the L shaped couch in Anna's family room. Catherine leaves the room for a few moments and comes back with a plastic bag. She loosens the drawstring and starts pulling out tiny little gold boxes and handing one to each one of us.

"Don't open them yet," she says.

"I can't believe you got us gifts!" says Nan, "I feel bad. I didn't get anything for you guys."

"Neither did I," I say.

"Me neither," says Anna.

When we all have our boxes, Catherine says, "Okay, open them."

I gasp dramatically when I open the box and see what's inside. It's a gold necklace with a little gold rectangle hanging from it. The word Cinnamon is written on the rectangle in sort of a cutesy print.

"I love it!" I shout. Then I get up and hug Catherine.

Nan has tears in her eyes.

"I'll always wear this," says Anna, "I'm never taking it off."

"Me too," I say, "I'll never take it off."

"Let's promise each other we'll never take these off. Ever!" says Nan.

"It's a promise!" says Catherine, "We're the Cinnamon Girls!"

We all put on our necklaces.

"How did you get that name again?" Anna's mom asks.

Nan begins telling her the story and we all listen, even though we know it so well. She explains how her brother was working at Denny's Restaurant a few years earlier, and how the they sell gum and mints at the cash register. She explains that the store manager let him buy a case of Cinnamon Certs at a deep discount. He kept them in his closet.

"Every now and then, I'd take a few rolls and give them to these guys," says Nan.

"And we'd eat them all of the time," adds Anna.

"This guy at school started asking us why our group of friends always smelled like cinnamon," says Catherine.

"So," I finish, "We named ourselves the Cinnamon Girls and it has stuck ever since."

Anna's mom laughs and tells us she loves the story. As I look at all my friends admiring each other's necklaces, I think to myself, 'These girls will be my best friends forever.' I feel so lucky!

Chapter 5

Maybe J.J. was right. Maybe Paul had given me a gift, letting me out of a marriage that was so passionless that I never wanted to sleep with my own husband. Or maybe that was something every woman whose husband dumped her rationalized.

The sting of knowing Paul was having sex on a daily basis, and according to J.J., probably filming it for future porn movies was terribly painful. Plus, I was now 38 years old and single. Thirty-eight was old! Forty was just around the corner. Did men want women who were 40? Two names popped in my head at this moment: Demi Moore and Ashton Kutcher. They gave me some much needed relief, and being older and single suddenly didn't feel like the worst thing in the world. Granted, I didn't have Demi's looks and body, plus, they were now divorced. Still, Demi had met Ashton when she was over 40, plus she looked better than ever, and now she was almost 50!

I could meet someone and fall in love, too. Maybe I'd find a guy I enjoyed as much as Brad Harrison, only with a more stable job and a desire for somewhat of a commitment. Yes, for the first time since Paul walked out on me, I felt a tinge of optimism about my love life.

But then, just as the sun was coming out, a major thunderstorm blew in. It was the night after Christmas. I had spent the holiday curled up on the couch with a bottle of wine watching *It's A Wonderful Life,* even though J.J.'s parents had invited me to their house, and Gina had begged me to come to New York. I was glad the damn holiday was over, and felt like if I could just get through New Year's, I'd be home free.

I was shopping for wine (of course) at Whole Foods and I ran into Mr. Manipulative, a.k.a. Stuart Manus, the boss of Paul's who always focused on us not having kids. It would be interesting to hear what he had to say, now that the subject of Paul and I having babies was off the table.

"Hi, Missy," he said, giving me a polite hug, definitely keeping his distance, and almost acting like I was ill or something, "I was so sorry to hear about you and Paul."

"Thank you, Stuart," I replied, "I appreciate that. How *is* Paul? Is he doing okay at work?"

"Yes, of course. He's sad, though. You can see it in his eyes."

Stuart's comment gave me an adrenaline rush like none I'd ever had before. Here was one of Paul's bosses telling me that my husband's eyes were sad! Maybe Paul was having second thoughts. Maybe he wanted to come home! I was about to burst. I wanted to tell Stuart to tell Paul that I'd take him back. I'd be here for him. We could forget all about Priscilla and her big boobs and work on fixing *us!*

"Stuart," I asked gently, "Does Paul miss me?"

"He wants to be your friend, Missy," said Stuart.

"He does?"

"Yes, and do you know what friends do? They support each other."

"I always supported Paul."

"Good," he said, patting my shoulder, "then support his decision to marry Priscilla."

"What?!"

"Be a friend and let him know you're happy for him."

I must have been standing there with my jaw on the ground because Stuart smiled and then said, "Okay?" and before I could answer him, he answered himself with, "Okay." Boy, Mr. Manipulative was on his game. "Well, nice to see you, Missy. You hang in there." With a smile, he was off.

Running into Stuart and learning of Paul's engagement sent me to new heights of despair and depression. My crying episodes subsided, as sadness turned to bitterness now. After throwing up one night, a result of Haagen Dazs overload, I stopped eating ice cream, but the rest of my bad habits continued. Over the next week, I continued slacking off at work, sleeping a lot, and drinking lots of wine.

Gina continued to call every day, which only made me feel worse. Not because I didn't love my little sis dearly, but because I didn't want to concern her with my pathetic wreck of a life, and because she kept asking me to come visit, which I truly did not want.

"What if I just don't tell you, and I hop on a plane and show up at your door?" she said one night.

"I'll be really mad if you do that, Gina," I said, "I'm serious. Please, honey, bake your cupcakes and keep enjoying your life. You don't need to be around Miss Loser."

"Miss, please shut up."

"What?"

"You heard me. Shut up! Stop feeling sorry for yourself. Yeah, you got screwed. So did I last year. I was engaged, remember? I got my heart stomped on three months before my wedding. Does that ring a bell? I've been where you are. I know that pain."

"I know you do, sweetie. That's why there's no need for you to go through it again with me."

"But I want to! Why won't you let me help you?"

"Because no one can help me," I said sadly, "Time just has to go by."

After I hung up with Gina, I couldn't have felt worse. I hated myself. My poor sister was just trying to be there for me and I wouldn't let her. And speaking of "being there for me," where had I been when her fiancé called off the wedding? Did I go visit her? Did I call her every day? Did I plan a fun trip for the two of us to take? No. I did none of those things. I was wrapped up in work and in closings and showings and listings. The only time I took trips were for real estate conventions and seminars. I suddenly felt beyond awful.

Gina and I had no one else but each other. Our dad had died when I was in high school, and our mom had passed away three years earlier, which was the last time I'd seen my sister. When it came to family, we had only a few distant (but wonderful) relatives who lived in Ohio and Florida, and us. Just us. And I hadn't been there for my baby sister when the man she thought she was going to grow old with had a change of heart and moved to San Francisco to work at a wine vineyard. Gina really needed someone and I wasn't there. I remembered J.J. urging me to go see her or to go somewhere with her.

"Take her somewhere fun. She must really be hurting right now," said my wise for her age assistant.

Even Paul was surprised that I didn't go to New York when it happened.

"My going there isn't going to change what happened," I'd snapped.

"Yeah, but Gina needs you," he said, "She needs her big sister."

I remembered feeling badly, but just too busy to make the trip. I just couldn't find the time. I felt guilty about it for a couple weeks, but when Gina started calling me and sounding better, I felt like she was okay. So, I did nothing. NOTHING. What I remember clearly is that a couple days after it happened, I sent her a black patent leather *Prada* bag from *Saks.* I thought an expensive gift would make her happy. Looking back, I felt like it was insensitive and stupid. Gina didn't need a new purse. She needed her sister.

It hit home right then what a shitty person I was. A shitty sister and a shitty friend. And maybe, just maybe, a shitty wife.

Chapter 6

There's something strange, yet very peaceful about waking up in the middle of the night and knowing you're the only person up. Friends, family and everyone in the community are all sleeping soundly in their beds. Outside it's dark and quiet and still. Everyone is resting. Except you.

On this particular night, at around 3 a.m., I felt like the only person in Chicago who was awake, with the exception of 911 operators, taxi drivers and late night partiers who were stumbling out of bars that had just closed.

I turned on the TV and began channel flipping. I watched an episode of *Friends,* the one where Rachel is waiting at Ross's gate with flowers, planning on telling him she's in love with him when he gets off the plane. To her dismay, she never expected to see him happily walk off the jet bridge with his new girlfriend. I sobbed.

Next, I watched *Family Guy.* I'd always criticized Paul for liking the show, telling him it was offensive and vulgar and distasteful. Now, though, for the first time, I was giggling and laughing, and finding it utterly hilarious. It was really funny! Why had I been so uptight about it for so long? What was wrong with laughing at something that was so completely inappropriate?

After *Family Guy,* I moved on to the movie *Rocky II*, but found it a little too inspiring for me at this point. Rocky was about to beat the crap out of Apollo Creed, and I wasn't in the mood to cheer him on. I was still feeling sorry for myself, so I didn't want to see anything that was remotely motivating. I didn't want to cheer, I wanted to wallow.

Next, I flipped to *Sex Games,* a porno movie on some premium channel. For a minute or so, I watched two girls and a guy having a threesome. I found myself literally becoming nauseous, thinking about how Priscilla's boobs probably looked just like these girls'.

Just when I was about give up and try to go back to sleep, I flipped to the movie, *An Officer and a Gentleman.* It was pretty close to the beginning. Zack and Paula were at the dance, meeting for the first time. My first reaction was that I'd never seen this movie as an adult, and had therefore never realized how hot Richard Gere was. And how cute was Debra Winger? As a teenager, I had always wanted to be her. Now, as a jaded, bitter, soon-to-be divorced, middle-aged woman, I *still* wanted to be her. Was that a sign that maybe I was softening?

Halfway through it, at around 4:15 a.m., I went from feeling more alone then I'd ever felt in my life, to realizing that watching this sweet love story was making me really happy. It was temporary, but at least I knew I was capable of feeling that emotion again.

I was mesmerized during the last scene. It was as if I was watching it for the first time, unsure of what was going to happen, even though I already knew. I watched Mayo walk into the noisy factory searching for Paula. Background music was blaring while the gorgeous guy in uniform strutted confidently to rescue his girl. My heart pounded, especially when he grabbed Paula's waist from behind and kissed her neck. When she turned around and realized her true love had come back to get her, my eyes welled with happy tears. She was so lucky! But she deserved it. She was sweet and so compassionate, and she loved him with all her heart!

Things had worked out for Paula and Mayo, and yes, this was a movie, but in my opinion, all fiction was based on truth. So, it occurred to me that whoever wrote this had to have had a similar experience. So didn't that mean that love like this was possible in real life?

Paul had always told me I was unromantic and that I was like a guy, uninterested in sentimental, tender moments. Practical and realistic were the words my mom used to describe me. Even Gina. She told me once that she couldn't believe I didn't cry during the movie, *The Notebook.*

"I cry at funerals," I told her, "I don't feel like it's appropriate to cry if it has to do with a fictional character's tragedy." I then assured her I was very sad when James Garner and Gina Rowlands were holding each other and dying together in their old age.

"There's a passionate, hopeless romantic inside that girl," Gina said of me once, "It will just take the right situation to bring it out in her. You'll see."

And now, here it was. I was captivated, completely taken in by a movie. Sitting here on the verge of divorce, dumped by my husband, an eighties classic was causing me to re-evaluate what love and passion and romance really meant. Did I really love Paul? Had I ever really been in love in my life? Maybe not. That thought was both depressing and exciting. Exciting because the prospect of finding true love someday was now real, now that the husband I wasn't sure I'd ever really loved had set me free.

It sounds a little crazy, but *An Officer and a Gentleman* gave me faith and optimism that love was possible, and that just as there were men out there like Paul, who would get involved with someone else before trying to fix what he had, there were also guys like Zack Mayo, who acted like men, who rescued the women they loved, and didn't take the easy way out when things got rough. That thought brought light and hope back into my core.

I turned off the TV and dashed to my jewelry box. Once there, I retrieved my big, beautiful engagement ring, the ring I'd taken off my finger just weeks earlier. I put it back on my left ring finger and then I got into bed, held my left hand to my heart and sobbed.

I think I was crying not because I missed Paul, but because I realized that when my soon-to-be ex-husband gave me this ring, I never really had the feelings a person was supposed to have. Unlike Debra Winger, I wasn't madly, desperately in love. I was going through the motions of life, getting engaged to the appropriate person, not the man who made the hair stand up on my arms with his touch, not the man who stopped my heart with his kiss, and not the man who I didn't want to live without.

My big, expensive ring didn't mean anything to me. It never really had. Yes, it was exquisite and sparkly and people were always commenting on how pretty it was, but what it was supposed to signify was missing. And that made me physically nauseous. I cried myself to sleep and when I woke up the next morning, I was in the same position, still holding the ring to my heart.

Chapter 7

Mid-twenties

Nan and her new husband are dancing their first dance to Elton John's "Can You Feel The Love Tonight." They're the only ones on the dance floor, except for the photographer who's bent down, snapping pictures of them. Nan and the cardiothoracic surgeon she married about an hour and a half ago are gazing into each other's eyes with big grins on their faces.

I'm sitting at my table watching them, and feeling so happy that one of my closet friends found love. One of my closest friends...whose shower and bachelorette party I didn't attend. My excuse for missing both was work. I'd told her I couldn't get away for either event. In reality, I didn't want to go. I was too ashamed. I didn't want to deal with my friends and the way they now looked at me, with pity and sadness.

"So, Missy, you walking down the aisle anytime soon?" Catherine's boyfriend, Roger asks me in a loud voice with a hearty chuckle.

I feel like telling the guy to focus on someone else, as well as to stop drinking because he's already so buzzed that he just spit on my face while he was talking.

I look at Catherine. She looks embarrassed by him. I think to myself there's no way she's going to marry this obnoxious drunk. At least I hope not.

I answer, "No, not in the near future."

"What about that sports marketing guy you were seeing?" Catherine asks me, "Are you guys still together?"

"No," I say with a fake smile, "We broke up."

"Why?" asks Roger.

Anna answers for me, "Because he liked her too much. Missy can't handle anyone who treats her well. She likes assholes."

"Anna!" says her boyfriend, Jake.

Anna looks at me and says, "Right?"

Deep down I know she's right, but I'm really angry about the remark.

Everyone's waiting for me to respond.

"Look, I'm really into my career these days. I'm focusing on that. I don't want to get married right now." I look directly at Anna and finish, "I'm assuming no one here has a problem with that, right?"

"You should spend more time with Catherine!" shouts Roger, "Maybe you could rub off on her a little and get her to back off about a ring!"

"Roger, shut up, please," says Catherine. She's gritting her teeth.

The song ends and we all clap.

Anna gets up and sits in the empty chair next to me. She puts her arm around me and whispers in my ear.

"I'm really sorry, Miss. I'm a little drunk."

"It's okay."

"No it's not. I'm a bitch."

I laugh, "Yeah, you are."

"A bitch who loves you and who's worried about you."

"Don't be, please."

"Hey, see that guy sitting at table number 7?"

I look across the room and notice a good looking guy, who just like me is dateless tonight.

"Yeah."

"He's cute, huh?"

"Sort of."

"He's a pilot for American."

"Oh."

"You interested?"

"Not really and please don't give me a hard time because I'm not," I say.

Anna laughs, "Fine. He's kind of gross, anyhow."

"Why do you say that?"

"I was talking to him earlier at the bar and he farted."

We both crack up and I realize that only best friends can have a conversation like the one we just had.

Chapter 8

"I love that movie!" cried J.J. the next day, "Such a classic."

"I'm surprised you've seen it."

"I watched it with my mom a few years ago. I really love the end."

"Me too!"

"Hey, why are you wearing your engagement ring?" she asked.

I looked down at my big, huge rock and then looked at my assistant, who was at the kitchen sink in our client's house doing last minute dishes before the open house.

"Do you know how much Paul paid for this?" I asked her, motioning to my left ring finger.

"Why does it matter?"

"It's worth thirty-six thousand."

She shut the water off, grabbed my hand to get a closer look and shouted, "Shut up! Are you serious?!"

I giggled.

"Seriously?"

"Yes."

"Do you know how many children you could feed in Haiti for thirty-six grand?"

"Is that helping?"

"Sorry." J.J. motioned to some crumbs on the kitchen counter and then said, "Can you believe what a pig this guy is? Doesn't he want to sell this place bad enough to wipe the counter after cutting his bagel? I mean, are we realtors or cleaning ladies?"

I shrugged.

"So, seriously, what's up with the ring?"

"I don't know," I said with a deep sigh, "Just feeling emotional."

"Listen," J.J. said with hesitation, "I'm not sure I should say anything, because I don't want to upset you any more than you already are, but..."

"What?"

She took a deep breath. "Well, Christian and I went to work out last night at *East Bank.* We have a friend who works there and she gave us guest passes...and...we...umm...we saw Priscilla.

"Oh my God! Is she cute? Did you talk to her?"

"She's okay. She looks like a stripper, you know, slutty looking, but kind of pretty. Bleached blonde hair, lots of make-up, and of course, those knockers."

"Did you talk to her? Was she nice?"

"Sort of. Christian asked her about her spin classes and told her he was interested in trying one, just to see what the girl would say."

"And?"

"Again, I don't want to upset you, but she was pretty cool. She gave Christian and me free passes for a class."

"Oh," I said, "But no offense, that's probably because Christian's famous."

"True."

"There's something else."

"What?"

"I got a glimpse of her ring."

"And?"

"It didn't cost thirty-six grand, I can tell you that."

"Really?" I said, suddenly feeling the best I'd felt all day.

J.J. nodded. "I'd say it's like a carat and a half max. And here's the best part. It's a marquis."

"Yuck!"

"I know, right? Didn't those go out of style in like 1990?"

I laughed.

"By the way," said J.J., "the guy who lives here is single."

"Yeah, but he's like 60 and he's a slob."

"54."

"Isn't that the same thing?"

J.J. shrugged. "So, how long are you going to wear your ring?"

"I'll take it off soon," I said.

"What do you think you're going to do with it?"

"I don't know. Any ideas?"

"Sell it. Buy yourself something."

"No, I want to do something good with it," I said, pushing my palms onto the kitchen counter and lifting myself up to sit.

"Like what?"

"I don't know yet. The thing is, what happened to me was horrible. Paul pretty much dumped me. And this ring...when he gave it to me and proposed, saying yes seemed right. I thought we were going to be together forever. Now, looking back, I'm not so sure I felt what a person who is getting engaged should be feeling. And that's bittersweet. So, since I don't need the money, maybe I could do something meaningful with the ring. I mean, maybe something good could come from it."

"Well, Christian and I are talking about getting married. You could give it to me."

"Why would you want to wear the ring of someone whose marriage failed?"

"Because it's a gorgeous piece of jewelry?"

"No, that wouldn't be right," I said.

"Look, I guess I agree. I wouldn't want your ring because I know you, and I know what Paul did to you. But, if I didn't know you and I saw your ring, I wouldn't care that your marriage ended and I wouldn't care *why* your marriage ended." She pointed to my ring and finished, "I'd want that big ring. Know what I mean? Maybe you should sell it, like on *eBay* or *craigslist* or something."

When I heard the word *craigslist* come out of J.J.'s mouth, I went numb.

"Okay, never mind, you hate that idea."

"No, I don't!" I exclaimed, "I *love* it!"

At that moment, the first guest of our open house knocked on the front door. J.J. hurried to answer it. I remained seated on the kitchen counter, my brain going a hundred miles an hour, feeling excitement and enthusiasm. For the entire open house, I had a hard time concentrating because an electrifying and meaningful plan was consuming my mind.

"What's going on with you?" J.J. asked me after the last person left, "You were like not here for the entire showing."

I gave her a wide grin. "J.J., I know what I'm going to do with my ring."

Half an hour later, we were back at my office, and J.J. was leaning over my desk while I showed her the ad I wrote for *craigslist.*

For Sale: 2.5 carat diamond engagement ring – 99 cents

I am selling my 2.5 carat H color grade, VS2 clarity cushion cut diamond engagement ring, which retails for $36,000 for 99 cents.

This is not a joke. *If interested, please send one page e-mail containing the following: How you met your girlfriend, why you wish to marry her, why you think you'd make a good husband, and most importantly, why you love her.*

Please include daytime phone number. I will grant interviews based on responses. Then I will choose the buyer of my ring.

Thanks.

"Miss, you are not doing this," said J.J.

"Oh yeah, I am," I smiled.

"What do you hope to gain from giving away thirty-six thousand dollars?"

"I want to believe in love again," I said sadly, "I want proof that it's out there. I want hope. I want a reason to think that someday it might be possible to find true love. And talking to people who are supposedly in love might provide me with the answers I'm looking for."

"No offense, but therapy's a lot cheaper."

"J.J., I'm doing this."

"Look, you don't have to spend tens of thousands of dollars on something that I can tell you for free. Love *is* out there. It's real. I mean, look at *me*!"

What happened next is quite unbelievable. The second J.J. spoke those words, Kiley Davenport, a realtor we worked with who was much better at spreading gossip than at selling houses, came running into my office.

"Oh my God! Have you seen this?" she exclaimed, placing an open *Sun-Times* on my desk.

Instantly, my eye was drawn to a picture of Christian kissing some woman on the lips. The caption underneath read, *"Second City star, Christian Maverick outside Rockit."*

J.J. hurried over and when she saw it, she gasped and put her hand over her mouth.

"Did you guys break up or something?" asked Kiley.

Both J.J. and I just looked up at her, neither of us knowing what to say or do.

"Is he cheating on you?" Kiley asked.

"I thought you were with him last night at *East Bank,"* I said.

When J.J. spoke, she was barely audible. "That was earlier. He said he was going out with friends. I went home and went to bed."

"Well, don't jump to any conclusions yet," I said, "Maybe it's just a good friend."

"Good friend?" asked Kiley, "His tongue is jammed down her throat. Looks like more than a good friend to me."

Right then, I realized that in the five years I'd known her, I'd never seen J.J. even remotely upset. Now she had a look on her face like she was about to burst into tears.

"Kiley, can we have some privacy?" I asked gently.

"Sure. Sorry, J.J.," she said, "That sucks." Then, unbelievably, Kiley actually picked up the newspaper from my desk and carried it out with her.

The second I shut my office door, J.J. lost it. "Oh my God! Can you believe this?" she said through tears.

"Seriously, give him the benefit of the doubt. Maybe it was just a platonic kiss that looks like more."

"Did that look platonic to *you?"* she shouted.

"No."

"Sorry, Missy, I'm not trying to be a bitch. I'm just in fucking shock."

"I know," I said sadly.

"I'm going to call him," she said, storming out of my office.

I sat there in a daze, staring at my computer, my *craigslist* ad still on the screen. I thought to myself, 'First me and now J.J.' My sweet assistant, full of life and hope, and untainted by heartbreak until this very moment…crushed. She was yet another victim of a relationship gone bad. She was another poor soul who thought things were okay and had just been rudely awakened.

I didn't have proof yet that Christian was actually cheating on J.J., but I was pretty sure the picture in the paper would cause them to break up. Christian was now in the ranks with Paul, a slimy cheater who didn't have the guts to end things with one person before beginning a relationship with someone else. What a jerk.

What had just happened to J.J. further confirmed how much I needed to see if there were any couples who were really, truly in love. I desperately wanted to meet people who claimed to be in love, so that I could judge for myself if there was anyone left in this world who had a chance of making it to a fifty year anniversary. So, it was at this moment, with determination and confidence, that I posted my *craigslist* ad.

Chapter 9

Within the hour, my inbox was flooded with letters from interested "buyers." I can't say I was surprised. After all, who wouldn't want a thirty-six thousand dollar ring for a buck?

It wasn't easy to do, and I felt like a kid dying to open the gifts under the tree in the days before Christmas, but I was able to resist opening even one response e-mail until I got home from work.

Once in the door at 6:30, I poured myself a glass of Pinot Noir and sat on the couch with my laptop, reading all the letters. And as I went through them, more e-mails kept coming. The whole thing suddenly seemed massively overwhelming, but that was okay. It was interesting to hear what guys who were supposedly so in love that they were ring shopping had to say.

"Hi, I've met my soul mate and I'm planning on proposing..." began one letter. I immediately hit delete. I decided to nix anyone who used the words soul mate or love of my life. It just seemed too cliché.

"I met my girlfriend about a year ago at a bar in Lincoln Park. We immediately connected and had the best sex." I hit delete. No way was I giving my ring to a guy who used the word sex in the second sentence of his story.

"I'd make a great husband because I'm a great guy. I'm easy to be with, I'm not moody, I'm an excellent cook, I'm thoughtful, I love chick flicks, I'm very organized, and I go down on my girlfriend four times a week." Delete.

"My girlfriend is so hot and she thinks I am, too." Delete. What are you, 12 years old?

"My parents hate her. That's why I'm marrying her. I have to show them that they can't control me." Delete.

"I desperately want children and I'm getting up there. Time's running out. It would be such a shame if I didn't reproduce. I'm a marine biologist with an IQ of 166. That's the reason I need to get married. It'd be a shame to waste that, huh?" Delete.

"I'm tired of the bars. I'm tired of dating. I just want to feel loved and secure. Plus, I need someone to clean my place and have dinner ready for me when I get home from work." Delete.

"If I don't marry Shawna, she said she's going to break up with me. Since she's the only girl I've ever dated who doesn't have a problem dressing up like a cop and using handcuffs on me during sex, what choice do I really have?" Delete.

I could not believe some of these people! What were they thinking? That being said, interspersed with the ridiculous, crazy, disgusting, creepy and outrageous letters were some seemingly heartfelt, sweet, sincere and normal responses. The first night alone, there were four guys I wanted to meet, and by the end of the week, I chose twenty three interviewees.

My devastated, depressed, newly single assistant (yes, the relationship was over the day the tabloid photo came out) was now fully on board with what I was doing. In fact, J.J. was so into it, she asked if she could help.

So, as we did our regular jobs of selling homes, J.J. and I now had second jobs: reading letters from and screening potential ring recipients, weeding out the jerks and idiots, and looking for the lucky guy who would ultimately get me to believe in true love.

Thirty-six grand: a high price to pay for confirmation and peace of mind that real love was ever present in my cynical, jaded world. Yet, since financially I had no worries, giving the ring away seemed like the right decision. It was logical, almost necessary in a way. Honestly, the monetary loss would make absolutely no difference in my financial world.

My temporary alimony checks were huge, and I suspected the reason for that stemmed from two things: Paul's guilt, and his desire to keep me happy and get rid of me quickly so he could get married again. Additionally, my successful career was more than paying my bills. Money wasn't even a slight issue for me, and hadn't been for a long, long time. And, since part of me felt like my two and a half carat diamond was worth less than a gumball machine ring as far as sentimental value, it seemed like a small price to pay for the potential of getting tremendous mental help.

That weekend, both J.J. and I cleared our Saturday schedules and set up shop at Starbucks to begin conducting interviews with the guys who'd sent e-mails I liked.

The first guy we talked to was Stan Goldblatt, 35, Architect. When he walked in, I was pleasantly surprised. Stan was cute. Not movie star gorgeous, but he had a warm way about him, a kind and gentle demeanor that made him attractive. Plus, he had a fit body. It was very obvious he took care of himself.

"What can I get you to drink?" J.J. asked him.

"Uh…coffee?" he said with a nervous smile.

"Please, order whatever you'd like," I said, "It's on us."

"Just a regular coffee, please," he said.

"No problem," said J.J., "You two sit. I'll go get it and be right back."

"Thanks," he said.

Stan and I made polite chitchat for a few moments, until I asked, "So, you're interested in my ring."

"Right," Stan replied with a nervous chuckle.

There was a moment of awkward silence, and then Stan asked, "So, are you divorced?"

"Getting divorced, yes."

"I'm sorry. Are you okay?"

"Yes, thank you."

"Mind if I ask what happened?"

"Actually, don't concern yourself with that. I'm going to be fine," I said with a smile, "Let's talk about *you*."

"Okay."

I took a deep breath and asked, "So, what's her name?"

"Who?"

"The girl you're going to propose to."

"Oh," he said with a nervous chuckle, "Caroline." When he said the name Caroline, Stan's entire face lit up. It was really cute.

"So, tell me about her."

He gave me a big grin. "She's the best. A total sweetheart. She's a social worker. Caroline is a very selfless person."

"What does she look like?" I asked.

"Does that matter?" he replied, suddenly seeming a bit offended.

"Well, actually, I just wanted to hear you describe her. I wanted to hear what *you* thought she looked like," I said, "Know what I mean?"

"Look, I'm sorry, I'm just nervous. This whole thing's a little weird for me. I mean, I want to buy Caroline a really nice ring and I can't afford one that's this expensive. But I want to know, what's the catch?"

"There's no catch, Stan," I said, "I just want to give my ring to the best guy I find. So, tell me what Caroline looks like."

"Caroline's the girl next door," he said with pride in his voice.

At this moment, up walked my shy, quiet assistant.

"How's the sex?" she asked, making me want to crawl into a hole.

"What!?" Stan practically shouted. Then he stood up. "Look, I think I should go. I'm not going to sit here and discuss my sex life with two girls I don't know. I'll buy my own ring."

"Stan, wait," I said, "Please…" I turned to J.J., "Can I talk to Stan alone?"

"Fine," she said with a pout. Then she turned to Stan and said, "I'm sorry if I offended you. I'm new at this."

Stan nodded.

"Stan, will you sit back down?" I asked.

"Sure."

"The thing is, my husband really hurt me. I guess I'm just looking for hope. I don't need the money, and I want the ring that I once thought meant something to me, going on the finger of a girl whose guy will make her really happy. Forever. Is that wrong?"

Stan didn't respond verbally. Instead, he got up, walked around the table and gave me a huge bear hug, almost to the point where it was overwhelming. Part of me was embarrassed and wanted nothing more than for him to let go of me. The people in Starbucks didn't need a visual of a girl who was falling apart. Yet there was a side of me who felt safe and secure, like Stan was my big brother. What a total sweetie. At that moment, I decided to let someone care about me, and that it was okay to be temporarily vulnerable, even in front of strangers.

So, as I stood there in the big embrace of a man I met no more than ten minutes earlier, I decided that Stan was definitely in the running to buy my big ring.

Chapter 10

I wish I could say that the next few interviewees were as nice as Stan. I wish I could say that, but I can't. After Stan, it was all downhill. In they came, nightmare after nightmare, one worse than the next.

First was Jordy Firth, 32, Commercial Real Estate Broker. The first thing he did that bugged me right off the bat, was walk in, look around, look right at me and say loudly, "Are you the divorced girl?"

I immediately looked around and noticed that every coffee drinker was looking at the divorced girl. I looked at J.J., who had a look of concern on her face that this obnoxious guy might hurt her delicate boss.

"Hi, I'm Missy," I said, extending my hand and deciding to get over it and move on, rationalizing that I was being overly sensitive.

J.J. went to get him coffee while Jordy and I talked about the weather. When she came back, Jordy began his story.

"I've been with Rhonda for six years. She's a honey," he said happily.

"How'd you guys meet?" I asked.

"Uh...why's that important?"

"I'm just trying to get to know what your relationship is like, and in your letter, you didn't mention how you two met."

"It's really none of your business."

"She's considering giving you a thirty-six thousand dollar ring for a dollar. I seriously think it's her business," said J.J.

"Fine," said Jordy, "Want to know how we met? I'll tell you." He took a deep breath. "Rhonda was married to my brother."

The three of us sat there in silence for about ten seconds, my jaw stuck to the ground.

"I know it sounds bad," he continued, "but I fell in love with her. What can I say?"

"I'm not trying to be a jerk," J.J. said to him, "But if you're Missy, do you want to give your big ring to a guy who stole his brother's wife?"

"I guess I see your point," said Jordy, as he put his head down.

"I'm glad," said J.J.

Jordy looked up and finished, "But you don't have to be so mean about it."

"I hope you don't think I'm being too judgmental, but this is what it is," I added. "For me to give away my ring, I need an untainted story, a story that's pure and genuine, a story that makes me cry, in a good way, and a story that moves me and tells me that the love is real. There's nothing about your relationship that speaks to me in this way. I apologize, but I'm sure you can understand how I feel. Good-bye Jordy," I finished, "I hope it works out for you."

I could have sworn I heard him murmur, "You're a bitch," as he got up and walked out.

The next idiot who came in was Chris Middleton. "Before we go any further," he said, "I just want you to know this was not my idea. My mom made me do this."

"But your letter..." I said, "it was so nice, so heartfelt..."

"Of course it was," he said, "My mother wrote it."

"Well, is any of it true?"

"No clue. I didn't even read it."

"Would you like to?" J.J. asked.

"Sure."

J.J. handed Chris the e-mail we printed out and he began to look it over. Then he began to chuckle. Then he began to laugh.

"What's so funny?" I asked.

Chris practically threw the letter in my face and said, "Most of this is bull."

I looked at the letter and then read part of it out loud. "Kathy is the highlight of my day. Every day. She's brought color back into my life, brightness back into my soul. I love her dearly..."

"Please stop," said Chris, "My mom's a writer. And I'll admit she's good. But she left out a pretty important detail."

"What's that?" I asked.

"The only reason I'm marrying Kathy is because she's pregnant."

"Seriously?" asked J.J.

Chris chuckled, bitterly, "Yeah. Seriously. Should have rethought that whole condom thing."

"Well then," I said, standing up and extending my hand to shake Chris's, "Great to meet you."

"Later," he said with a casual wave. Then he headed for the door.

Chris was actually the highlight of our day, compared to some of the other guys we interviewed. Interspersed with some really nice, decent men, whose stories just honestly seemed a little too vanilla for me to consider them as my ring buyer, were a few more nightmares.

One guy was in the middle of telling us how in love he was with his girlfriend, when he got a call from a prostitute, confirming their 4:30 appointment (which was weekly!) He actually offered the information, saying his girlfriend knew about it and was fine with it because she understood it was all sexual, "a biological need" and nothing else.

Another guy told us he quote, "didn't hesitate to give his girlfriend a few smacks on the ass when she deserved them," unquote.

When I asked the next guy, Charlie why he loved his girlfriend he answered, "Read the letter."

"I did, but I want to hear more."

"Please, just read the letter."

J.J. obliged. "Sara's the girl I loved even before I met her. Her warmth and her touch and her kisses are like oxygen to me now..."

My assistant looked up at Charlie, who was standing there with his head down, "This is beautiful. Please, tell us more. Don't be afraid."

"I'm not afraid," said Charlie, "I just don't know what to say. Just read the letter."

It suddenly dawned on me what the issue was. "You didn't write this, did you?" I asked.

"No," he said sadly, "My girlfriend did. She's going to kill me if I don't get the ring."

"You're not getting the ring," said J.J.

"I know," said Charlie.

"Don't you have anything to say about her on your own?" I asked.

"Actually, I do. Honestly? She's a complete bitch."

"Then why are you marrying her?" I asked.

"I have no idea," he responded, "Why the hell am I with a girl who treats me like crap?"

"Why are you?" I asked.

"I mean, my girlfriend ordered me to come here and meet you and get the ring."

"She's a good writer, though," said J.J.

"Sounds like you have some thinking to do," I said.

Charlie stood up. "Actually, I really don't. Everything is so clear to me now. I'm dumping that hoe!" He then shook my hand and added, "Great meeting you girls. Good luck with your ring contest." He smiled and walked out the door with his Grande Mocha Frappuccino.

"I can't take this anymore," said J.J., "It's exhausting!"

"Only one more for today," I said, and at that moment, I looked up and saw a guy walk in whose appearance mesmerized me. I wasn't really sure why. He was good looking, with dark skin and beautiful dark brown hair, but it was more than looks. He had these big brown eyes that made me feel like I knew him. They were kind, familiar almost.

It had been two and a half months since Paul left, and until this very moment I hadn't noticed one guy, hadn't thought about a guy in any type of romantic way, and hadn't had one sexual impulse. Now, all I could think about was how it would feel to rip this guy's clothes off and be naked with him. It was bizarre.

"You must be Parker," J.J. gushed like a junior high-school cheerleader.

The guy extended his hand. "Yes, Parker Missoni."

"Nice meeting you," J.J. said with enthusiasm, "I'm J.J., and this is my boss and ring owner, Missy Benson."

When I shook hands with Parker, I could actually feel myself melting like snow does on a sunny mid-March day, and the smile he was giving me was saying he was aware of this. And what a nice smile it was... He had this big lower lip that touched his tooth ever so slightly when he grinned. It was warm and it was kind and let's be honest, it was sexy as hell!

"Parker, can I get you something to drink?" asked J.J.

"No thanks, I'm good."

"Okay...well I actually have to make a phone call. Will you two excuse me?" she asked us both.

"Sure," I said. I would realize later than my assistant sensed my crush and wanted to give us some privacy.

"So, Parker," I began, as I nervously shuffled through some papers to find his letter, "I got your e-mail. I really enjoyed hearing what you had to say." I wanted to add, "But had no idea you'd turn out to be such a hot babe." I didn't, though.

"Thanks," he smiled.

"So, your girlfriend's name is Lilly?"

"Right."

It was so bizarre because at this moment, I felt insanely jealous of Lilly. She was going to marry this adorable guy with his benevolent smile and gentle demeanor, who had written a letter about her that was so heartfelt and so endearing, he was possibly going to end up getting a free engagement ring. Lilly was most likely gorgeous, smart, and successful. How could she not be? After all, she'd landed Parker.

I glanced down at the letter. "It says here that you met Lilly on a ski trip in Deer Valley."

"Yeah, I was in the singles line for one of the chair lifts and I got paired up with her. Our first conversation took place riding up a mountain. It was kind of cool."

"That's really nice," I gushed.

"Hey, can I ask you something? Why are you doing this?"

I was startled by Parker's sudden subject change. "What do you mean?"

"I mean, I'd like to know why you're giving away your ring. There's got to be a reason."

"There is."

"Tell me."

Suddenly, Parker was bugging me. So much for the gentle demeanor. He was in my face and acting a little too nosy.

"Actually, all you need to know is that my marriage didn't work out and I'm looking to give my ring to a guy who I think deserves it, and someone who will make his wife really, really happy. Forever."

"So, why'd you get divorced?" he asked.

"I'm sorry, did you not hear me? I just pretty much told you I'm not getting into details."

"Did the guy like cheat on you or something?"

"It's personal!"

"It's not *that* personal. It's not like I asked you what your favorite sexual position is," he joked, "It's just a simple question."

I stood up. "You know what? This isn't going to work. I already know you're not the right person for my ring."

"Look, I know you're the divorced girl and everything..."

"Why is everyone calling me that?"

"What?"

"Nothing."

"I'm sorry about your divorce. I really am. It must be hard. But I have to be honest with you. You're way too uptight."

"You don't even know me."

With his smile (that I still thought was killer, despite the fact that he was annoying the hell out of me) he said, "Actually, I do. You're really pretty, and I bet you're really successful in your real estate business."

"Wait a minute! How do you know what I do for a living?"

"I grocery shop at Henry's. I recognized you from your ads on the shopping carts."

"Oh."

"Anyhow, you're hurting, and that's making you defensive, and for lack of a better word, kind of bitchy."

"Please leave."

"I didn't mean to upset you," he responded, "although I feel like you're probably always pissed off these days, and believe me, I'm sure you have a good reason to be that way, with the divorce and all. But at some point, you have to let it go, right?"

"Thanks for the armchair psychotherapy. Goodbye. Have a nice life."

"Just think about it."

"See ya."

As I watched Parker Missoni walk out the door, I realized I was furious. But, at the same time I felt a happy, giddy almost. The guy who angered me beyond belief had actually brought red blood back into my cold, jaded veins. And for that reason, it was hard to hate him. In fact, it was hard not to secretly adore him.

Chapter 11

Senior year of high school

"Hi! I'm home!" I shout when I walk into my house after a long day of school and then my afterschool babysitting job. My mom and Gina both come running to the door. Gina's holding a dozen pink roses wrapped in cellophane.

"Look what you got!" she says.

"A certain someone dropped them off earlier," Mom says with a smile.

My heart starts to pound. They're from Greg, the guy I've been seeing for about three months.

"You're so lucky!" says my cute eight-year old sister, who's bursting with excitement, partly because pink's her favorite color, but more so because she's in love with my boyfriend.

I smile, "Yeah, I am, aren't I?"

"He's lucky too," says mom, kissing my cheek, "You're both lucky to have found each other. He's a very nice boy."

"And hot!" says Gina.

We all burst out laughing.

"There's a card, too!" says Gina.

I take the card off the cellophane, leaving the roses in Gina's hands. I read it. It says, "To the best three months I've ever had. I love you, Greg."

"What does it say?" Gina says.

"I bet you want to know, huh?" I joke.

Gina emphatically nods.

I start playing a game. "Not going to tell," I say teasingly.

"Aw, come on!"

"Nope!"

Gina tries to grab the card out of my hand and I start to run. She starts chasing me around the living room. My mom stands there giggling. I finally stop running, kneel down and give it to her. "Okay, but don't tell anyone!"

Gina reads it out loud. I look at my mom. She gives me a big smile, but like always, beneath it you can see her sadness. I wonder for a second if that look is ever going to go away. Do widows stay sad for the rest of their lives?

My mom is so pretty. It's been almost two years since Dad died and she hasn't been on a single date. A few weeks earlier, I overheard her and her best friend, Linda talking at the kitchen table. Mom thought I was watching TV. Linda asked mom if she could set her up with this wealthy attorney named Louis. Mom told her she wasn't ready.

I miss my dad so much I can't stand it. Still, after all this time. I miss him the same as the first week he was gone. Maybe more. But what's even worse is seeing my mom. We don't really talk about it that much, but I can tell she's still in so much pain. And part of me feels guilty about what's going on right now. I just got roses from a boy I'm dating, and where's HER guy? Buried in a cemetery a couple of suburbs from where we live.

Gina hugs me as tight as she can. "You're the coolest, prettiest girl in your school, and I get to be your sister!"

I giggle, "You're pretty too. And I get to be YOUR sister."

I look up at my mom and she winks at me.

"I'm hungry," says Gina, "Can we eat now?"

"What's for dinner?" I ask.

"Chicken parmesan and Caesar salad," says Mom.

"I made the salad," says Gina, "Plus, guess what's for dessert?"

"No! You didn't!" I tease.

"Yup! I did."

"You made your famous chocolate chip and Rolo cookies??"

Gina giggles.

I turn to my mom and say, "Mom, I think maybe we should skip dinner and get right to the cookies."

Gina looks really proud at this moment. It's really nice to see.

"The cookies can wait. Let's eat," says Mom.

I follow them into the kitchen, and suddenly I have this strange feeling about my eight year old sister. I have this wonderful intuitive thought that she's going to grow up and become a famous chef. It makes me smile, despite all the sadness that's around me in this house.

Chapter 12

"Who the hell do you think you are, putting an ad on *craigslist* and giving away the engagement ring that cost me thirty-six thousand dollars?!"

Those were Paul's first words to me on the phone after I said, "Hello."

"How do you know about that?" I asked.

"Not that I owe you an explanation, but embarrassingly enough, I found out at work! From a partner, no less. Michael Fane's brother-in-law has a friend, who I guess answered the ad, wrote a letter, and then got picked to be interviewed by you."

"Which idiot, jerk or creep was it?" I wanted to ask. Instead I went with, "Who was it?" while trying to absorb the fact that the odds of my soon-to-be ex-husband finding out what I was doing with MY ring (I stress the word MY) were slim to none, and that it had actually happened.

"I don't remember. I guess you told him on the spot he wasn't getting the ring and he left. I think he told Michael's brother-in-law you weren't happy that his wife-to-be was pregnant. Something like that."

I could not believe this! So now *I* looked like the bad guy? "Actually, the guy's name is Chris Middleton and his *mommy* wrote the letter for him. He was a fraud. He told me the only reason he's getting married is because his girlfriend is pregnant. So, don't be so quick to judge. I don't even know why I'm explaining this to you. The ring is mine and I can do whatever I want with it."

"The ring is hardly yours," Paul snapped, "The divorce isn't final. I may ask for the ring back in the settlement."

"Oh please! What are *you* going to do with it? I'd say you could give it to Miss Huge Boobs, but from what I heard, you already bought her a ring."

"That's right, I did."

Now I found myself fuming and wanted to hit something as hard as I could. I was making a fist and clenching my teeth. What right did he have to take this attitude with me? He was the one who pulled the plug on our marriage. He was the one who cheated and sprinted out to buy another diamond ring. The nerve of this guy!

"Well, great then!" I shouted, "Enjoy it!"

Paul chuckled vindictively, "There's the temper I know and love."

"Is there a purpose for this phone call, Paul? Because in case you forgot, I work and I need to be getting back to that."

"Yes," he said, "I want you to stop this whole ridiculous contest or whatever it is, and cash the ring in. We can split the money."

I laughed bitterly, "Yeah, right. I think I'll do what you say because you've been so upfront with me, so honest and so fair."

"I always loved the way you resort to sarcasm when you're angry. I miss that."

I couldn't take it anymore. "Fuck you, Paul!" I shouted. Then I hung up. In all the years I'd been with my husband, I'd never said those words to him. Never. But things were dramatically different now. I wasn't the same person anymore. I felt like a total stranger to myself, doing and saying things I would never have thought existed in my persona.

My tolerance had been pushed to the limits and I was one angry, pissed off, scorned wife. Can you say *Betty Broderick?* I was now understanding her mentality, although I was sure I would never actually kill Paul and Priscilla. Still, there was a sense of being dumped, thrown away, discarded, pushed aside, whatever you want to call it that made anger envelop my soul.

I wasn't claiming to have been the perfect wife, and was now realizing lots of things about my not-so-perfect self. That being said, Paul let go of us without discussing it with me, and moved on to start another life with someone else, who happened to be young and beautiful. And that was a feeling I wasn't sure I'd ever get over.

"What's going on divorced girl?" asked J.J., walking into my office.

"Please don't call me that."

"I just heard you say, 'Fuck you.' Paul, I assume?"

I nodded. "He knows about the *craigslist* ad."

"So what? What's he going to do about it?"

At this moment I got a text from Paul. "Be prepared to hear from my lawyers. You are *not* giving away a thirty-six thousand dollar ring."

Without even giving it a second thought, I texted back, hitting the keys as furiously as I could, "Oh yes, I am. And I guarantee that the guy who I give it to will be more of a man than you'll ever be."

Unfortunately, when J.J. and I went to Starbucks later in the day and interviewed a few more guys, I felt like maybe what I'd texted Paul wasn't true. Finding a guy who was worthy of a free thirty-six thousand dollar ring was certainly posing a challenge. The only person who had given me hope was Stan Goldblatt, the first guy I'd interviewed. The hugger. Stan seemed like good husband material. But my gut wasn't saying he was the one. But, he really was sweet and seemed genuine. So, if Stan was out there, I figured there had to be more guys like him. I'd find my prince. Or I should say, another woman's prince. I had to.

But today, the frogs continued to come in. I interviewed Simon, a very religious guy, who hadn't mentioned in his letter that the girlfriend he was planning to propose to would actually be his sixth wife. After Simon came Rick, who asked me if I wanted to get together later for a drink, and then Joe, who was playing poker on his iPhone the entire time we were talking. Joe actually made me feel like I was interrupting each time I asked him a question. I wish I had a dime for every time he held his index finger up to me and said "hold on," so he could take his turn.

It wasn't until the last interview of the day that I felt a glimmer of faith. His name was Tony Lionetti and he was adorable! He was only five foot eight, but he had a fit body, and his dark, Italian look worked so well for him. Tony was sweet, but not in a boring kind of way. He was magnetic, one of those people everyone wanted to be around because he was so pleasant and easy going.

"So, Tony," said J.J., "tell us about your girlfriend. What's the best thing about her?"

Tony smiled, "That's a hard question. Let me try to answer it by telling you a story," he began, "Claudette's a second grade teacher. Last year, one of her students was diagnosed with a rare form of leukemia. Obviously, everyone who knew the kid was devastated. And the family basically had to move to Indiana for the year while the kid had treatment."

"That's so sad," I said.

"My amazing, giving, selfless girlfriend drove two hours each way every single weekend to visit him. I'm not lying when I tell you she never missed a weekend. I went with her a few times. She tutored him in the hospital, she read to him, and she brought him letters from the other kids.

Claudette is the kind of person I want to marry, a person I respect immensely, and someone I look up to enormously. Her endless acts of kindness and selflessness make me want to be a better person because she always sets the bar so high. Seriously. She's the one–the one I want to spend my life with. I want to give her a wonderful, happy life by being the father of her children and by being a devoted, loyal life partner."

After hearing what were probably the most inspiring, hopeful words I'd ever heard in my life, I was on the verge of tears. Happy tears.

I looked at J.J. She was crying. "I'm so sorry," she sobbed, "That was beautiful."

Tony laughed, "I didn't mean to upset you."

J.J. stood up and hugged him, while I sat there thinking, "Finally! A guy who may be a real life Zack Mayo!"

Chapter 13

Joe's Market, a quaint, gourmet grocery store in my neighborhood sells frozen salmon that tastes really good if you marinate it, and then either bake or grill it. For years, I'd been buying and preparing it for Paul and me. Now, in my cynical, embittered state of mind, however, I had an issue with the fish, which was that it came in packs of two pieces. I felt like the executives at *Joe's* were discriminating against single people, or I should say "the divorced girl."

If a person who lived alone wanted salmon, he or she had to buy it for two, even if like me, they would only eat one piece. I mean, was the store punishing me for being single now? Were they rubbing it in my face that I had no one to give the other piece to? When I shared my theory with J.J., she told me I had delusional paranoia and that the owner of *Joe's* was divorced, anyhow, so that theory couldn't possibly hold water.

Despite the unfair packaging, I continued to buy the salmon. I would grill both pieces and then save the second piece for the next night, and every single time I did that, as delicious as the meal was, I felt like the biggest loser on earth. Would I be cooking for two and eating the leftovers the next night until I was eighty and moving into a nursing home?

I poured myself a glass of white wine to soothe the sense of loneliness and self-pity that seemed to be encasing my soul these days. Just as I took the first bite of the salmon I was eating today, the other piece already wrapped in tin foil, my phone rang, and I saw it was Harvey Firestone, my divorce lawyer.

"Hi Harvey," I said, trying to sound cheerful, but knowing full well he was calling with bad news. In the short time I'd been working with Harvey, I'd learned that if he called me, something was wrong. There was never any good news with him. Although, was it really his fault? Was there ever any good news while going through a divorce? I'd be willing to bet no divorce attorney in history ever called a client and said, "Hi, I have great news," and really meant it.

"Hello there, Missy!" he replied in a fake jolly tone. My theory was now confirmed.

"Hi, Harvey, how are you?" I said to my lawyer, who I didn't know very well. I'd sold Harvey a house several years earlier, and because I remembered feeling safe and almost protected by him, and because he had a great professional reputation around the community I'd hired him as my attorney.

"Fine, thank you. Do you have a minute?"

"Sure," I answered, looking down at my salmon and really wanting to reply, "Actually, I have all the time in the world. I'll be sitting home again tonight eating salmon, drinking a couple glasses of wine, and then plopping myself in front of the TV, channel flipping between *The Voice, The O'Reilly Factor,* and *Two and A Half Men* re-runs. Then, I'll stumble upstairs, get into bed, cry a little bit, and then fall fast asleep hoping that when I wake up, all of this will have been a dream. Paul will be sleeping next to me and I'll wake him up and tell him how much I love him, and that we should try for a baby again. Then he'll make love to me and it will be really nice, and I'll feel loved and cherished and so will he. But obviously that won't happen.

What *will* happen is, I'll get up, get in the shower, go to my job where people make me feel smart and idolize me, and then I'll come home again tomorrow night, feel like crap, and eat the other piece of salmon. So, yes, I have a minute."

"Look," said Harvey, hesitation in his voice, "I got a call from your husband's attorney today."

"Okay," I said. I already knew it was about the ring.

Harvey took a deep breath. "The ring. He wants it back."

"I know I'm not a lawyer, Harvey, but the ring was a gift from Paul to me. It's mine. Won't that hold up in court?"

"Probably not. The thing is, they're claiming you had the ring re-set a few years ago and added some diamonds, increasing its value from significantly. Is that true?"

"Uh...yeah..." I said. The next thing I did was take a huge gulp of wine.

"I'm afraid that now makes the ring marital property."

I drank another sip of wine, took a deep breath and began, "Harvey, my husband dumped me. He's marrying another woman. He's already bought her an engagement ring. The one thing keeping me going through this entire hideous, disgusting, humiliating, almost unbearably horrendous time is what I'm doing with that ring."

"Really, Missy, giving a ring like that to a perfect stranger...that's not a very responsible decision. I question it. I truly do. And I'd strongly advise you against it."

"Thanks for the advice, but I'm not changing my mind. Tell Paul I will buy his half. Tell him to come up with a price."

"Well...the thing is...that's not acceptable to him. He wants the ring so you can't have the contest."

"What?! Why does he care what I do with it if I pay him for it?"

"I'm not sure, but..."

"Look, I want the ring and I'm not changing my mind. It might seem ridiculous to you, maybe even crazy, but I can assure you, I know exactly what I'm doing. So, your job is to fight and get me my ring. If I lose it in court, I can accept that. But I'm not going to roll over and give in to Paul on this one."

"Missy, please be reasonable," he urged.

"You're either with me or you're not. If you're not, I need to know that."

There was a silence on the other end of the phone that was long enough for me to pour myself more wine and take a sip. When Harvey finally spoke, his voice was soft and sad. "Sorry, Missy, as your attorney, I'm advising you to sell the ring and split the money. I can't see it any other way."

"Harvey, I truly appreciate your opinion. I really do."

"I'm glad."

"But I have to pull a Donald Trump on you."

"What?"

"Harvey, you're fired," I said, trying to sound like Donald. Before Harvey could respond, I hung up. Then I started laughing, and for the first time in what seemed like ages, I felt self-confidence and tremendous pride. I suddenly had a surge of energy I hadn't had in years. I was full of self-respect and dignity. I actually felt better about myself than I could ever remember. Maybe I was completely nuts, I wasn't sure. What I did know was that I had just stood up for myself. I was sticking to what I believed in. Give Paul back the ring? Give up the only thing that was keeping me sane right now? No way! The contest was on. I wasn't backing down. And for those reasons, I really liked myself.

I stood up, took my salmon and wrapped it up with the other piece, while singing Celo Greene's *F You* as loud as I could and dancing. This felt amazing! I had self-esteem. I wasn't letting Paul or Harvey or anyone else tell me what I could or could not do with *my* engagement ring. I was giving that big thing to a good guy, and no one was going to stop me.

Yes, so far, I'd only met a couple men in the contest I was considering, and yes, I was actually going to have to read more letters and get more guys into Starbucks for interviews. But, somewhere out there was a great guy–a guy who would be a loving, caring, devoted husband. I was sure of it.

It wasn't creepy Chris Middleton, the guy whose mother wrote a letter so that he'd get engaged to his pregnant girlfriend, and it wasn't disgusting Jordy Firth, who is planning to marry the woman he stole from his brother. It wasn't Joe, the iPhone poker playing gambling addict, and it wasn't Parker Missoni, the sexy guy with the kind brown eyes who made me weak in the knees and angrier than a caged bull at the same time. Maybe it was Stan, maybe it was Tony, or maybe it was another great guy. That remained to be seen. But he *was* out there. Somewhere.

The next thing I did was call J.J. "Hi!" I said when she answered.

"Hi, what's up?"

"Will you go out with me tonight?" I asked.

"Go out where?"

"I don't know, out. To a restaurant, to a bar, dancing, whatever."

J.J. didn't answer, and I was getting a kick out of the fact that she seemed stunned.

"I need to party," I continued, "Socialize. Drink. Have fun!"

"Um...okay."

"Come on! Get more excited! We're going to have a blast!"

"Did you get on anti-depressants or something?"

"No, I just fired my attorney. I feel great!"

"What?" she exclaimed, "Why? Did Paul back down about the ring?"

"No. I'll explain when I see you. Just get ready and I'll be down there around nine."

"Where are we going?"

"Pick someplace, anywhere where there's wine, loud music, and guys."

"Well, congratulations, divorced girl, for moving on."

"Please don't call me that," I said. What J.J. couldn't see on the other end of the phone was that I was smiling so wide, my cheeks were hurting.

Chapter 14

Hub 51 was the latest Chicago hot spot, and when I walked in, it felt that way. The upscale bar and restaurant had an elegant feel, but its décor was comfortable, too. The high ceilings and exposed whitewashed brick gave it an airy loft-like feel, and the lounge-like furniture made it seem homey.

The place was packed with wall-to-wall twenty and thirty- something professionals, each with a martini in hand, and heavily engaged in those bar-type conversations, the ones that are seemingly focused and meaningful, which everyone knows is just an act. I mean, how serious of a conversation can you have with someone you met 40 seconds ago?

When I shared this theory with J.J., her response was, "Let's be honest, they're looking for Mr. Right." The girl was already on her second lemon drop martini and we'd been there for thirty minutes at the most.

"That's okay," I replied, "Maybe they're looking for love."

"Wow, is the ring contest turning you into a romantic?"

"Hmm..." I replied, "Let's just say I'm a little more open minded than I was a few weeks ago. How about you, J.J.? Do *you* have an open mind? Are you ready to move on?"

"I don't know. No one's ever hurt me as much as Christian did. I'm not even remotely over him. Then again, getting out there and meeting people helps. I mean, maybe what I need to get me over the backstabbing, unscrupulous, heartless cheater is some great guy."

"What's a great guy, in your opinion?"

J.J. began, "Someone who gets me. Someone who cares about what I say."

"And listens..."

"Someone who notices things."

"Who appreciates things."

"Someone like..." J.J.'s eyes were now transfixed on something behind me.

"Someone like what?" I asked, "Finish."

Her eyes never left what seemed to be mesmerizing her.

"What are you looking at?"

Softly, she replied, "Someone like him."

I turned around and saw a very nice-looking, young guy smiling at my assistant. I swung back around and looked at J.J. "You like him?"

"Yeah," she gushed, "He's cute, huh?"

"Yeah!" I replied with genuine enthusiasm, so happy that J.J. wasn't wallowing in sadness at the moment.

"He's coming over here," she exclaimed under her breath.

I was about to turn around when she reprimanded me like a teenager would to her mother. Two seconds later, I heard the guy say, "How ya doin'?"

"Great," she replied casually.

"Yeah, me too," grinned the cute guy. He appeared to be about J.J.'s age, mid-twenties. He was shy, but had made the effort to walk over here to meet her. For that, I liked him immediately.

"Glad to hear it," J.J. smiled.

All three of us sat there smiling until I finally broke the silence. "Hi, I'm Missy," I said, extending my hand. We shook hands.

"Jake," he said with a grin.

"This is J.J.," I introduced. And that was it. At this moment, I might as well have been invisible. The two of them locked eyes and began to talk. Both seemed so taken with each other that nothing or no one else in the room existed. It was cute.

"So, who are you here with?" J.J. asked him.

"Actually, don't laugh, but I'm here with my grandfather."

J.J. burst out laughing, "Really?"

"I told you not to laugh," he said.

"Sorry."

"Here he comes," said Jake.

When I turned and looked at the person walking toward us, I almost fell off my bar stool. It was John Concerto.

"Missy?" said my soon-to-be ex-husband's boss, who I knew without fail would grab my butt at some point this evening. Although, now that I was estranged from Paul, I was hoping the thrill was gone for him and maybe he'd take a pass on the butt grabbing.

I faked enthusiasm. "John, hi!"

"You look amazing! Separation is doing wonders for you!"

When I looked at J.J., she was giving John a dirty look.

"Do you know my grandson?" John asked.

"Um...we just met him," I answered, "This is my assistant, J.J. McNealy. J.J., this is John Concerto. He's the managing partner of Paul's law firm."

"The one who grabs your ass all the time?" she blurted out.

I gasped. John burst out laughing and Jake put his hand over his mouth.

"Guilty," said John after he calmed down from his laughing attack.

"Dude, I take kick boxing classes three days a week," replied J.J., "Do it again and I'm going to uppercut your jaw and hook your left cheek pretty good." She looked at me and added, "There's no excuse for groping anyone, let alone the spouse of a guy who works for you."

"She's right," said John. He turned to me. "Missy, I apologize."

"Thank you, John," I said, "I appreciate that."

"That was cool, John," said J.J. with a smile.

"Yeah," said Jake, seeming relieved.

Another martini later, while the lovebirds continued chatting, I found myself in a deep conversation with the man who I would normally cringe at the sight of, the man who would constantly, inappropriately put his hands on me, and the man who had always seemed arrogant, full of himself, and gave new meaning to the word cocky.

I was now seeing John Concerto, 68 year old grandfather of J.J.'s new love interest in a whole new light. Yes, he was very full of himself and acted like he was thirty, but there was more to John, a side of him I'd never gotten to know. He was extremely intelligent, very charming, and had a surprisingly good sense of humor I'd never appreciated.

"Look, Missy," he said, his voice a bit slurred, "Let's be honest. Paul's a great catch. He could have any woman he wants."

That comment made me seethe.

He continued, "That being said, I really mean this: You are a beautiful woman." He put his hands on my shoulders and finished, "Gorgeous, in fact."

"Thanks," I smiled.

"But even more importantly, you're really smart. You have drive and determination, and because of that, you're successful, and you always will be."

Now I felt tears welling up in my eyes. It was such a great feeling to get the stamp of approval from a man as well known, as wealthy, and as high up on the corporate ladder as John. I felt like Warren Buffet was complimenting me.

"Thanks, that means so much to me."

"You're going to be fine," he said.

"I think so. For the first time since Paul left, I really think so." I suddenly felt strangely like John and I were becoming friends. And when I thought about it, it was a perfect scenario. Why not have an older friend? John was like a mentor to me. He could guide me, offer me advice.

"And if you ever need anything," he said, "I'm here for you."

I hugged him. "Thanks so much," I whispered. Wow. I really hadn't given him enough credit. John was truly stepping up to the plate in such a time of need for me.

It was at that instant that I felt his hands cup my butt. I gasped and pulled away.

"What?" he said with a chuckle, "You know me. I can't resist!"

"You're disgusting!" I shouted, "What makes you think you have the right to touch me??"

"Oh, Missy, come on. I'm harmless. I just like to have a little fun."

J.J. stood up, "You were warned my friend." She went to punch him, but Jake held her arms back.

The room began to spin. I was buzzed, and in the middle of what could have been a bar fight between a twenty-seven year old woman and a sixty-eight year old guy. If I wasn't so pissed off that I'd let my guard down, only to be rudely awakened by this pervert, I'd have thought this whole scene was hilarious. But I wasn't laughing. I decided to be vocal about it.

"You're a pig and you make me sick!"

I looked at J.J., whose big smile felt like an endorsement of what I'd just said. Jake was still holding her arms back, with a look on his face of both concern and amusement. And when I looked at John, his head was down. The next thing I heard was a familiar voice behind me saying, "Hostile. Totally hostile. You haven't let go of the bitterness yet, I see."

I think I knew whose voice it was before I even turned around. Standing there was none other than Parker Missoni. Parker…the guy who made my entire body shake at our interview, the guy who infuriated me with his nosiness and his way too direct demeanor, and the guy who I loved to hate and hated to love.

Maybe it was the martinis, but he looked even better than he did at Starbucks. I was horrified by what he'd just seen, and instantly angered by his candid comment. So, why was I so unbelievably thrilled to see him? I couldn't deny it. He was outspoken, rude, and way too blunt for my taste. But boy, he was adorable.

Chapter 15

"I'm not even going to begin to try to explain this to you," I said to Parker, trying to maintain a confident game face, but truthfully wanting to crawl into a hole. Out of the corner of my eye, I could see and hear J.J. giving John a lecture, with Jake still semi-holding her arms back.

"Okay, that's cool," he said with a chuckle, "I may be a little twisted, but I actually find that kind of psychotic confrontation cute. In a strange, demented way, it's a little bit of a turn on."

"Do you even know what tact is? You are the most outspoken person I think I've ever met."

"I take pride in that, actually. I don't like bullshit. 'Tell it like it is,' I always say. It's so much better that way. Cut through all the crap, know what I mean?"

"You infuriate me!" I said, secretly admiring what he'd just said, in addition to adoring his deep, brown eyes. I loved that they were now familiar to me.

Up walked J.J. "Just so you know," she said to Parker, "That guy she just yelled at is her ex's boss, and he just grabbed her ass."

Parker chuckled, "Really?"

She ignored Parker and turned to me. "Listen, Grandpa's going home. Do you mind if I leave with Jake? He's meeting people at another bar. He wants me to go with."

"Um..." I looked at Parker.

"She doesn't mind at all. She's going to stay and have a drink with me," he answered for me.

"I am?" I asked.

"Cool," said J.J. Then she hugged me. "You're still staying over, right? Of course you are."

"Uh..."

"You can't drive home. I'll text you in like an hour and we'll hook up back at my place."

"Okay," I smiled, "I guess." This was all happening so fast. J.J. was out the door in an instant, and now, here I was alone with this guy. I was scared, but part of me was thrilled, to the point where I wanted to do cartwheels right in the middle of the place.

The minute she was out of sight, Parker looked right at me and said, "Getting your ass grabbed by some old guy can't be fun. Sorry I called you hostile and bitter. He deserved what you said."

"Wow."

"What?"

"You actually know how to apologize."

"I have a lot of other really good qualities, too."

"Are you hitting on me?"

"Yes."

"What about Lilly?"

Parker put his head down, and then looked up and said softly, and with much more seriousness, "We broke up."

In my head I was high-fiving myself. "I'm so sorry," I said with my best fake sad face.

"I bet you are," he said.

"What's that supposed to mean?" Could he read my mind?

"You're totally thinking that I'm a jerk and I deserve it." Phew. Not a mind reader.

"Parker, don't quit your day job and become a psychic. You're way off."

"Really?"

"What *is* your day job, by the way?"

"I'm a physical therapist, mostly for kids."

"You are not!"

"Okay, I'm lying."

"Are you really a physical therapist?"

Parker chuckled, "Why is that so unbelievable?"

"It's just so altruistic of you."

"So you pretty much assumed I was a selfish asshole."

I looked at him, hoping he couldn't see through me and detect how much I wanted to rip his clothes off. "Can we start over?" I managed.

He smiled, "Sure." Then he extended his hand and said, "Hi, my name's Parker. Parker Missoni. I'm a physical therapist and I'm single."

I shook his hand and felt a little silly for giggling like a teenager. "I'm Missy Benson, the divorced girl."

"You're so much cuter when you cut out the tough girl act."

"You don't even know me."

"I thought we were starting over."

I smiled, "Right."

An hour later I found myself engrossed in conversion with Parker, exchanging life stories. He told me all about growing up in the city, how his dad was a dentist, his mom a dental hygienist, his older brother and sister the good kids, while Parker was the one who got in all the trouble.

"Why doesn't that surprise me?" I joked.

"The good news is, I turned out okay."

"Are you sure?" I said with a laugh.

Parker laughed.

"So, why did you and Lilly break up?" I asked, "And who broke up with who?"

"Well, that's a tough question. Technically I broke up with her, but that was after she slept with some other guy."

"Really?"

Parker nodded.

"How'd you find out?"

"I suspected something was up. I know it's not cool, but I read her texts while she was in the bathroom because I really wanted to know. Turns out, the guy sent her one saying she left her thong in his bed."

"Seriously? He texted that?"

"Along with other sexual stuff. Kind of gross."

"I'm sorry. I really am."

"The ironic thing is, Lilly had been pressuring me to get engaged for months. That's why I was ring shopping." He added with a smile, "If that's what you want to call meeting some rich, divorced chick at Starbucks to try to get a free ring."

"It's actually ninety-nine cents. How old are you, Parker?"

"36."

"Why was Lilly pressuring you? Are you one of those guys who's afraid of marriage?"

"Every guy's afraid of marriage. But honestly, the idea doesn't repulse me like it once did. I mean, I can actually picture myself married and not feel physically nauseous."

"That's encouraging."

"So, I was actually going to bite the bullet and propose to Lilly. I think I checked her texts because I had a gut feeling something wasn't right and I wanted to check things out before I did anything. Turns out, my gut was right on."

"I'm really sorry."

"It's okay. I really do want to get married someday. And even more so, I'd love to have kids."

When Parker said the word kids, my face turned white.

"Do *you* have kids?"

"No."

"Why not?"

"There you go again, asking personal questions to someone you barely know."

"Why is that personal? You don't want kids, or your ex didn't want kids, or you didn't want kids with *him,* or you had problems having kids... Why is it such a big deal to talk about it?"

"Because it is."

Parker gave me a gentle smile, "Just try."

I took a deep breath and then said, "I had a miscarriage like six years ago. It was really late into the pregnancy, like six months."

"That's awful," he said, "I'm really sorry."

"Thanks."

"So that was six years ago... What happened after? I mean, did you try to get pregnant again?"

"Well, I wanted to try again right away and Paul didn't. We argued about it all the time. And then I finally gave up and stopped asking him. And then, like a year later, he wanted to start trying again, and I didn't."

"Why not?"

I took a deep breath. "This is really hard for me to talk about."

"Just answer the question. Say it and then we'll stop talking about it."

"I think I was afraid. I'd finally gotten over it and I didn't want to risk it happening again. Honestly, I fucking chickened out."

My head was down and Parker bent down, putting his face under my chin. "Hey!"

I looked up at him.

"It ain't over, girl! You're young. You can have lots of babies. Even better, with some guy you really love!"

I broke into a huge grin.

He smiled back at me, and for an instant I felt like we were best friends. And I knew Parker could tell.

"You want me to kiss you, don't you?" he asked.

The room was spinning. "Yes," I answered, "but I can't."

"Why not?"

I stood up. "Because I've got to go." Then, without even looking at Parker, I dashed out the door as fast as I could. I could hear him calling my name, but I kept running.

Once outside, it took me no more than three seconds to hail a cab. As it sped away from the bar, I looked back and saw Parker running outside and looking around for me. I took a deep breath, feeling relieved, as though I'd just escaped.

I texted J.J., "On my way back to your place. Are you there?" Then, as I waited for her response, the cab speeding up State Street, I began to think, 'Why would someone who was starving, flee an apple orchard? Why would a person be in such a hurry to dash outside of her warm, heated home on a sub-zero winter day? Why would anyone who needed water sprint from the well?'

Right then, I put my face in my hands and I wept, not because I was upset. Quite the opposite reason, actually. I cried because I was happy. Terrified, but really happy. A person who thought her life was over was running from someone who had just made her realize her new life was just beginning.

Chapter 16

Age 27

I can't believe I'm at this party. A girl I work with, Randi Gurian, begged me to come with her because some guy she likes is supposedly here and she didn't have anyone to go with. Randi is really sweet, and I like her a lot, but right now I'm ready to kill her because I don't want to be here.

I feel like I'm getting a sore throat and I'm really tired. I just want to go home and go to bed. I've been working my butt off lately because there's this contest in the office and if I sell one more house in the next two weeks, I'll win a trip to Mexico.

Randi is talking to two really nice looking guys. I'm standing here with a beer in my hand that I don't even want, thinking about how many good looking guys are here and how much I don't even care. I'm wishing that I cared about men as much as I care about my professional life.

I'm so good at what I do. I really know how to sell houses. I know how to make people feel good about the asking price, I know how to make them comfortable with such a big decision, and when it comes to sellers, I know how to get them to have faith that I'll get them a good price. I'm such a talented salesperson, so engaging, so self-assured, so personable. So, why can't I act the same way in relationships? I know the answer but I can't bring myself to think about it. Ever.

I glance over at Randi again. She genuinely looks like she's having fun. I'm glad for her. Why can't I be more like her?

"Excuse me," I hear someone say.

I turn around and standing there is this absolutely gorgeous guy who appears to be around my age. He looks like a model, almost pretty, like he belongs in an Abercrombie catalogue.

"Yes?" I say.

"I've been watching you and I wanted to meet you, so I asked a few people who you were. I heard your name's Missy."

"Yes," I smile.

"I also heard you don't get into relationships. Is that true?"

It's without a doubt true. "Well, that's a little harsh," I flirt, "If I met a really great guy, I'd have to be stupid not to consider a relationship with him, right?"

The guy gives me a big grin. I can tell he can't really think of a clever response, but he's so good looking that his lack of wit is *instantly forgotten. He is seriously one of the best looking men I think I've ever seen, and ironically, because of that, I'm not that attracted to him. His looks are intimidating.*

I continue to compensate for his lack knowledge of flirting. "Are you a great guy?" I ask him.

"Yes," he grins, "May I take you to dinner tomorrow night?"

He really is cute. Maybe he's just shy. Maybe he'll get a little less vanilla and a little more interesting on a dinner date.

"Hmm…" I say.

"Look, with me, what you see is what you get. I'm 29, I'm from Chicago, I'm an attorney, I went to Harvard undergrad, Stanford for law school. I have three sisters, and my favorite dessert is cherry pie and ice cream.

"Do you like the pie hot?"

He chuckles, "Yeah."

I think to myself how funny life can be. The last thing I wanted to do tonight is come to this party, and now I just met this guy and my gut is telling me he's going to be significant in some way. Some really big way. Two words: gorgeous and wealthy.

I don't want to jump into bed with him, but part of the reason is because I don't want to jump into bed with anyone except Brad Harrison, a musician I've been having regular sex with for the past several months, years maybe, but I can't even begin to admit that to myself.

When I say regular, I mean that we are sleeping together on a regular basis. I certainly don't mean regular in the sense that the sex is regular. The sex is anything but regular. It's crazy and dramatic and a little violent. He throws me around and blindfolds me and holds me down and drips candle wax on me and licks dessert (like cherry pie and ice cream) off of me.

It's so unlike me to be in a purely physical relationship with someone. I'm feeling like a borderline sexual deviant, but there's something about Brad that's changed my attitude about casual sex. He seems to bring out sexual impulses I never even knew I had. Each time we get together, the sex gets better and better, and I'm always surprised because I didn't think it could get better, but it keeps happening.

So now, seeing this drop dead gorgeous guy who any woman would feel lucky to land, I'm not sure how to react. He sure does look good on paper: a handsome, Harvard grad, a charming attorney who actually asked people about me. My mother is always telling me to marry someone who loves me more than I love him. This guy really seems smitten. Maybe he's the one. Although, if he's the one, shouldn't I feel more?

The truth is, Brad or no Brad, I haven't really been able to feel anything significant for ANY man. Maybe I'm just not meant to feel the way people feel in movies. Maybe no one feels that way and they just lie and tell you they do. Or maybe, just maybe, a horrible thing that happened in my past is shaping who I am. It happened almost seven years ago and I keep waiting for the guts to love someone and to forget about an unthinkably terrible thing I did.

I decide to put the past behind me, just for tonight, and focus on this man who is interested in me. I decide, just for tonight, that maybe I deserve something more than hot sex with Brad. I decide that just for tonight, I'm going to try to like myself, just like I do professionally, and realize that I deserve someone like this.

I turn to the Kevin Costner double and give him a grin. "What's your name?"

"Paul," he says, extending his hand, "Paul Benson."

Chapter 17

"Door is open. Let yourself in. I'm in bed. Not alone☺." That was the text I got back from J.J. Although a bit shocked that she would take Jake home for a sleepover the first night she met him, I was happy for her. She'd been so miserable since her break up with Christian, having to deal not only with a broken heart, but also with the sting of constantly seeing him and his new girlfriend all over the tabloids. It seemed like she was always trying to hide her sadness and act happy, but I'd caught her teary-eyed at her desk several times, which was so uncharacteristic of her.

I was still extremely focused on my own breakup, but acutely aware of how much pain my young assistant was in. Yes, J.J. had been with Christian for less than a year, and didn't have to deal with a divorce, but did that make her breakup easier than mine? No way. It was very clear she was hurting. And although I found a bit of comfort in the fact that the two of us were going through things together, it was still difficult to see my usually upbeat, gregarious, free spirited assistant so down in the dumps.

So, when I walked into her apartment and saw both the guy's and her clothes scattered around the living room rug, I found myself anything but judgmental, and I wished I had had the guts J.J. did, to be sleeping in Parker's arms right now instead of the t-shirt and sweatpants J.J. put out for me on her couch.

I fell asleep watching TV, the remote in one hand, and a bag of *Sea Salt & Sweet Potato Crinkles* in the other, until I was awakened at dawn by a loud noise. I sat up quickly and saw none other than Christian Maverick, totally naked and looking for his boxers, which I happened to notice were right under the couch.

"I'm sorry I woke you," he said, "I tripped."

Looking back, the funniest part about this whole scene was that Christian didn't even try to cover himself up. I truly believe he loved himself and his body so much that he didn't care who saw it. He actually seemed to take pride in showing it off.

"They're right there," I said, pointing to his purple underwear with one hand, as I used my other to cover my own face.

"Thanks," he smiled, leaning down and grabbing them off the floor. "Missy, right?" he asked.

"Yes," I answered, deciding to keep my eyes closed and face covered for awhile.

"Nice to see you again," he said.

"Same to you," I murmured, speaking under the hand that was covering my face.

"I'm sure you think I'm a huge jerk, but I'm not. I really love J.J. I'm just…"

Now I looked at up at him. Naked or not naked, this guy needed an earful. He had his boxers on and one leg in his jeans.

"You're just what?" I asked, "A cheater, a liar, a coward? Which one?"

"Oh, I get it. You think you have the right to judge me because you're this divorced girl and you hate all men."

"Why does everyone call me that?!" I shouted.

"Hey!" shouted J.J., walking into the room, "Don't call her that!"

"Did you hear what she said to me?!" said Christian.

"I don't care! She's my boss *and* my friend!"

Christian continued getting dressed. "I don't have to take this, you know."

J.J. rushed over to him, "Listen, can't we all just get along?"

I could tell J.J. was getting upset and that was the last thing I wanted, so I said, "Christian, I apologize for calling you a cheater and a liar."

"And a coward," he whined.

Ugh! This guy was bugging me! I took a deep breath. "And a coward," I repeated.

"Fine," he said.

I looked at J.J. She mouthed "thank you" to me while Christian was putting on his socks.

"So, are you guys back together?" I asked, desperately trying to keep the sarcasm out of my voice.

"Yup," said Christian, proudly putting his arm around J.J.

"Try to control your happiness," she said, glancing at me nervously.

"What about your new girlfriend?" I asked him.

"They broke up," said J.J.

"Yeah," he stammered, "she was just too clingy and too needy." He turned to J.J., "Don't believe what the tabloids say, baby. She's telling everyone *she* dumped *me.* It's a lie."

When J.J. said, "I believe you, honey," I wanted to puke. Christian was lying. I was sure of it. He'd been dumped and now he wanted J.J. back.

"Can you believe we ran into each other last night at the bar at the *W Hotel?*" she said to me.

"Fate," added Christian, "That's what that is."

He looked at me and I just nodded at them.

The second Christian was out the door, J.J. looked at me and said, "Don't say anything!"

"What happened to Jake?"

"I liked Jake," she said, "I really did. We were having a nice time. Jake's great. But then I saw Christian and that was it. My heart stopped. I was a mess. He was so happy to see me, and he started crying right in the middle of the bar."

"That's so touching."

"Please don't judge me. I think he deserves another chance. So he fucked up. So what? Everyone makes mistakes."

"Look, I care about you. And I have a bad feeling about this guy. So, all I'm going to say is, be careful."

"I will," she said.

I had to admit it was really nice to see her like this, happiness back in her face, pure joy back in her core. So, I decided to let it go for now and give Christian the benefit of the doubt, even though I knew deep down the guy was the devil.

"So, what did you tell Jake? I mean, did you just leave him there?"

"Jake was cool about the whole thing. When I left with Christian, he was talking to his friends and having a good time. It's all good."

"I'll bet."

"Um…can we talk about Parker? What about Lilly?"

"They broke up," I smiled.

"You like him, don't you?"

"Yeah," I smiled.

"Did anything happen?"

"No, but I wanted it to. He tried to kiss me and I ran out of the bar."

"Dude, why?!"

"I'm scared of him, and why are you calling me dude?"

"You're scared of him because you like him."

"I know."

"Oh my God! What time is it?" exclaimed J.J. She looked at the wall clock and said, "Shit! I have a showing at 8:30! The out of town couple!" She ran into her bathroom, shouting, "I'll make it, Missy! I promise! And we'll talk more about Parker later!"

"See you later!" I shouted, hearing the shower go on. Then I quickly got dressed, thinking that it was 7:45, and how the hell was J.J. going to shower, get ready, and make it to the showing (which was in the suburbs), all in 45 minutes? Wasn't my problem, I said to myself. Although, yes, it *was* my problem, since it was *my* client and J.J. worked for *me.* Deep down, though, I knew my assistant would work it out.

She'd text or call the couple, show up late, and then charm the heck out of them, and they would forgive and forget the tardiness because J.J. will have put them in great moods with her upbeat, energetic, happy demeanor. And eventually, they'd buy something from one of our listings. And that's the reason J.J.'s bonus went up significantly every year.

Two minutes later, I was on the road, headed back home to shower and start my day as well. Like J.J., I had appointments and meetings and phone calls to make, and I also had a closing to attend. But I had two other jobs in addition. One was to continue reading letters and screening potential ring buyers, the other: find a new divorce attorney A.S.A.P.

Throughout the day, I called and left messages with eight divorce lawyers in Chicago, referrals from people I worked with, from a couple of former clients, and from my hair colorist. I set up meetings for the following day with the two who made me feel particularly comfortable. I was hoping to soon have a new attorney representing me, one who understood me, one who was on the same page as me, and one who was a lot less judgmental about my ring giveaway idea than Harvey Firestone was.

Around 3:00, my head still pounding and my eyes half-shut, I was having a hard time focusing on a sales plan I was putting together for 770 North Maple Avenue, a home I was planning to list for $1.3 million dollars, which was $300,000 less than the seller thought it was worth. In the present economy being what it was, however, the big question was, how badly did they want to get rid of it? Since they'd already purchased another home for $1.9 million, they'd told me they'd feel lucky to get $1.3.

All of a sudden, I got paged.

"Missy Benson, call on line four...Missy...call on line four..."

I picked it up. "This is Missy, how may I help you?"

"What happened last night?" asked the caller.

My heart was pounding, because I knew exactly who was on the line. I took a deep breath, "Hi, Parker."

"Are you feeling better today, Cinderella?"

"Not really," I giggled, "My head hurts and I'm exhausted, courtesy of three lemon drop martinis."

"Four."

"No, I really think it was three."

"So, what happened last night?"

"I've just got issues."

"Well, I'm thinking we should talk about them. Want to go out for dinner with me tonight?"

I was so shocked I didn't know what to say. So, I sat there frozen.

"Hello? Still there? It's just dinner."

More silence on my end.

"Look," he continued, "I have an idea. Why don't I come up to the suburbs? We'll go to Wildfire and we won't drink. We'll just have a good meal. And then we'll get some dessert, chocolate chip cheesecake maybe. And we'll talk and hang out. We'll get to know each other a little better. That's all. Nothing more."

"I do like their cheesecake."

"Where do you live? I'll pick you up."

"No, that's okay. I'll meet you there."

"Okay. 7:30?"

"Sure."

When I hung up the phone, I thought about how tired I was, how much more work I had to do today, how I was planning to get to bed early, and how I had to be up at the crack of dawn to go downtown for divorce attorney meetings tomorrow. Was I crazy for making plans tonight? Maybe so, but I couldn't deny the intense thrill I was feeling. I was more excited for tonight's date than I'd ever been about *any* date. And that included the ones I had with Brad Harrison!

Chapter 18

I walked into the restaurant about 5 minutes late. There stood Parker by the hostess stand, smiling at me, his big lower lip grazing one of his front teeth. Dressed in a pair of faded jeans and a plaid button down, he looked really cute.

We walked towards each other.

"Hi," I said, realizing I was shaking a little bit.

Parker gently kissed my cheek, which I thought was interesting (and heart stopping.) "Hi."

"Hi," I said again.

"Our table's ready," he replied. He seemed a little nervous, too, which was kind of funny to me.

"Right this way," said the hostess.

Parker motioned for me to walk in front of him, and I followed the hostess to our booth in the back.

We sat down and a waiter came over almost instantly and asked if we wanted anything to drink.

"Ice tea, please," I said to the waiter.

"Iced tea?" Parker asked.

"Yup. No drinks for me tonight."

"Don't trust yourself?"

"There's the bluntness I can't get enough of."

Parker chuckled and said, "Touché."

"For you, sir?" the waiter asked.

"I'll have what the lady's having."

Dinner went really well. The conversation was light and funny and fun and interesting, and even though I was nervous, as anyone would be on a first date (especially a first after-divorce date), I felt strangely comfortable, too. It was as if I was having dinner with an old friend.

"So, you started telling me last night...your sister owns a cupcake bakery in Manhattan?"

"Yep."

"That's so cool. Are you guys close?"

"Yes and no. I love her dearly, but I don't see her half as much as I'd like to."

"Why not?"

"Cause I'm an idiot."

"That's harsh."

"Well, I am. Over the years, I've just turned into a workaholic who never has time for her family."

"What about your parents? Do you see *them?"*

"My dad died when I was 16 and my mom passed away a few years ago."

"Oh, I'm so sorry."

"Yeah. It's weird having no parents. I really don't know anyone my age who has lost both their parents."

"How did they die?"

"My dad died in a car accident and my mom actually died of pneumonia. It was a really fluke thing. She was such a healthy person, and one day she got sick and her body just couldn't fight it off. She died three weeks later."

"Wow. I'm so sorry."

"You said that already," I smiled.

"Sorry. I can't even imagine. I'm so close to my parents. Not sure I'll be able to handle their deaths."

"Well, I hope it doesn't happen for a long, long time."

"Hey, you have something in your teeth."

"What?!" On impulse, I put my hand over my mouth and Parker chuckled.

I took out a make-up mirror from my purse, looked at it, and sure enough, a big piece of lettuce was hanging out in the middle of my two front teeth. "God, how embarrassing," I said, trying to keep my mouth closed while I retrieved it. "Gone?" I asked my date with a forced grin.

"Yes."

I put the mirror away. "I thought we were in the middle of a serious conversation."

"We were. Having food in your teeth is a pretty serious thing."

I laughed.

"Do you always tell your dates when they have food in their teeth?"

"Only if I like them. If I don't, then I don't really care."

"Again with the brutal honesty," I said with a laugh.

Parker made me feel like he and I had known each other for years, like he was an old friend. Yet, I also found myself insanely physically attracted. It had started at Starbucks, when I didn't even like his personality. When I saw him at Hub 51, it was even worse. And tonight, well, I pretty much had a strong urge to rip off his clothes. It was crazy! And exciting.

Unlike Paul, Parker wasn't drop dead gorgeous. He was nice looking, but it was something else. It was his eyes. They were deep, dark brown, and they were incredibly sexy at the same time. The look in his eyes was telling me he'd give me anything I needed.

I was sure he'd be an incredible lover, warm and tender and gentle. And his lips, especially that bottom lip. I wanted to kiss that lip. Both his lips, actually, and I'm not talking about a gentle smooch. I had this urge to devour his mouth, and I wanted to put my hands all over his body. I kept envisioning what it would be like looking at his eyes while his body was on mine. It was nuts.

How would Parker feel about a non-emotional, purely physical relationship with the divorced girl? I wondered. He could be my post-marital Brad Harrison. After all, I wasn't ready to date anyone, but maybe good, old fashioned, meaningless, out of the ballpark great sex was what I needed right now.

Maybe this was the time for a no-strings attached relationship. After all, wasn't that what people going through a divorce were supposed to do? Have meaningless physical affairs at the beginning? That seemed so much more doable to me than going on dates, making polite conversation and ending the night with a peck on the lips at the front door, wondering if you said the right things.

"Can I ask you something?" Parker asked.

"Sure."

"Why are you so nervous?"

"Don't flatter yourself. I'm so not nervous."

"Okay," Parker chuckled.

"But let's just say I'm a little bit nervous."

"Just hypothetically."

"Right. Hypothetically, why would I be nervous? Gee, I have no clue. Maybe it has something to do with the fact that this is my first date in about eleven years?"

"I don't think that's the reason."

"Then tell me, smart ass," I said with a giggle, "What's the reason?"

"If I tell you in my straightforward way that you now know and love, you have to promise you're not going to get pissed off, or even more so, you have to swear you won't get up and run out of here."

"I swear," I said.

"I think you're thinking about what it would be like to have sex with me."

"That's what you think?"

"Yup."

"Please, you are so far off."

"I don't think so."

"Well, to tell you the truth, Parker, the thought did cross my mind to use you as my boy toy."

"No thanks."

"What?!"

"Yes, I'm passing up sex with you."

I stood up.

"You swore you wouldn't run out of here."

"Damn!" I said, sitting back down.

Parker had a big grin on his face that made me smile.

"So, tell me, why don't you want to have sex with me?" I asked, "Do you find me unattractive?"

Parker did something at this moment that I will remember for the rest of my life. "Give me your hands," he said. Then he took my hands across the table. "Would I like to take you home with me and put you in my bed right now? A hundred percent yes. But, I want to take my time with this, with us, especially because of where you are right now."

"You really like me, don't you?"

"Yeah," he smiled.

We sat there smiling at each other and then Parker said, "I have a confession to make. When I first met you, I felt really guilty because I was attracted to you, and here I was trying to buy your engagement ring for Lilly. Looking back, I think that's when I realized it wasn't right with her."

"I have to tell you something, too," I said.

"What?"

"When I was interviewing you at Starbucks, I was really jealous of Lilly."

Parker said nothing. Instead, he just sat there with a slight smile on his face, looking into my eyes. I gazed back at him, too nervous to look away and scared to death about having just been so honest.

After what seemed like a long time, he said softly, "Should we get the check?"

No more than six minutes later, I was pulling into my garage, and my date was pulling in right behind me. We got out of our cars, and Parker walked toward me. There were no words, only desire.

Our first kiss took place right there in my garage. The second I hit the remote to close the garage door, he took my face in his hands and began kissing me, and I thought my entire body was going to explode. His lips felt soft and warm, he smelled great, and his hands on me felt delightful.

A hunger was building in me, a hunger for lust and sex and nakedness that I hadn't had in years. No matter how hard I kissed him, I wanted more intensity. I couldn't get enough of his lips and his tongue and his smell and his arms and just him. It was like I wanted to breathe him in.

"Let's go inside," I said, urgency in my voice. Then, I took his hand and led him into my house. We made our way to the couch in the family room and continued to kiss for what seemed like hours.

"Hey, Missy?" Parker said in between kisses.

"Yeah?"

"I'm glad your husband dumped you."

"You give new meaning to the word honesty," I said with a giggle.

"I'm not glad for *you.* I'm glad for *me.*"

I responded by kissing Parker as hard as I possibly could. The hunger was getting more intense. We kissed and kissed for a long time, but that's as far as it went.

When we were both exhausted, I put my head down on Parker's chest. I felt safe and secure and for lack of a better word, loved, if only temporarily. I closed my eyes and rested, thinking maybe Parker wasn't the only one who was glad I got dumped. Maybe the divorced girl was glad, too.

Chapter 19

"Hi, I'm here to see Richard Wexler," I told the receptionist on the 46th floor of the posh downtown office building where the law firm of *Stern, Meisner and Wexler* is located.

Richard Wexler was the second of the two attorneys I had appointments with today, and I was really looking forward to it because there was absolutely no way in hell I was going to hire the first lawyer I'd met with. Her name was Patricia Reese and at first she seemed more than competent. It was obvious Patricia knew how to argue a case. She wasn't a pushover. She seemed really headstrong and I got the impression she'd be great at negotiating a good settlement.

The problem was, when I told her about the ring, her response was the same as Harvey Firestone's: hand over the ring, sell it and split the proceeds.

I tried to explain my rationale for wanting to do things my way. "You're a woman, Patricia," I said to her, "Can't you understand how I feel? I want this ring to go to a good guy. I want something good to come out of all of this."

"Look, Missy," she responded, "I'd like to have your business, believe me. And I think I can get you a great settlement. But this ring thing is ridiculous."

The second she said "ridiculous," I stood up.

"Thanks for your time," I said coldly. As I was walking out, I heard her say, "Mrs. Benson, please don't go."

I turned around, only to say, "It's *Ms.* Benson, soon to be *Ms.* Margaret, which is my maiden name that my new divorce attorney will include in my divorce decree when I hire him or her."

Patricia stood there speechless while I walked out, my head held high and my self-confidence just as good as it had been when I fired Harvey Firestone. Only now, I wondered if I'd ever find a lawyer who would side with me on something that probably seemed "ridiculous" to most people, but mattered to me immensely. I almost felt like if I didn't follow through with giving my ring to a worthy guy, it would be impossible to move on. Maybe I was crazy, I wasn't sure, but I wasn't giving up.

So, as I waited for Richard Wexler to come into my life, I said a prayer. "Please God," I prayed silently, "Let Richard, who I've never met before understand how I'm feeling."

"You must be Missy," I heard a voice call out. I turned and there stood a slightly overweight, but kind of cute middle-aged man.

"Richard?" I said, standing up and extending my hand.

"Yes," he answered with a smile, shaking my hand. "Come on back." He motioned for me to walk ahead of him.

As I made my way down the hallway of the law firm, Richard right behind me, I had this weird feeling that my search was over. There was something very comfortable about this place and these people, and I got this warm, safe feeling.

When Richard and I sat down in his office and began talking about my divorce and my *craigslist* ad, however, warm and safe turned to cold and uncomfortable, and basically, I once again felt defeated.

"I'm going to be completely honest with you," said Richard, "Aside from a sure loss in court over this thing, you would have to be completely nuts to give away something with that kind of value. I'm positive that as time passes and as feelings of loss and sentimentality fade, you'll see things more clearly and from a more practical point."

I was just about to go off on Richard when I heard a knock at the door.

"Come in," he said. The door opened and an absolutely beautiful African American woman appeared in the doorway.

"Sorry to interrupt. May I borrow that box of Kleenex?" she asked, pointing to the box on Richard's desk.

"Sure," said Richard, leaning over his desk to grab the tissue box. He handed it to her and said, "Please don't tell me your client is crying, and if she is, she must be tearing up with happiness from all the money she was just awarded."

"Richard," said this not only beautiful, but classy and poised, as well, thirty-something woman, "I don't care how much money my client ended up with. She is grieving. Her divorce was final today, and while she might be very happy, ecstatic even, with her monetary settlement, this poor woman is mourning. She's suffering. Her marriage of twenty-six years is legally over today. What's wrong with you? What are you, the tin man? Where's your heart?" She turned to me. "I apologize for interrupting. Lawyers often forget about feelings and they only see dollar signs, and honestly, I'm sick of it. Good luck." She gave me a polite smile and closed the door.

"I'm sorry," said Richard, "Where were we?"

I looked at Richard, feeling like a four year old kid whose parents just told her they're taking her to Disney World and said, "Please don't take this personally, but I think I just found the perfect attorney for me."

Richard looked confused for a second until the light went on that I preferred to work with the kind-hearted woman who had just poked her head into his office, the lawyer who measured feelings into the mix of divorce, rather than seeing it solely as a business deal. Not that I didn't care about coming out ok monetarily, but for me, I needed someone who would fight for principles as well, and the woman I'd just gotten a glimpse of seemed like she would fight.

"Wait here," he said, "Let me see if Denise can speak with you."

"Thank you," I said.

Richard left his office and came back two minutes later. He handed me a business card and said, "If you can wait in the reception area for about fifteen minutes, Denise Williamson said she will be free then, and happy to speak with you."

"Thank you, Richard," I said, standing up and extending my hand to shake his, "Again, I hope you won't take this personally."

Richard smiled and shook my hand. Then he said, "I went through a divorce last year. Trust me, it's really important that you *love* your attorney."

As I sat happily waiting for Denise in the lobby, I realized how right Richard was. I was already in love with Denise. She looked more like a supermodel than a divorce attorney, but it was obvious she was smart. She'd get me my ring. Or at least she'd try. I was sure of it.

Less than a half hour later, I was in her office, telling her about *craigslist.*

"Wow, that's really something," she responded.

"So, what do you think?" I asked her.

Denise didn't answer right away. She was pensive, just sitting there for awhile, staring at me.

"If you could have your husband back right now, would you take him back?"

"No!"

"Are you saying that because you know you can't have him and you're being defensive, or do you really mean it?"

"I think I mean it. I've had a few months to digest things and I realize now how abnormal my life with Paul was. We led very separate lives. And looking back, it was lonely. I'm lonely now, but it's different. I'm not living a lie, and I feel good about that."

"Here, sweetie," said Denise, handing me a Kleenex. That's when I realized I was crying.

"Missy, what do you hope to gain from giving away such an expensive piece of jewelry?"

"You look like Halle Berry," I answered.

"Answer my question," she said gently.

I looked at Denise, my eyes still filled with tears. "Hope," I whispered, "That's what I want. Hope."

Denise gave me a gentle smile and said, "I was married for three years. My husband left me for another woman. It's been five years now. They have two children and from what I've heard they are very happy. And me, I'm alone still. I don't even have a boyfriend."

"That's a horrible story. Are you okay?"

"Yes. I really am. And guess what? I still have my ring. It's sitting in a drawer because I have no idea what to do with it."

"Will you represent me or not?"

"I can't guarantee I'll get you your ring."

"Will you try?"

"Yes," she grinned, "I will."

Chapter 20

Age 33…

I'm sitting at my desk surfing the internet, looking into different diets and how they affect fertility. I'm getting more and more desperate every month. I've tried everything. I've quit drinking alcohol and caffeine, I've used ovulation kits, I have sex with my husband five times a week (which honestly is like a full time job with no benefits,) and I'm not lying or trying to be funny when I say that for the past three months I've been standing on my head after sex for 15 minutes. And still, no babies.

Paul and I have both been tested and nothing seems to be out of the ordinary. So, why a 33 year old healthy woman and her 35 year old healthy husband can't make a baby is an enigma to me. Although, I have my suspicions and it has to do with God not really having faith in my mothering ability. But I don't let myself go there.

I look around me. All my friends are having babies or are pregnant, some with their second and third child. Nan has two kids already, Catherine has one, and Anna is pregnant with her first. She and her husband decided that as soon as she passed the bar, they were going to start trying to have kids. She passed the bar three months ago. Bingo. She's knocked up.

What's wrong with me? According to my doctor, nothing. "Keep trying," he says, "It will happen." When I asked about fertility treatments, he advised us to wait a year before pursuing anything. Eight months we've been trying.

Four months to go and then I'm running to a fertility specialist. I want to be a mother!

My phone rings. It's Anna.

We chat for awhile and she tells me how she just had her ultrasound and heard the heartbeat. I'm so happy for her, but deep down I'm so envious I can barely breathe. And I hate myself because of that. I also have some self-loathing because I've never met even one of my best friends' children. Not even one. Never laid eyes in person on Nan's two children, or Catherine's child. What a shitty friend I am.

I rationalize that I'm busy working, and when I go home for the holidays, I'm too focused on spending time with my mom and my sister to stop by and say hi to anyone. But deep down, I realize how terrible that is.

"I have something to ask you," says Anna, "The three of us are planning another girls' trip in June and I want you to come. We're going to San Francisco."

I immediately decline. "Sorry, I wish I could but June is one of the busiest months for me."

"So fucking what?" says Anna, "So June's busy. I'm sure the real estate market's not going to fall apart for four days without you there."

"I know, it's just..."

"Come on, Missy," Anna says, her voice filled with sarcasm, "Quick! Think of another excuse."

I sit there not knowing what to say.

Anna's tone lightens. "You know, once you signed up to be one of the Cinnamon Girls, didn't you know it was for life? Come on, Miss, take a trip with us. The three of us have been to Mexico, New York City, Cape Cod, San Antonio... We even went to London two years ago. Come with us. Just one time. You'll love it. I guarantee you'll never miss one of our trips again. Ever. We miss you!"

"I miss you guys, too," I say, "Let me think about it."

"Okay," she says, "But I know you won't go."

"Really, I'll consider it."

"Right," she says.

"Hey, Anna?"

"Yeah?"

"I really am happy about your pregnancy."

"I know you are girlfriend."

"I'll think about San Francisco."

Anna almost seems defeated. "Sure you will," she says. Before I can defend myself again, she says, "Oh shit! Here comes by boss. I've got to go."

I sit there with the receiver still up to my ear, thinking of how bad a friend I am because I'm not even considering going to San Francisco. I know my mom will tell me to take the trip. So will Gina. Even Paul will tell me to go. He likes the Cinnamon Girls. He's always asking why I don't make more of an effort to see them.

"It seems like you guys were so close in high-school," he said to me once, "And you still wear that necklace that says Cinnamon."

Paul's right. I do still wear my necklace. I wear it a lot, actually. It gives me an identity in a lot of ways. It says that I am someone's friend, and that people care about me, that I'm loved, that I'm part of something. I wish the necklace had magical powers, and that it could convince my brain that all those things are true.

At this moment I get a text from Anna. "Please come to San Fran. Your friend, Anna, nickname Chubby."

The trip… I really should go. When am I going to start enjoying myself and doing fun things? When am I going to reconnect (other than standard phone calls on birthdays and Christmas cards) with my closest friends? I really should go.

On the other hand, I need to focus on my job. I need to concentrate on getting pregnant. That's what I tell myself. Deep down, though, I know exactly what I'm doing. I'm trying to erase a little secret buried in my past by keeping my distance from the people who love me the most in life: my three best friends.

Chapter 21

"I don't know if I can do this anymore," said J.J., now on her second Frappuccino and seeming almost defeated, "I'm so sick of these guys who clearly don't deserve your ring."

"Just two more for the day," I told her.

"I mean, that last guy, was it necessary for him to tell us that he still brings his laundry home for his mother to do every Sunday?"

"I think the guy before him, Carl was worse," I said, lowering my voice to imitate the weirdo, "The man handles all the finances and the woman handles the kitchen. That's the way it's always been and that's the way it should be."

J.J. started laughing and joined in the imitation, "Cathy knows that and that's why our relationship works."

I continued imitating Carl, "Cathy knows her role."

In her own voice, J.J. replied, "Cathy needs to run away from this guy as quickly as possible."

I agreed. But it wasn't just Carl. The day had offered disappointment after disappointment after disappointment, and I wasn't sure how much more I could take. Yet, coming off the date I'd had with Parker the night before, coupled with the fact that I now had the best divorce attorney on earth, the compassionate, caring Denise Williamson, I was energized and optimistic, despite six complete idiots, one who told me that he couldn't stand his girlfriend's kids, but that they'd be "in college and out of the picture soon."

Other highlights included a guy who had to excuse himself to check in with his parole officer, and perhaps the funniest, a guy who had a germ phobia. After shaking my hand, he pulled out a sample bottle of hand sanitizer. I wouldn't have thought much about it, except that after he used some on his hands, he proceeded to take a piece of cloth from his pocket, squeeze sanitizer on it, and then wipe his seat, his coffee cup and *my* coffee cup.

Oh, one more story. One of the guys asked, "May I see the ring?"

"Sure," I replied, pulling out the photo I showed to all the guys.

"What's this?" he said, "I want to see the actual ring."

"I don't have it with me," I answered, "I don't feel right about carrying it around. But, if I decide you might be the right person to buy it, I'll show it to you at our next meeting. Is that all right?"

The guy stood up and got in my face. "No! I want to see it right now!"

With a nervous giggle, I replied, "But I don't have it."

"How do I know you're not lying about this whole thing? Maybe this picture is bullshit! Maybe there *is* no ring."

J.J. intervened, "Why would we waste our time doing this if there was no ring?"

"I don't know, but I don't trust you girls. I'm out of here. I'm going to report you to *craigslist* and the Better Business Bureau! Plan on hearing from them!"

As he walked out the door, J.J. shouted, "Okay, but we're not a business!"

So, two hours later, to say the two of us were tired and frustrated and losing hope was putting it mildly. But in an instant, things changed. The first thing that happened to change the karma of our afternoon was a text from Parker.

"Do you have a new lawyer? Do you have a ring buyer? I have a bad case of Missy-itis."

"Yes, no and what are your symptoms?" I texted back.

"Warm all over, can't stop smiling, and craving more Missy."

I giggled, thinking how great life had just become. Yes, Paul dumped me, but in all the years we were together, would he have ever texted (or said or e-mailed or written) anything even remotely as romantic and witty as this? That would be a firm "no."

I showed J.J. the text.

"Do you realize if you marry him, your name's going to be Missy Missoni?"

"Glad you brought that up since I'm really thinking about marriage right now."

All of a sudden I heard a voice. "Excuse me, are either of you two Missy?"

I looked up and standing beside me was a really cute guy who looked just like Will Smith. I tried not to act too star struck. "Yes, that's me," I said with a grin, "Are you Derek?"

The hottie extended his hand and said confidently, "Yes, Derek Graham."

I shook his hand. "Hi."

J.J. pushed her way in and gushed, "Hi! I'm J.J., Missy's assistant."

Derek smiled and shook her hand.

He and I sat down while J.J. went to get him a Grande Frappuccino.

"So, tell me about Cassie. How'd you two meet?"

"It's a great story," answered Derek. "Actually, we got in a car accident. She was at a stoplight and I hit her from behind. She got out of her car and started shouting at me, and man, she was mad."

Derek's voice suddenly got higher, as he imitated his girlfriend. "'Are you crazy?! Are you on drugs?! What were you thinking?!'" At this point, he chuckled and went back to his normal voice. "She's standing there just going off on me, and all I could focus on was how sexy-angry she looked. She had her hands on her curvy hips and I noticed her high cheek bones and her big, beautiful lips. She's shouting at me, and all I could think about was how much I wanted to kiss her.

Deep down, in my gut, I knew that beneath her rage, there was a soft, sweet girl who would really like me if she got to know me. She was focused on her car at that moment, and I was focused on how lucky I was that I ran into her. Literally. I fell in love with her right then and there."

"That's interesting..." I said, wondering at this point if Derek was genuine. Hoping so, actually.

He went on, "Finally she asked me if I was going to say something. I smiled and said, 'I'm sorry Miss. Truly. Let me make it up to you. May I take you to dinner?'"

"What did she say?" I asked.

"She goes..." Again Derek changed his voice to imitate his girlfriend. "'Take me to dinner? Are you nuts?! What I need is a rental car while mine's in the shop! I have a job. I have responsibilities! I don't have time for dinner, especially with a person like you!'"

I was thoroughly entertained at this point. "Really?" I asked him.

"Yeah," he said with a laugh.

"So, what happened?"

"I ended up convincing her not to call the police and report the accident. I told her that if she'd go out with me, I'd pay for her car and loan her mine while hers was being fixed."

"And she agreed?"

"Yup. I took the bus to work for over a week."

"Wow, that's really something."

"Yeah, lucky," he said with a wink.

J.J. came back with his drink and Derek answered some more of our questions about his girlfriend and about their relationship. He was very entertaining and his stories were funny, hard to believe almost, but Derek seemed like a real guy. Talking to him was so easy and comfortable, and I really felt his genuine love for his girlfriend.

"What is it about Cassie that you love the most?" I asked him.

"Her ass!"

My facial expression must instantly have gone from happy and hopeful to shock and dismay. I say that because Derek immediately apologized. "Missy, I was just kidding. I didn't mean to offend you, I'm sorry."

"Then why'd you say it?" asked J.J.

"The truth is," he said, "I do love Cassie's butt. It's sexy." Derek's tone suddenly got serious, a side I hadn't seen until now. He continued, "This relationship is so much more than that. I'm divorced. Cassie's divorced. She has a little boy named Kenneth. He's nine. He's such a great kid, because Cassie's such a great mother. She's so many things. She's smart and funny and sassy, and her heart's the size of Chicago. And yeah, the first time I saw her, I was focused on my physical attraction to this angry, sexy woman. But we've been together for three years, and even though the attraction is as strong as it has ever been, it's so much more.

I want all of her. I want to marry her in a church, in front of God and in front of all of our family and friends. I want her to have more kids. With me! I want us to be together for the rest of our lives."

At this moment I was sold. I knew instinctively that Derek was a good guy, and *the guy.* There was no question in my mind, and I felt hope like I hadn't felt in ages.

We had to say good-bye to Derek because the last interviewee for the day was waiting. Otherwise, I think the three of us would have sat there talking for hours. Derek was just one of those people whose story-telling ability and personable demeanor was infectious. He made me laugh, and he had this way of drawing me in to everything he'd talk about.

Since the last guy we spoke with ended up trying to talk us into becoming Jehovah's Witnesses, we quickly dismissed him. Not that I have anything against freedom of religion, but he wouldn't let it go, to the point where he told me he didn't think he wanted my ring unless I converted first.

After he left, I realized the search was over. There were two ring finalists. One was Derek Graham, the tall, dark heart-throb who had a passion for curves and sass. The other: Tony Lionetti, the nice, wholesome Italian boy who loved his sweet, giving school teacher girlfriend.

Just before we left, I got another text from Parker. "Can I cook dinner for you Saturday night?"

I showed it to J.J., who replied, "Ahh...the divorced girl has a date."

I laughed.

"Missy Missoni..." she continued, "It has a nice ring to it."

Chapter 22

Parker lived on the second floor of a charming vintage brownstone on Wells Street in the city. As I rang his buzzer, red wine bottle in hand, I found myself really nervous, in a good way, though. Excited to see him again, but scared of the reality that intimacy (okay, let's not sugarcoat it–sex) could be in my near future. I, Missy Benson could very well end up naked with someone new for the first time in more than a decade. And that was terrifying.

"Be right there!" Parker shouted over the intercom. Seconds later, he opened the door and when I saw him, I literally melted. He had on jeans and a brown wool Polo sweater with a white t-shirt underneath. It was indisputable. He was just so cute.

"Hi!" he said with a smile. Then he kissed me on the cheek and said, "Come on up!" I followed him up a flight of stairs and inside his apartment.

The whole place was filled with a strong smell of something baking. I wasn't sure exactly what it was, but it was undoubtedly Italian.

I took a deep breath in to get more of it. "Something smells really good."

"Homemade pizza," he said, "My grandma's recipe."

"Homemade?" I smiled, "Impressive."

Three seconds I'd been in his place and I was beyond touched. This adorable guy had made me something homemade. It was endearing. I handed him the wine, which he thanked me for with a soft, gentle kiss on the lips.

"Let me take your coat," he then said, extending his arm to for it, "I'll show you around."

I gave him my coat, which he placed over a random wooden chair that was close to the entryway, and the tour began.

As a realtor, I'd probably seen over 10,000 homes in my career, and I had staged and fixed up thousands of single guys' condos to get them ready to sell. If Parker was moving tomorrow, he'd never sell this place. It was warm and comfortable, just like him, but it truly was a bachelor pad that needed some touching up.

The wood floors were nice, but they desperately needed refinishing. All of his furniture looked like it came straight from his college apartment. Hanging on the walls were several sports pictures, including a group picture of the Chicago Bears in 1985, a 12x16 photo of John Paxson making the championship basket in the NBA finals in 1991, and a World Cup poster from 1994, the year it was held in Chicago.

The place wasn't dirty, though, and when I told Parker I was impressed by that, he informed me that he'd recently hired a cleaning woman who had just been here yesterday.

After the quick tour of his pad, Parker poured me some wine in a wine glass he told me he bought that day. Then he instructed me to sit at his kitchen table (which was already set and had lit candles on it) and relax. He took the pizza out of the oven and then he served me! And it was truly delicious.

Parker drank *Moretti* beer and I drank more wine, and we ate and talked and had the best time. We talked about my business and he told me he'd never dated anyone as wealthy as I was.

"How do you know I'm wealthy?"

"Well, let's see. You're giving away a thirty-six thousand dollar ring..."

I smiled. "Fine, I have money. It doesn't really matter, though. I never spend any of it."

"Why not? What are you waiting for?"

"I don't know. I just work all the time."

"Well, what do you like to do for fun?"

I was speechless. I had no answer. I took another bite of pizza crust. Parker was still waiting for me to speak, but I had nothing to say.

"Missy, you need a hobby, girl! That's what money's for. To spend. To enjoy yourself. To have fun."

"Parker, can I ask you something?"

"Sure."

"Why did you really want my ring? I mean, you have money, right? You could have bought Lilly a ring."

Parker smiled, "Yes, I do have some money saved, and I could have gone out and bought Lilly a diamond. But the thing is, I felt like what you did was really, really romantic, and I wanted to be a part of that."

"Getting a ring from the divorced girl whose husband dumped her is romantic?"

"Why do you call yourself the divorced girl?"

"Because that's what I am."

"That's hot," he joked.

I laughed.

"But seriously, having this contest, or whatever you want to call it, truly is romantic. Face it, the divorced girl is looking for love. Maybe not directly for yourself, but you're interested in validating that true love exists. And that's what's romantic about it."

"It's funny. Paul used to tell me I was the most unromantic, unemotional person he knew."

"Well, maybe it had something to do with *him,* because clearly, whether you want to admit it or not, you're into romance."

All I could do was smile and shake my head.

"What?" he asked me.

"You get me."

Parker just smiled, and he and I sat in silence for a few moments, looking so directly into each other's eyes, it was as if our souls were having a conversation. It was unbelievably strange. And very sexy.

Parker finally broke the silence. "So, since we now know you're an idealistic dreamer, what's your favorite movie?"

With a grin, I took a deep breath. "If you'd have asked me that up until a few weeks ago, I'd have told you *The Godfather.*"

"And now?"

"Don't laugh, okay?"

"Promise."

"*An Officer and a Gentleman.*"

He exclaimed, "I love that movie!"

"You do not."

"Yes, I do!"

"Really? You don't think it's corny?"

"Nope."

At this very moment, the divorced girl was falling hard.

"Tell me yours," I said.

"My favorite movie?" he asked.

"In the romance genre."

He thought for a moment and then said, "Have you ever seen *Something's Gotta Give*?"

"I think so. Is that with Jack Nicholson?"

"Yup."

"That's a great movie."

Parker cleared his throat and then in a deep voice, imitating Jack Nicholson, said, "I'm 63 years old and I'm in love for the first time in my life."

"That's good dialogue," I said softly.

"Come here," he said.

I got up from my chair, sat on his lap, put my arms around his neck and hugged him for a long time. It felt safe and warm.

He gently pulled away, and looked right into my eyes. I couldn't understand how I could feel so intense with someone I didn't know very well. I realized at this moment that I had probably never looked at my own husband this way. I felt a comfort I wasn't sure I'd ever felt. "You're finally here," I wanted to say to this man I barely knew.

He took my face in his hands and began kissing me. It was at this moment I realized the gratitude I felt for being the divorced girl.

Chapter 23

Parker's lips were on mine, his strong arms were wrapped around my waist, and my fingers were spread out in his soft, dark hair. It was even more electrifying and breathtaking as it had been a few nights earlier, and I truly could have kissed him for days. My outlook changed suddenly when he tried to take off my shirt.

"Parker," I whispered, "Don't."

"Why?"

"I'm not ready yet. Is that okay?"

Parker smiled at me. "Yes, I understand. Instead of staying here and having the best sex of our lives, I have a great idea."

I giggled.

"It's still early. Think you might want to go out?"

"Where? To a bar?"

"Yeah, it'll be fun. Or, we can stay here and get naked. You pick," he joked.

I did want to get naked with Parker, but I'd chickened out. So, after a four minute cab ride, I found myself at Shannon's, a little Irish pub in Lincoln Park. Parker led me to the back of the bar where karaoke was going on. A cute, petite twenty-something blonde girl was up on the little stage singing *I Will Survive*. There were about 20 people dancing in front of her and cheering her on. She was actually really good.

Parker looked at me and shouted over the loud music, "What are you going to sing?"

"You think I'm getting up there?" I shouted back.

"Sure, why not?"

"Because I can't sing!"

"Be right back!"

Parker disappeared for a few minutes and came back with two beers. "I just put my name in!"

I laughed. "Looking forward to hearing you!"

"I'm really good!" he shouted.

"I'm sure!"

I didn't give Parker enough credit, because when he got on stage and sang Bruno Mars' *When I Was Your Man,* I was stunned at how talented he really was. He had a great singing voice, plus, he had a stage presence that was really natural. He seriously looked like a professional entertainer.

When I told him all this later, he just laughed. "I actually come here a lot. I love to sing in front of a crowd." Then he asked, "What's it going to take to get *you* up there? How about another cocktail?"

"There's not enough alcohol on the planet to make me get up and sing in front of people. It's just not my style."

We stayed and listened to a few more singers, among them a heavy-set older guy who sang Stevie Wonder's *For Once in my Life,* a really funny Asian kid who sang Styx's *Too Much Time on my Hands,* and a cougar-looking woman who sounded exactly like Katy Perry when she sang *Waking Up In Vegas.*

Then there was this cute, young guy who sang John Mayer's *Daughters.* It made me smile because he reminded me of Brad Harrison (my sex-crazed ex boyfriend.) Brad was a much better singer, but this guy had a way about him that made me think about the guy who was capable of seducing me with so much as a certain look in his eyes. I wondered for a brief second, as I did so often these days if Brad was still traveling around Chicago, singing in various clubs.

A few minutes later, Parker got called back up. I didn't realize he had put his name in again, so I was thoroughly surprised, but entertained, nonetheless.

"This song is dedicated to the romantic Missy Benson," he announced. Everyone clapped and I think I turned ten shades of red. Parker smiled at me, and I heard some music begin that I didn't recognize. All I could tell was that it was slow and sounded like an oldie. He began to sing.

"Me and Mrs. Jones...we got a thing going on...we both know that it's wrong, but it's much too strong to let it go now. We meet every day...at the same café, 6:30 I know I know she'll be there. Holding hands, making all kinds of plans...while the juke box plays our favorite song..."

At this point, the entire audience (including myself) joined in and blared out with him, *"Me and Mrs. Mrs. Jones...we got a thing goin' on..."*

Parker continued, *"We both know that it's wrong, but it's much too strong to let it go now..."*

As I stood there swaying to the music, listening to this adorable guy sing, and singing along during parts of this awesome oldie one hit wonder, I realized something. Yes, I was a soon-to-be divorcee, a cliché, whose husband moved on without discussing things with me. But what wasn't a cliché was that life really does go on.

I was having fun, I was living, I was on a date with someone I never would have met had I still been trapped in a marriage that just wasn't right. What a wonderful gift I had been given, the freedom to find a new life, to find happiness, because I was released from something that didn't really work.

As a result of Paul leaving me, and subsequently having no use for my ring, I had put an ad on *craigslist,* looking for a ring buyer, and looking for love, but not for myself. In that process, I'd sure met some nut cases, but I had met a few really good guys as well, and I'd met my two finalists.

There was Tony, the cute, sweet Italian boy next door whose parents were immigrants and whose family values seemed to be nothing but honorable and commendable. Then there was Derek, full of life, vibrant, funny, and passionate.

I couldn't wait to get to know both guys better, delve into their relationships, and confirm that love was real, and that it would last, unlike my failed marriage.

The other person I'd met as a result of the events Paul had set in motion was the physical therapist currently up on stage, smiling at me and channeling his inner Billy Paul while singing the one hit wonder, *Me and Mrs. Jones.* And just as he did with everything else in life, including shopping for engagement rings and cooking and kissing, Parker sang with passion. Watching him was truly taking my breath away. So, without Paul making a move, I wouldn't have had any of this.

When the song was over, the crowd erupted in applause, and Parker hammed it up with a big bow. He also threw a couple kisses into the crowd. Then he came off stage and back to me.

"How was I?" he asked excitedly.

All I could do was throw my arms around him and hug him tight. I could hear Parker laughing over the beginning of the next song, Michael Jackson's *Man in the Mirror.*

In the cab ride back to his place, I asked him, "Why did you pick that song?"

"Me and Mrs. Jones? I love it. It's a classic."

"I like that song too, but I never understood it."

"What do you mean?" he asked me.

"Well, he and Mrs. Jones really love each other, right?"

Parker seemed intrigued. "Yeah, so?"

"So, they're okay with meeting every morning and that's it?"

"Yeah, but that's all they could do." Then Parker sang, *"Cause she's got her own obligations. And so... do I..."*

"I know, I know...but still, why didn't they do something about it? She could have left Mr. Jones. Gotten a divorce."

"Don't you think they thought of that?"

"I don't care. If they loved each other that deeply, they should have made sure they were together. They shouldn't have just kept things the way they were, and settled for just seeing each other every morning for breakfast."

"Oh, it was breakfast?"

"Yeah, 6:30."

"I thought it was 6:30 at night."

"Whatever time of day it was, they should have tried harder to have something more than one meal a day together. Don't you understand that?!"

Parker grinned.

"What? Don't you agree?" I asked.

"You? Not a romantic?"

All I could do was smile.

When we got back to Parker's place, he asked me if I wanted to stay over.

"Parker, I told you, I'm not ready."

He gently took my shoulders and said softly, "Missy, I want you in my bed. I won't touch you, I promise. Even though you're passing up the best sex you'll ever have in your life."

"How do you know it's the best?"

"Because girls have told me that?"

"And I'm sure they all mean it."

Parker laughed. "Listen, I just want to sleep next to you. Are you comfortable with that? Do you think you want to sleep next to me tonight?"

"Yes," I answered, giving him a gentle kiss on the lips. Then he got me a pair of basketball shorts with a drawstring and a Bears t-shirt to wear to bed.

Lying there wrapped in his arms, I whispered, "Parker?"

"Yeah?"

"Thanks for the best date I've ever had."

"Really?"

"Yeah."

"You're welcome."

"Hey Parker?"

"Yeah?"

"Will you tell me a story to help me fall asleep?"

He kissed my cheek and whispered, "Just go to sleep."

"Please?"

"A story, really?"

"Yes."

"What are you, like five years old?"

"Yes, and I like stories about princesses."

"Princesses?"

"Yeah."

"Again, you're not a romantic at all."

I laughed.

A moment later, Parker began softly, "Okay, here goes. Once upon a time there was this dude…he was really, really short."

"Okay…" I giggled, "Is there a princess involved here?"

"Just listen."

"Okay, sorry."

"So this short guy…he was a wealthy prince who was supposed to marry this princess, which was arranged by his parents, the king and queen…"

That was the last thing I heard. As I was falling asleep, I was smiling. I can honestly say I'd never felt more comfortable and more at ease than I did at that moment in my life.

Chapter 24

Age 34…

I'm making love with Paul. It's 10:00 at night and I'm thinking about how much work I have to do. I'm also wishing I could turn on the news. I'm obsessed with finding out whether Chicago will be the city chosen for the 2016 Olympics, and I want to hear some commentary on the subject. Paul is kissing me. I'm kissing him back and I'm trying to get into it, but I can't.

Why do men put so much emphasis on sex? Why is it so important to them? Maybe it's me. When it comes to sex, I could take it or leave it. Although, I wasn't always this way…

At this moment, Brad Harrison pops into my head. I think about how much I used to crave him like a drug addict craves drugs. I'd be out at the bars with my girlfriends and I'd drag them all to the offbeat place where Brad's band was playing that night. I'd sit and watch him sing and I'd wait for him. I'd sit there until 2:00 a.m. Then he'd come home with me and we'd make love until the sun came up. That's the only time in my life I can ever remember feeling really, really sexual.

Paul whispers, "Baby…you're so hot…" and I start breathing heavy. It's fake, though.

"You feel so good," I whisper. I'm lying. Sex with Paul doesn't feel good. It feels obligatory. It feels phony. I'm practically rolling my eyes in my head, hoping he'll have had enough soon so I can check my e-mail.

I feel guilty about feeling this way, but the way he's been speaking to me lately gives me the right not to want him touching my body. He's been so mean to me, so short-tempered, so edgy. He keeps asking me to go off the pill and try to have another baby and I keep putting him off. I keep telling him I need more time. The truth is, though, I've decided I'm never getting pregnant again.

I hear his cell phone ring and I'm ecstatic because I know he'll get it. It will be one of the young lawyers from his office working late and he'll be putting out a fire for the next thirty minutes. When he gets off the phone he won't want to continue having sex. He'll grumble and complain about how much he hates work and then he'll go to sleep.

"God damn it" Paul shouts. As I predicted, he gets up to answer his phone.

"Yay!" I shout silently.

Chapter 25

Tony's Shoe Repair was started by Tony's dad, Alberto Lionetti, forty three years earlier. He started his business in Chicago, but when he and Mrs. Lionetti had kids, they decided to move to the suburbs. So, they moved their business there, too.

When I walked into the shop, a pair of broken Prada sling- backs in hand, Tony, (one of my two ring buying finalists) was ringing up a customer.

He smiled, "Hi Missy, I'll be right with you."

"Okay, thanks," I said.

A cute little bald-headed man (who I knew right away was Tony's dad) was behind the counter working intently, so much so, that he never even looked up.

While I waited, I watched Tony, this sweet, affable guy who had spoken about his girlfriend, Claudette with such respect, such admiration, and such love.

Tony seemed happy to be here working with his dad (or his "Paps," as he called him) and that pleased me. After all, I had to make sure that the guy who was getting my ring was content in his professional life. Because one thing I knew from my own failed marriage was that a happy union was impossible if the guy was miserable at work.

Yes, Paul had a high-paying job as an attorney, but all he ever did was complain about it, and that made it hard for me to respect him. And like him. The entire time we were married, it seemed like we had the same conversation over and over again.

"Why don't you look for another job?" I'd ask.

"Are you crazy?" he'd reply, bitterness in his voice, "There's no firm that would pay me what I'm making now."

I'd say, "So what? You can take a pay cut. We can certainly afford that with what I'm making. And if you're happier at another firm, why not?"

"Missy, please..." he would say, "If you want a baby, babies cost money. We need the money."

"Well, we don't have a baby yet," I'd say through gritted teeth, feeling like Paul just delivered a cruel jab, "If I ever get pregnant again, we'll worry about it then."

"What an irresponsible attitude," he'd mutter.

The all too familiar dialogue was frustrating, but at some point, frustration turned to apathy. I had listened and listened and listened to Paul telling me how unhappy he was and I just couldn't listen anymore. So, I turned off. At some point, I just stopped caring. If Paul hated his job, and he wasn't willing to do anything about it, than it was *his* problem, not mine.

What I was starting to realize, though, was that maybe I could have been more understanding, more sympathetic for a longer period of time. Because, after all, Paul being unhappy was *my* problem too. I would never know what might have been had I gone about things with my husband in a different way. What I did know, though, was that men who were happy at work were happier at home.

So, I had to make sure Tony liked doing what he did. I wanted there to be little chance he could wake up in 10 years realizing he hated his job, and then choose to get a girlfriend to try to make himself happier. If he was fulfilled in his work, his marriage had better odds for success, in my opinion.

Tony had told me in our initial meeting at Starbucks that he had gone to college at DePaul University and had studied European History and Psychology. He had made a deal with his parents that he would go off and study for four years, earn his degree, and then come back and work for the family business, and eventually take it over if he chose to do so.

Did Tony love being a shoe repairman? I couldn't tell yet, but one thing I sensed was that he was doing what he thought was expected of him, and he didn't appear to be bitter or have issues with it.

"Hi there," Tony exclaimed, coming out from behind the counter to shake my hand. I then saw his dad's head pop up.

"Paps, this is Missy Benson. Missy's my realtor," he lied, "Missy, this is my father, Alberto Lionetti."

"Nice meeting you," I said with a big grin.

Mr. Lionetti looked at me and replied in his very thick, loud Italian accent, "Same to you." Then he addressed his son. "Why you need this? You moving?"

"Paps, please…" said Tony.

"You no like where you live now? You get married soon. Then you and Claudette…you buy my house."

"Paps, why would I want to buy your house? You still live there. And did you forget about grandma, who happens to live there, too?"

Mr. Lionetti laughed heartily and replied, "Then we all live there together! The family!"

"Right, Paps, that's just what I want to do," Tony said with a warm chuckle, "Live with you and mom and grandma while I'm a newlywed. That would be really great for my sex life."

This is the point when I think I fell in love with Mr. Lionetti. "Ah…I forgot who I was speaking to—Mr. Smooth, Sexy guy…ladies man…chick magnet…" Then he started saying all this stuff in Italian that I didn't understand, but I could tell Tony knew what he was saying.

"Paps, please…" said Tony in between chuckles.

I burst out laughing, and at that moment I felt like I already knew so much about this family. It didn't take a lot to see how close they were. The love was so abundantly obvious.

"So, are these the shoes?" Tony said, taking the Prada's out of my hand.

"Yes," I said with a smile, almost role playing.

Tony and I had planned out this whole scenario. I wasn't really here to get my sandals fixed. In fact, I had broken the strap myself, purposely, just this morning. I was here for the purpose of implementing step number two in my ring giveaway contest: watch Tony is his workplace and meet his soon-to-be fiancé.

It was just before 5:00. Tony had told me over the phone that his mother would be in at 5:00 to pick up his dad, like she did every day. Also, today was

Wednesday, and every Wednesday Claudette came with her, and they would all go to Tony's parents house for dinner. Obviously, Tony didn't want his family to know the real reason I was here, so the plan was he would introduce us and explain that he had just retained me to show him some condos.

As Tony wrote up a ticket for the shoes, in walked the women. Mrs. Lionetti was beautiful and very petite. Her white hair was pulled up into a tight bun and she wore frosted pink lipstick that was very flattering. She reminded me of a ballet dancer, very graceful, quiet, and delicate. That is, until she spoke. Then it was like a lion's roar coming out of a little dove's body.

"Hello my love!" she burst, speaking loudly and in the same exact accent as her husband. She then embraced her son.

"Hi mom," said Tony, a big smile on his face.

The next thing I saw gave me goose bumps. Claudette, very tall and thin, with dark black hair that hung down well past her shoulders and the longest eyelashes I think I've ever seen, hugged her boyfriend and said softly, "Hi, sweetie."

It was amazing to watch Tony turn from his usual upbeat, outgoing persona to complete and utter mush. I felt like I could actually see him melting, his vulnerability exposed so completely, right there in front of everyone. How one hug could completely transform someone so quickly said it all. Tony truly loved this woman. It was very touching to see.

At this same moment, I could hear Mrs. Lionetti saying, "Hello, darling," to her husband of forty some years.

I felt unbelievable warmth and tenderness all around me. And it made me miss my family.

"Honey, this is Missy Benson," Tony said to Claudette, "I just hired her to show us some condos."

Claudette shook my hand and with a smile said, "Nice meeting you." Then she turned to Tony. "You're buying a condo?"

"Yes, and I want my woman to approve."

"Thank you," she answered with a warm grin.

"Who's buying a condo?" shouted Mrs. Lionetti, "Tony, why you need a condo? If you don't want to rent anymore, you come live with us!"

"That's what I said!" shouted Mr. Lionetti.

"No thanks!" shouted Tony with a chuckle.

"Thank God," Claudette whispered to me.

I smiled. It seemed like Claudette was already part of the family, even without a ring.

"You come to our house for dinner," I heard next. I looked up and realized Mrs. Lionetti was speaking to me.

"Oh..." I began, "Um..." I then looked at Tony.

"Yeah! That'd be great," he said with a grin.

"Yes! We'd love to have you join us," said Claudette.

I looked at Tony. "Are you sure?"

"Yeah," he said. Then he said with a laugh, "But I'm telling you now, you're in for a shock. If I were you, I'd drink lots of wine."

Chapter 26

When Tony opened the front door and I walked into the Lionetti's modest but clean, warm and welcoming home, the smell was amazing. I felt like I was in a five star Italian restaurant. It was funny. It instantly brought back memories of the night I'd walked into Parker's apartment, and of the pizza smell. The Lionetti's house was also really loud. It was like being at a party.

"Okay, Missy, brace yourself," Tony said with a warm smile. He then brought me into the family room and introduced me to his extended family, which included his Aunt Isabella, her husband, Uncle Vito, and their children, Sal and Sonny, who were teenagers. Tony's mom and dad were talking to the adults and Claudette was having a conversation with the kids, although she was doing all the talking and they were answering questions by nodding, their eyes never looking away from the flat screen hanging above the fireplace.

"Now, don't get scared or anything, but come with me," Tony joked.

"Tony!" his mother scolded.

"What? She's a little scary," Tony answered.

Tony's dad laughed, "She not so bad."

"What's going on?" I asked.

"You'll see," said Claudette.

One of the teens finally broke away from the TV, looked at me and said, "Prepare yourself! She's a ball buster!"

Everyone burst out laughing.

"Sonny!" said Mrs. Lionetti.

"Come on, Aunt Donatella, you know it's true!"

Mrs. Lionetti couldn't help but laugh.

"Who this?" I heard all of a sudden. When I looked up, I saw a woman who I knew was Tony's grandmother. The room instantly became silent. This woman was little, just like Mrs. Lionetti, but believe it or not, her presence was even more powerful than her daughter's.

"Grandma, this is a friend of mine, Missy Benson," said Tony, "Missy, this is my grandma Selina, my mom's mom."

"It's so nice to meet you. Are you the chef? Everything smells so delicious," I said, feeling like a complete idiotic American with no interesting ethnic background.

Everyone in the room was silent and it seemed as if each was waiting for Grandma's reply with baited breath. And Grandma seemed to know this. She hesitated for dramatic effect.

"Gram?" said Tony with a nervous chuckle.

"You married?" she asked.

"Mama, please," said Mrs. Lionetti. Sal and/or Sonny cracked up.

"It's okay," I said to everyone. Then I addressed the Don. "Actually, I'm going through a divorce."

"Hmm..." she said, "That no good."

"I know," I said humbly.

"Divorce bad. Single girl, getting older..."

"You're telling me?" I exclaimed, inexplicably not uncomfortable. "Divorce sucks."

The teens burst out laughing and I think everyone else's jaws were on the ground.

Grandma hesitated, everyone (including me) holding our breath to hear what was coming next. When Grandma spoke again, she smiled. "You pretty girl. You seem smart. You find someone else. I know it."

"Wow. Now I've seen it all," said Tony.

I looked up and Claudette winked at me.

"Thank you," I said to my new favorite grandma.

"Let's eat!" exclaimed Sonny, "I'm starved."

When I'm in the mood to pig out, my favorite restaurant is Mama Carlina's Veal House. The Italian place serves the food family style, with two different appetizers, salad, two kinds of pastas, steak, veal and then two desserts. Grandma Selina surpassed Mama Carlina's with the amount of food she served, and as for the taste, I have to say, it was THE BEST meal I think I've ever had to this day.

The meal consisted of loud conversations, lots of drama, and much laughter. Grandma and the women were constantly getting up to bring more food to the table, and the teens were pretty much shoveling food into their mouths for a long time.

I loved loved loved this family! Yes, they certainly had their arguments and opinions, most of them with headstrong, willful personalities, but there was also an air of warmth and affection that made me certain these people had each other's backs. They were a solid family with a powerful, durable bond.

At one point, when no one else was listening, Tony leaned over to me and said, "Well, this is my family. Nothing fake, nothing superficial. This is us. What you see is what you get." He seemed proud and I loved that.

I thought about my own small family. Growing up, dinner at my house was quiet and calm, my mom and me and Gina, trying to be happy, and so often desperately aiming to get through a meal without focusing on the empty chair that was once my dad's. But, just like the Lionetti's, my family was loving and caring and kind. Yet it was vastly different. There was a perpetual sense of sadness in my home growing up. There was no sadness here. And that made me happy and hopeful.

Throughout the night, I also watched Tony with Claudette. There was immense courtesy, such respect in the way he spoke to her, asking her how her day was, and inquiring about some of her students. I sat there wondering, 'At what point do married couples go from this type of verbal exchange to malicious banter, condescending tones and defensive arguments?'

I had once spoken to Paul like this. Would Tony and Claudette end up conversing like *we* did in the last few years of our marriage? It literally made me sick to think about that possibility because they seemed so perfect, so untainted.

"This really is delicious," I said to Grandma Selina, "Thank you again."

"You need to eat more. You too skinny," she answered, handing me a plate of spaghetti, "Men no like bones. They like meat!"

"Well, she's not going to find another husband if she porks out," joked Sonny, "That's for sure."

"Sonny!" snapped Aunt Isabella, "You apologize!"

"No," I laughed, "He's right!"

"You no listen to him," said Grandma, "He's a punk!"

"Hey!" said Sonny.

Sal laughed.

"Shut up," said Sonny, punching his brother in the shoulder. Sal punched back and they were seconds away from a fist fight. Grandma stopped it by taking a huge serving spoon off a nearby plate of veal and sticking it in between them, threatening to "cut off their balls if they didn't stop."

Over coffee, I managed to have a private conversation with Claudette. Grandma Selina and the other women were doing dishes and the men had all retired to the family room to watch the Bulls game.

"We'll do this," Mrs. Lionetti had said to me and Claudette, "You girls go relax and talk." So there I sat, drinking coffee and fulfilling my purpose of being here by grilling Tony's soon-to-be fiancé.

"So, how did you and Tony meet?" I asked her, already knowing the answer, but wanting her version.

"It's not very romantic," she said with a smile, "But it's nice. My cousin plays baseball with Tony. And we all go to the same church. So, I guess we're in the same circles. I met Tony at my cousin's house one night. There was something about him that just made me feel comfortable, like home."

"That's really sweet," I said, "But was there a spark?" I didn't want to give my ring to a girl who was passionless!

Claudette turned a little red when she answered, "Well, yeah, there was. I think Tony's really cute. But, the attraction comes from so much more than his looks. There's a way he looks at me sometimes, and it stops my heart."

Yes! Yes! I was sold! I felt like Claudette might have just cinched the ring right then and there.

"Has that ever happened to you with a guy?"

Parker!! "Yes," I smiled, "It has." Recently.

"So, please tell me you're going to find us a condo," she said with a giggle, "I love these people a lot, but I really don't want to live here."

"Will you promise me something?"

"Okay," she smiled nervously.

"Down the road, after you've been together for years and years and things get a little rough, please don't forget how you feel about each other. And please don't forget how to speak to one another, with politeness and respect and understanding."

"That's good advice. Can I ask you something?"

"Sure."

"What happened with you and your husband? I mean, was he cheating?"

"It's kind of funny. That's the first thing everyone assumes when a woman says she's getting divorced. And actually, yes, he was cheating. But I realize now, that was just a symptom of our problems. I think our relationship faded away long before the other woman. It was dying a slow death. His girlfriend just helped kill it completely."

I wasn't sure if she was just tired, but Claudette's eyes looked teary when she spoke. "I love Tony so much. But how do I know that's not going to happen to us?"

"You don't, but I have some advice that I think can help prevent it from happening. No matter how much you really, truly love Tony, you have to nurture the relationship. You have to treat it like a plant, or a pet, or even a child. Cherish it, care for it, foster it. Keep it alive. Make him feel loved. Make him feel important and respected and appreciated."

"Thanks," she said with a smile.

Sitting here drinking coffee with an untainted woman in love, who was about to embark on the journey of marriage, and giving her advice that only a woman in my shoes could give felt really, really good. I was getting smart and insightful, and able to understand and accept my mistakes. I felt a sense of empowerment that felt great.

Chapter 27

Age 34

"You're doing just great, Missy," says Doctor Rafferty after she's just examined me, "You're body's healing perfectly and before you know it, you'll be pregnant again."

"When do you think I can start trying?" I ask.

"I'd say wait another month or so, just to be on the safe side."

"Thanks," I say sadly.

Dr. Rafferty looks at me with her kind, tired eyes, and I think to myself I'm sure she's been up all night delivering a baby. She says, "Listen, I see this all the time in my job. Millions of women miscarry and most have babies soon after. You'll see."

When Paul gets home from work that night, I tell him what the doctor said. I tell him I think we should start trying in exactly a month.

"Let's not rush things," he says, "Just take the time for yourself. You need to heal first."

Fury rises in me like never before. "Are you fucking kidding me?" I shout.

Paul's shocked by my outburst. "What?"

"I don't want time to heal. I want a fucking baby!"

Paul gets up from his chair, sits next to me on the couch and tries to put his arm around me. I pull away, stand up and storm upstairs. He follows me.

"We'll have a baby, Miss, I promise. But I think we need time. That's all I was saying."

I turn around to face him. Tears are streaming down my face. "You don't know how this feels!"

"Yes, I do!" he shouts, "It was my baby too that you lost. It was OUR baby!"

I'm now sobbing. "It wasn't inside of you. Or I should say, SHE wasn't inside of you, kicking you and living in you and growing in you until SHE died!"

Paul hugs me on the stairs and I cry in his arms for a little while. "I'm so sorry this happened," he whispers.

When I can't cry anymore, I say softly, "I'm really tired. I'm going to bed."

"I'll come too," he says.

"That's okay. Finish watching the game. I'll be asleep in about two minutes."

Paul has this look in his eyes. It's a look of disappointment. I've actually seen it before. In fact, I think I've seen it hundreds of times before. Paul wants more of me. He craves the love and attention I never give him. It's so obvious.

A good wife would make an effort to give him what he needs, to shower him with love, to make him feel important, to be his partner, his life teammate. A good wife would say, 'Yes, come upstairs with me and let's just lie in bed together and hold one another.' But I'm not a good wife, and I don't really care that I'm not a good wife. All I care about is my dead baby.

"Okay, good night," he says.

"Good night, Paul," I say. Then, I gently kiss his cheek, and he seems as happy as a little puppy that just got the tiniest piece of food.

Paul walks back downstairs and I walk the rest of the way up. I reach my bedroom and burst into tears again. I try to cry quietly because I don't want Paul to hear me and come up here. I want to grieve by myself. I want to continue to be miserable and sad and devastated and hurt by myself. I don't want to talk about it with Paul anymore. In fact, I don't want to talk about it with anyone anymore.

I love my mom and Gina, but I wish they'd stop calling every two minutes to see if I'm alright. Clearly, I'm not. And Anna and Nan and Catherine… they all keep calling, too. I wish I could change my number and never take anyone's calls ever again. I just want to feel sorry for myself and I'm tired of everyone telling me I'm going to have another baby soon. I'm not! I know I'm not. I'm not because I don't deserve it. God doesn't give babies to bad people.

I crawl into bed and fall asleep. In the middle of the night I'm awakened by Paul spooning me. Instead of a wife who loves that her husband wants to hold her in the quiet, darkness, I am a coldhearted, desolate woman who just wants to be left alone in her misery.

"Paul," I whisper, slithering out of his arms, "Can you move over? I'm hot."

He rolls over, lifts his head up, fluffs his pillow, and lies his head back down.

At this moment, I feel just like my dead baby: dead.

Chapter 28

"This is going to be hilarious!" exclaimed Parker as we walked down the street. It was late. It was almost 10:00, and we had just eaten dinner at Sushi Samba in River North. Now we were headed toward Market, a hip bar and restaurant in the south Loop.

"How fun is this?" Parker continued.

"It's pretty fun," I said with a giggle.

I loved Parker's enthusiasm. He was being so cute about the little game we were about to play involving my second ring finalist, Derek Graham and his girlfriend, Cassie. Derek told me he took Cassie out for a nice dinner every other Saturday night, when Cassie's son, Kenneth, spent the night with his father. Derek had been doing this religiously for three years and said it kept the fire burning. He told me he was planning on "dating" Cassie for the next fifty years. He had said that even if they were ninety years old, and even if their dates had to be in the dining room of a nursing home, he would still make sure they had dates.

Tonight, he'd taken her to Prime for dinner. Our plan was that he would suggest they go for a drink and/or dessert at Market, where they'd just happen to run into an old friend of his: me.

"So, should we go over the plan again?" I asked Parker.

"No, I get it. Derek's going to come up to you and say you look familiar. You're both going to realize you used to work together at Starbucks in the late nineties..."

"Right. The one on North Avenue and Wells. That's the one Derek really worked at."

"And then we're going to get to know Cassie and watch them interact."

"And ask more questions about their relationship," I finished.

"Pretty manipulative, don't you think?"

"Yes, but it's for a good cause."

Parker smiled, "Showtime!" He opened the door and motioned for me to walk in ahead of him.

Once inside, I noticed that the bar was packed. It wasn't a huge place, however, so I could see everyone who was here. Derek and Cassie had not arrived yet.

I ordered a lemon drop martini and Parker got a beer. And while we waited, we giggled and laughed, only the way a new couple can. Yes, I was here for business, and needed to focus on getting to know Derek and Cassie, but I felt like a lovesick teenager who couldn't wait to climb into the backseat of my boyfriend's car and make out.

"You look really hot tonight, Mrs. Jones, "The outfit, the hair...the necklace..."

I smiled, "Just so you know, this whole ensemble..." I motioned to myself, "I did it for you."

"I like that," he flirted.

Our drinks came and our nauseating infatuation-based conversation continued. I told Parker I was looking forward to running my fingers through his soft hair again, and he told me that if I'd let him touch my boobs, he'd tell me another bedtime story.

I laughed. "It's a pretty good deal. Let me think about it."

"How long are you going to deprive yourself?"

"Deprive myself? You mean of sex with *you?"*

"Yes. You know I'm irresistible."

"And so full of yourself, it's frightening!"

At this moment, I was tapped on the shoulder. "Missy?"

I turned around. There stood gorgeous Derek. Next to him was a large boned, beautiful, sexy woman who I knew was Cassie.

"Oh my God! Derek?"

Parker was trying not to laugh, and Cassie was just standing there wondering who we were, a polite smile on her face.

Derek then hugged me. "Nice to see you!"

"You, too!" I faked, "How long has it been?"

"At least fifteen years," he said. Then he turned to Cassie, "Baby, this is Missy Benson. She and I used to work together at Starbucks."

"Like a million years ago!" I exclaimed.

"Missy, this is my girlfriend, Cassie."

I shook her hand. She was just as sassy as Derek had described, and filled with confidence. She had attitude, but in a good way. She seemed a little bit territorial, but it was justified, and it wasn't in a bad way. She didn't seem intimidated or jealous or insecure by Derrick hugging me, just a little guarded.

Like Derek, Cassie was African American. She had a sparkle to her face that made people want to look at her and be around her.

"This is Parker Missoni," I said, "my...uh...friend."

"Boyfriend," Parker said boldly, stepping in and extending his hand to shake Derek's and then Cassie's. He continued speaking to them like I wasn't even there, "This is our third date. Actually, though, we met two other times before we had any dates. First at Starbucks and then at Hub 51."

"Sounds like a boyfriend to me," declared Derek.

"Me too," added Cassie, "But if you don't want him, I'll take him, Honey!"

Everyone laughed and I instantly loved Cassie. She was bubbly and giggly, but not obnoxious. Her voice was actually kind of soft and pretty.

"Easy, baby," said Derek, "Your man's in the house."

"Oh yes he is," she flirted. Then she kissed Derek and I don't mean she gave him a peck. They pretty much began tonguing it. Parker and I looked at each other and exchanged a huge grin.

This couple was adorable! There was so much lust in the air and after three plus years, I thought that was commendable. But now I wanted to know about the emotional part of the relationship. To get my ring, they had to have it all. Their physical attraction scored them some points, but I needed to make sure they were friends, too. My thirty-six thousand dollar ring and I were looking for lust *and* true love.

When they were done kissing, Derek told us they had just had dinner (which we already knew) and asked if we wanted to join them at a table for dessert.

"Sure," exclaimed Parker.

"Sounds good," I said.

I watched Cassie as she walked to the table. Her body was very curvy, but she wasn't fat. She was just one of those women who attracted men who liked big boobs and lots of curves.

Once at the table, we all agreed on ordering coffees and two desserts to share–the signature dessert, cotton candy with caramel and cheddar popcorn, and ricotta cheesecake with almond biscotti crust.

I had instructed my accomplice to talk to Derek about sports so I could have my own conversation with Cassie. So, when the guys started talking about the Blackhawks, I had my chance to really get to know the woman who was possibly going to end up with *my* ring on her finger. The problem was, though, Cassie began pounding *me* with questions.

"You're divorced, aren't you?" she asked.

"How did you know?"

"When I hear a girlfriend refer to her man as her *friend,* I can sense the apprehension. And only divorced girls have that kind of vibe going. I know because I'm divorced also."

I already knew that, but I said sympathetically, "Oh, I see."

"It's all for the best. I have a beautiful boy named Kenneth." She unzipped her purse and pulled out his school picture. "He's nine."

"Aww, he's adorable."

"How about you? Do you have kids?"

"No."

Parker butted in at this moment, "Don't ask her that, Cassie," he said with a chuckle, "It's too personal."

I laughed and said to Cassie's concerned-looking face, "No, it isn't."

Parker took my hand under the table and then the guys went right back into talking sports. I could hear them discussing Patrick Kane's teeth (or lack thereof).

"Question, Girlfriend," said Cassie, "When are you planning on letting go of your fear and letting this man love you? Because honey, he loves you."

"It's really soon, Cassie," I said, "I seriously just got separated, like two minutes ago."

"I understand. I do. When I met Derek, I was a mess. I was recently divorced and I didn't trust anyone. And here's this guy, who just rear-ended me, mind you, asking me out for dinner. I was like, 'Are you for real? Why would I want to go out with someone who I don't know at all, but who I *can* say for certain is a horrible driver?"

I laughed, and right then I felt guilty. This was a story I already knew. I was being such a fake to Cassie. But, I wasn't faking when I laughed. It really was a funny story, no matter how many times I heard it.

She continued, "But something made me give him a chance. Something made me trust. And it was hard. It takes guts to take another chance. But, it's worth it. Just do it," she grinned, "you'll be so happy."

"I hope so," I answered.

"You know what Derek said to me a couple years ago? He goes, 'My biggest fear is that I may hurt you. I don't want to hurt you and I'm scared I might.'"

"He said that?" I asked.

"Yep, and do you know what my answer was?"

"What?"

"I said, 'Then don't. Just don't. Don't hurt me. Period. There. Now you have nothing to be scared about. It's pretty simple.'"

"And what did Derek say to that?"

"He said 'Thank you for solving my problem.'"

Both of us burst out laughing.

"What's so funny?" asked Derek.

We kept laughing until there were tears in our eyes.

"Hey, Parker," Cassie said, "Are you scared you might hurt this gorgeous woman?"

Parker looked right into my eyes when he answered. "I can honestly say, with one hundred percent certainty that I will do everything in my power never to hurt this woman."

As I stared back into his warm, kind brown eyes, I suddenly realized that Cassie was right. It was time. Time to trust again, time to take a chance again, time to open my heart. And at that moment, with my smile exploding and my heart filled with hope, I decided to let myself free-fall into Parker. The time had come to get into his bed and do more than just sleep.

Had we gotten up and left Market right then, things might have turned out differently. I'll never really know. I'll never be sure what course of events would have taken place had Derek not decided to order another cup of coffee. Because fifteen minutes later, when our evening was winding down, something made me turn my head and look over at a nearby table. And that's when I saw the infamous Christian Maverick lip-locked with a girl who wasn't my assistant.

Chapter 29

I had such a bizarre reaction to witnessing Christian cheating on J.J. I didn't make a big deal out of it, in fact, I didn't even tell anyone at the table what was happening. All I said was, "Do you guys mind if we go? It's kind of hot in here."

"Sure, no problem," said Derek.

"Yeah, I'm ready too," said Cassie.

Then, everyone got up and we walked out. I hugged Derek and Cassie good-bye, and the second their cab sped away, Parker looked at me and said, "Wow, they're awesome. How do they compare to the Italian couple?"

I couldn't even answer him.

He went on, "I mean, it's probably a tough decision, huh? You've got the cute Italians and their big, ethnic family, and then you've got Derek and Cassie, older, divorced, a child involved... But both couples seem pretty much in love..."

I interrupted, "Parker, can you please stop talking?"

He chuckled, "Okay, why? I mean, this is fun. Tell me more about Tony and Claudette. Maybe I should meet them."

"Parker!" I shouted, "Stop!"

"What's wrong?"

"I just saw J.J.'s boyfriend tonguing it with a girl."

"Christian?" he asked, "I knew I recognized that guy."

"Yup. That was Christian Maverick."

"Not good."

"No, it's not."

He asked, "Are you going to tell her?"

"What kind of friend do you think I am? Of course I'm going to tell her!"

"Okay," he said, "Don't freak out on me. I was just asking."

"Well, you shouldn't have asked. Yes, I'm going to have to be the person who breaks her heart. Again..."

"*You're* not the one breaking her heart. Christian, the two-timing asshole is," he replied. Then he put his arm around me, but I moved away. Parker looked like he was hurt. Softly, he said, "I'll flag down a cab."

I stood there freezing cold, my eyes stinging with tears, not from sadness, but from the burning pain of anger. I couldn't believe Christian had done this to J.J. for the second time! I suddenly hated him as much as I hated Paul and every other man on the planet. I was even having a problem with Parker at this moment, to the point where I wouldn't talk to him the entire cab ride back to his place.

Before he stuck his key in the door, he looked at me and said, "Missy, I'm really sorry about J.J. That sucks. But not all men are like that. The guy's a jerk. She'll find someone better. You'll see."

"Can you just open the door? I'm fucking freezing," I answered.

He nodded sadly and obliged. Once inside his place, he said, "Look, if you don't want to stay here, I can drive you home."

I was already making my way into the kitchen, almost frantically searching for an open bottle of red wine. "No. I'm staying."

Parker followed me. "Okay."

"Where are the wine glasses?" I asked.

"In the dishwasher, I think."

Parker just watched me, not knowing what to do while I poured myself a glass of wine and then chugged it. Finally, he said, "What are you doing, Missy?"

"Um...drinking?"

"I see that. But why? Because you're upset?"

"Because I feel like it. Do you have a problem with that?"

"No, but I have a problem with you acting like a total bitch to me when I haven't done anything."

"Yeah, not yet," I said with a bitter chuckle, "But it's early. Give it some time. Trust me, you will."

"Look, you're upset and I don't want to get into a fight with you. Let me put you to bed."

Here's where I turned into a complete psychopath. I put the mostly empty wine glass down on his kitchen table, took two steps toward him and put my arms around his neck. Then I gave him a huge drunken smile and said softly, "Yeah, I think you *should* put me to bed." I began kissing him on the lips, but he pulled away.

He chuckled nervously. "Wait a minute, what are you doing?"

"It's time, Parker," I said, trying to sound seductive, "I want to have some fun, don't you?" I began kissing him again. Again, he pulled away.

"Not like this, Missy. Not tonight. Not when you're in this state of mind." He took my arms off of him but I put them right back around him.

"I think I can make up my own mind about when I want to have sex, don't you?" I asked, "I'm a big girl." I was thinking I sounded sexy and seductive. Looking back, I sounded more like a drunken idiot.

Parker took my arms off of him again and smiled kindly, like he felt sorry for me. "Come on, let's get you to bed."

This is where I went ballistic. I shouted, "You don't want to have sex with me?!"

Softly, he answered, "No. Not tonight. You're not in a good place right now."

Thoughts of the night I tried to seduce Paul, the night he announced he was leaving me for Priscilla came flooding back. I couldn't handle it. Rejected by Paul and now *this* guy?!

"What's going on here?" I shouted, "Is it me?! I'm throwing myself at you, giving you an open invitation to fuck me and you're saying you don't want it?!"

"Of course I want it. Just not tonight. I don't want this to be the memory of the first time we're together."

It was like I couldn't even hear him. "Fuck you, Parker!" I shouted, tears now flowing down my face. I said, "fuck you" again, but this time it barely audible because I was crying so hard.

Parker tried to put his arms around me, but I pulled away. "I'm out of here!"

"No, I can't let you leave," he said sadly, "You're drunk and too upset."

"You can't *let* me leave?! Yeah, right." I then started searching around the apartment for my keys, but they were nowhere in sight.

"I hid your keys," said Parker.

I looked up at him. "You can't keep me here!"

Parker was very calm when he replied, "I have to. I'm sorry."

"I hate you," I said coldly.

"No, you don't."

I looked into his big brown eyes and I knew deep down he was right. I didn't hate him. I hated myself.

Chapter 30

Early the next morning, I woke up fully dressed in Parker's bed. I was alone. I vaguely recalled giving in to his adamant stance that I stay over, and I remembered lying down on his bed, still extremely angry, but feeling tired, defeated almost, both by Parker holding me prisoner for the night and by cheating men all over America.

When I lifted my head off the bed, it was pounding and I felt hung over physically, but I felt a lot worse about the events that had taken place shortly after eating yummy caramel popcorn and ricotta cheesecake with Derek and Cassie.

Up until then, it had been a perfect evening. Parker and I had had sushi and had flirted shamelessly with each other. We'd then gotten to know Derek and Cassie, and I had felt so sure that they had everlasting love. And then, in a flash, my whole outlook changed. I'd seen the devil, Christian, kissing some bimbo.

When I thought about it, it was almost unbelievable. I mean, what were the odds in a city of millions of people and thousands of bars and restaurants that I would just coincidentally happen to be seated fifteen feet away from my young assistant's cheating boyfriend?

And then the way I'd reacted to it, taking my anger and frustration out on Parker, who had been nothing but kind and honest from day one. I had been mean to him with the goal of punishing him because he was male and nothing else. And then, I'd tried to seduce him, use him, almost.

I was beyond horrified by my drunken behavior and didn't have the slightest clue what I was going to say to him, other than two necessary words: I'm sorry.

In addition to having a headache, I was nervous and edgy, and my heart was pounding out of my chest. After all, I liked Parker! What if he decided to dump me after my psychotic episode? If I were him, I'd get rid of me after the way I'd acted. And fast.

When I walked into the other room, I heard snoring, and realized Parker was fast asleep on his couch. I watched him for a minute. God, he was adorable. He was one of those guys who looked pretty while he slept. He just looked gentle. And nice. He *was* nice! He was a genuine person with a good heart who just wanted to be loved. (And get some rest, obviously.)

The night before, he was having a great time and I ruined it. And as unreasonable as I became, Parker had kept his composure and put me to bed. And then he slept on the couch. I cringed as I suddenly recalled seven hours earlier, telling him as I got into bed that I didn't want him anywhere near me.

I put my head down in shame. I could not have felt worse. I was just about to wake him up when I decided to go a different route. I tiptoed into the kitchen, got a pad of paper and a pen, and wrote him a note.

Parker,

I thought I'd let you sleep. I'm so sorry for the way I acted last night. You didn't deserve it. You didn't do anything wrong. I'll call you later.

M.

I put the note on the coffee table, took one last look at sleeping beauty and headed for the door. I felt as if I was escaping, and I felt cowardly, but I did it anyway.

Then, as I put my hand on the doorknob to open the front door, I realized I had no keys. Parker had hidden them!

"Shit!" I whispered.

I then spent the next fifteen minutes searching Parker's apartment for my car keys. Amazingly enough, I ended up finding them in the pocket of his coat, which was hanging over the chair by the front door.

One last stab of guilt and shame hit me and then I was gone. And at 8:15 on a Sunday morning, I knew exactly where I was going next: to the home of J.J. McNealy, undeserving victim of cheating boyfriend. I had to tell her what I saw. It was only fair. I'd want to know, and I knew she would, too.

With two Grande lattes, a cinnamon scone and a piece of blueberry coffee cake, I rang her doorbell. Three rings later, she finally answered and buzzed me in.

"Is everything okay?" she asked, "Did you have a fight with Parker?"

J.J. looked really tired. "Let's sit down," I said.

We sat on the couch.

"I was out really late last night," she said.

"Sorry, I just really wanted to talk to you."

"No, I'm glad. I can handle being awakened if there's coffee and cake involved."

I smiled sadly. "I don't know how to say this…it's really difficult."

J.J. took a sip of coffee and then said, "Missy, I have something to tell you, too."

Knowing whatever she had to tell me would never be as painful or upsetting as *my* piece of news, I said, "Okay, you go first."

"I think you should go first," she said.

"Mine's pretty bad," I told her.

"So is mine."

"Should I be worried?"

"Yes," she answered, "Should I?"

"Yes," I said with a nervous giggle.

"What should we do?"

I took a deep breath and then suggested, "Let's say it at the same time."

"Okay," she agreed, "One…two…three…"

At the exact same time as I said, "Christian's cheating on you," J.J. exclaimed, "Priscilla's pregnant."

Both of us gasped in unison.

"Are you sure?!" she asked, "How do you know?"

I was trying to focus on her, but my head was spinning. I managed to answer, "I saw him last night, kissing someone a few tables away from me." Then I burst into tears.

"Missy, I'm so sorry," said J.J., "I wanted to tell you before you heard it from someone else."

"Same with you," I said through tears.

J.J. hugged me and I cried in her arms for a long time. "This is so unfair," I said through tears. "Priscilla's having the baby I couldn't."

"I trusted him," J.J. said, "Fool me once, shame on you. Fool me twice, well, I'm just an idiot."

I managed to calm down after awhile and I ended up staying there with her for an hour and just talking. She explained how she found out about Priscilla's pregnancy. She had run into Jake, who had apparently just started working for his grandfather, John Concerto (the butt grabber.) Jake told her his new office was two doors down from Paul's.

"He doesn't trust Paul," said J.J., "He thinks the whole thing with Priscilla is pretty slimy."

"I love Jake," I replied jokingly, "Have I told you that?"

"Know what's ironic? He has a girlfriend now."

"Isn't that the way it always is?"

"Yup," she smiled, and that's when her phone rang. "Oh my God! It's Christian!"

"Get it. Talk to him," I said, standing up, "I'm going home."

"What should I say?" she asked.

"Say whatever you want," I answered sadly, "Just make sure the word good-bye is loud and clear."

I hugged my cute assistant with her sad, tired eyes and her battered heart, and told her to be strong. She said hello to Christian as I walked out of her place.

Once on the Kennedy expressway, headed back to the suburbs, Parker called me. I wanted to pick up so badly, but I didn't. I couldn't. All I could do was think about the baby who was growing inside of my husband's fiancé's belly. Paul was going to be married and he was going to be a dad.

I burned with anger and pain and envy. It could have been me, had I not turned off like a water faucet somewhere in the middle of our marriage. Right now, *I* could be having Paul Benson's baby. *I* could still be Paul Benson's wife. The reason we weren't together was because of *me.* That was becoming more and more clear with each passing day.

When I got home, I got right into bed and pretty much stayed there the rest of the day and into the night, wallowing in depression, self-pity, and self-hatred. I knew at some point I'd have to talk to Parker, but I kept putting it off, choosing isolation, misery, bad TV, and bouts of crying instead.

Around dinner time, I checked my messages. There was one from Parker, saying he was worried about me and to please call him and let him know I was okay, one from J.J., who was crying so hard I couldn't understand what she was saying, and one from my attorney, Denise.

"Hi Missy, this is Denise Williamson. Please give me a call at your convenience, today if possible. 312-975-9980. Thanks."

I wondered why my attorney would be calling me on a Sunday, and realized right then it was something important. Before I returned her call, though, I had to call J.J. Her call seemed urgent, and I was disappointed in myself that I'd put my phone on silent, not thinking she might need me today after her conversation with Christian.

"Hi," I said when J.J. picked up.

"Hi, where have you been?" she asked, "Are you okay?"

I immediately knew J.J. was better, judging by her tone of voice and the fact that she was asking about me.

"In bed all day," I answered, "J.J., you sounded hysterical on your message. Are you okay?"

J.J. told me she broke up with Christian, and that instead of apologizing or trying to save the relationship, he said some really cruel things to her, to the effect that he was glad he didn't have to sneak around anymore.

I hated the guy so much at this point I wanted to kill him! But part of me thought maybe Christian had made things easier for J.J., bowing out of the relationship and leaving her without a choice. In other words, thank God it was over this time!

My next call was to Denise. "Thanks for getting back to me," she said in the sweet, comforting voice that made me hire her.

"I wanted to let you know that I received a letter with a court order from your husband's attorney. They want the ring held in escrow until a decision is made on who gets to keep it."

"What?!" I shouted, "I have to give them the ring?"

"Well, actually, I convinced them to let *me* keep the ring. Our firm will hold it in escrow in a safety deposit box at our bank."

"Okay, thank you for that. But, I still can't believe this."

"Missy, don't be upset about it. Nothing's final yet. I'll do my best to get your ring in the settlement. But for now, we have to comply with the court's decision."

"Fine," I said, pouting like a four year old kid.

Denise and I arranged to meet at Salt N Pepper on the North Side of the city early the next morning so that I could drop off the ring. Right before we hung up, she asked, "Are you okay? You don't sound good."

"I'm not good. I had a really bad night last night, and today I found out that my husband's fiancé is expecting. I guess the hits just keep on coming." It was at this very moment that I got another call. It was from a number I didn't recognize. "I'll see you in the morning, Denise," I said, "Thanks again."

"No problem," she said gently, "Feel better."

I hung up and took the other call.

"Missy?" said a voice that was soft and weak, almost.

"Yes?"

"It's Cassie."

I was suddenly very confused. Cassie? Cassie who? This person didn't seem like the Cassie I'd just met last night. The Cassie I met was bubbly and loud and confident. This person seemed meek and timid. Plus, how did Cassie get my phone number and why would she be calling me?

"I don't understand," I said softly, "Cassie, Derek's girlfriend?"

Right then, I heard her sobbing and I had a really bad feeling.

"What is it?" I urged.

"It's Derek." More crying.

"Cassie, what's wrong? Tell me."

Through tears, she managed, "Derek died today."

Chapter 31

I froze. What? Was I hearing things? Did she just say...? The room began to spin.

"Are you still there?" Cassie said.

"Yes," I managed.

Cassie had stopped crying, but her voice was still fragile. "He was in a car accident." With a soft, sneering giggle she added, "I always told him what a bad driver he was, but this time it wasn't his fault. A drunk driver hit him. A drunk driver hit him and killed him on a Sunday morning at 9:30."

"Oh my God, Cassie..."

"He was on his way to church. Ironic, isn't it?"

"I don't know what to say."

"You're probably wondering how I got your phone number."

Now I realized that somehow Cassie had found out the truth about how I knew Derek. "Well...um..."

"I know about the ring, and about *craigslist*. I know everything."

I had no idea what to say. Was Cassie calling to tell me she was upset about the contest? Was she going to start screaming at me for lying to her and conning her? I was really scared.

"Do you hate me?"

"God, no! Will you come over, Missy?" she asked.

"Of course. Where do you live?"

Cassie gave me her address, and at 8:30 that night, I was headed back downtown to her apartment, which was in Lincoln Park. I don't really recall the drive, I just remember feeling like I had to get to her. She needed me. I could tell. And let's face it. I needed her, too.

I wanted to know more about what happened. I wanted details. I wanted to know why a person was drunk on a Sunday morning at 9:30. And the weirdest thing, I wanted to make sure it really was true. Because I refused to believe that sweet, kind, honorable, romantic, beautiful Derek was dead. There was no way.

When Cassie opened the door, she threw her arms around me and hugged me for what seemed like a long time. She was squeezing me really hard and she was sobbing. When she stepped back and said, "Come in," I was shocked at how different she appeared than just one night earlier. The vibrant, sexy woman with sass almost seemed transformed. She was shaky and scared, almost lifeless herself.

"This is my sister, Renee," she said. Cassie's sister, who appeared a little bit older got up from the couch, shook my hand, and patted it with her other hand.

"Please, sit down," said Cassie, motioning to the couch.

I sat next to Renee, and Cassie sat in a recliner across from me.

"So, what happened?" I asked.

"It was a head on collision and he died instantly," she explained, her eyes almost too cried out to tear up again.

"The guy who hit him is a repeat offender," added Renee, "I can't even believe he was on the road."

Cassie went on to tell me how she always went to church with Derek, but today, her ex-husband had to bring her son home because he had plans. So, instead of being in the car with Derek, she was at her apartment waiting for Kenneth to get home.

"That's the silver lining," said Renee.

I completely agreed. As upset and angry as I was that Derek was dead, I was suddenly thankful. Had it not been for Kenneth's dad's sudden change of plans, they might have been in the car.

"So, my sister and I want to know more about this whole ring thing," said Renee.

I smiled sadly and looked at Cassie, "He was going to propose."

"I know," she said. Then she pulled out a piece of paper from her pocket and handed it to me. It was a copy Derek's original e-mail to me. I knew what it said, but I read it again, anyway.

Dear Missy,

My name is Derek Graham. I'm divorced. That means I messed up the first real romantic relationship I ever had in my life, my marriage. Not all of it was my fault, but I certainly take responsibility for some of it. I could have been a better husband, a better friend. I could have cared more, and I could have tried harder. That's what I'm going to have to live with. But, the good news is, I've learned from my mistakes and I'm still learning every day.

I'm now with beautiful, sexy, Cassie. We've been together for three years and I can honestly say I've never loved a woman like this before. I think part of it is that I'm different. I'm a better man. Maybe I'm smarter, or maybe Cassie just brings it out in me. She has this way of highlighting every good quality God gave me.

So, I've decided it's time to commit to a life with her. I'm going to do so much better this time....

I couldn't even finish reading. It was just too sad. Derek didn't have a "this time" anymore. He was gone. It sickened me.

"I'm really sorry I lied to you last night," I said, "I hope you know that my intentions were good."

Cassie smiled. "You don't owe me an apology," she said, "You're wonderful. You're not a bitter divorced girl, you're happy and optimistic, and filled with hope and love."

"I wasn't always that way."

"The past doesn't matter. Now is what's important."

I put my head down. Cassie came over to me, put her arm around me and we just sat there for a little while.

"I'm so sorry for your loss," I said to her, "I didn't know him very well, but I know he was good man, and I know he truly loved you."

Cassie nodded.

"I interviewed dozens of men," I told her, "There were two couples I was making a decision between. One of them was you guys. And if I had one wish, just one wish, I'd wish that I could give that ring to Derek right now to give to you."

"The ring from your failed marriage," said Renee.

Her comment surprised me, seeming almost offensive. I understood it, though.

"Yes," I replied to both of them, "It was a ring from a divorce, which might turn some people off. But, the thing is, I wanted to give my ring away was because I was looking for hope. I put the ad on *craigslist* because I wanted to meet the men who were getting ready to commit to women for the rest of their lives. I wanted to regain hope and faith in love and marriage." Tears began to fall on my cheeks as I went on, "And when I saw you and Derek together, I thought I accomplished that."

"You did," Cassie said.

"Did I? Maybe. But look what ended up happening. Derek didn't mess it up, you didn't mess it up, but some drunk driver messed it up."

Cassie took my hands in hers and said, "I loved Derek more than I've ever loved anyone in my life. And I don't think I'll ever feel that way again. But I don't regret for one minute the time we spent together. Nothing's forever, Missy." She stood up and said, "Come with me. I want you to see something."

I followed her to the hallway that led to the bedrooms. Cassie opened one of the doors and motioned for me to step in. It was dark, but I could see nine year old Kenneth sleeping soundly in his bed. He was covered with a Chicago White Sox fleece blanket.

The boy was beautiful. I watched him for a moment, thinking about how devastated he probably was, how he'd most likely gone to bed weeping for his friend, and how much pain he'd be in for a long time.

But seeing the purity and innocence only a young child possesses caused a sense of calm to come over me. Kenneth had his whole life ahead of him. There was a chance he would grow up to be an amazing individual doing great things. He would never forget Derek. I was sure of that. Who could? But he would continue to grow and meet other people who would end up as his loved ones. And of course, he had his wonderful mother, who God spared today. And that thought was somehow overwhelmingly comforting.

When I walked out of the room, Cassie gently closed the door and said, "Nothing's forever, Missy. My marriage didn't last forever, but I got Kenneth. And Derek, well, we never had children, but I got to love him for three years. Three years. And I will never regret that, ever. I don't really think people find love too often like the love Derek and I had."

This woman was amazing. Here, her boyfriend just died today and she was comforting *me.* I hugged her. "You're an incredible woman," I said, "I'm proud to know you."

"Thank you."

"I'm sorry I can't stay and talk longer. I think I should go home. Will you please text me and let me know when and where the wake is going to be?" I asked.

"Yes," she said, "Let me give you my number and you can put it in your phone."

It was right then that I realized I had forgotten my phone. I searched my purse for a minute, hoping I'd thrown it in there and not remembered, but I knew that wasn't the case. I had been so upset and in such shock that I'd run out the door without it.

Cassie wrote her number down on a business card. Then I said good-bye to Renee and headed out.

"Thank you so much for coming to see me," Cassie said at the door.

"Please call me if there's anything you need."

"I will," she smiled. As I was walking out, Cassie called out my name. I turned around.

"Derek really liked you."

"I liked him, too."

"He said you and Parker belong together."

"Really?"

She nodded.

I hugged her one last time and then I left Cassie and her sister standing wearily at the door of her apartment, the letter from Derek now tucked back into her pocket. From that moment on, all I could think about was what a tough road she was about to face, a road entirely different from what I was experiencing.

Divorce versus death. From personal experience, I could tell you divorce was biting, cutting, hurtful, like a deep stab in the back. But death of a spouse had to be so much worse.

I thought about my dear, sweet mom, and how she must have felt when my dad died. As painful as it was for both my sister and I, my mother must have had gut-wrenching sadness that would nearly kill someone. That was evident by the look of permanent sadness in her eyes that she had unsuccessfully tried to hide until the day she died.

Both divorce and death were devastating, and both were guaranteed to leave a woman with frightening emptiness, but death had to take things to a new and more depressing level. That I knew.

Cassie had no choice in what happened in her relationship. She never saw the end coming. Until this moment, I'd thought the same about my marriage, that I was shocked and that I never dreamed Paul would leave me. Now I realized there were signs that I missed. Lots of them. Little things I didn't see because I didn't want to see them. I turned my head, when what I should have been doing was opening my heart and trying to talk to my husband. I should have tried to save what we had. I had a choice and subconsciously or not, I made it. Cassie didn't have that choice.

Chapter 32

Age 38…

Dinner's on the table and I'm alone. Again. I'm annoyed that Paul is again working late. He said he'd be home at 7:30. It's now 8:22. Where is he? I text him and ask. He texts back that he got hung up and will be home around 10:00. "Sorry," is how he ends the text.

So, again, I eat alone. I drink wine with my chicken piccata and I read the Chicago Tribune. I read the headlines. I think to myself that there are a lot of people who are worse off than me and that I should stop feeling sorry for myself that I am having dinner alone. Again.

I flip to the Lifestyles section and read a small article about Christian Maverick, my assistant's new boyfriend, being seen jogging on the lakefront. He really is cute, but seems a little full of himself. Nonetheless, J.J. is really happy right now, so good for her.

My eye then gravitates to an article about a woman who had in-vitro and just gave birth to eight babies. I think to myself, she is nuts! I certainly would never want eight babies. I just wanted one. Just one. "Was that too much to ask for?" I ask God.

God answers me by the ringing of my house phone. I get up and answer it. It's a sales call.

"I'm not interested, and please take me off the list," I say politely. I hang up and I'm not sure who I feel worse for, myself all alone in my house, or the woman who has to make cold calls at night. I decide I feel worse for her.

I finish dinner, do the dishes and then go through the mail. It's pretty much all junk mail and bills, except there's an envelope that appears to be a greeting card addressed to Paul. It's not his birthday, so who would be sending him a card? There's no return address, but the writing makes me sure it's from a woman. Weird. I put it in "Paul's pile" and make a mental note to ask him about it.

It's now 10:38. I'm lying in bed reading the book, The Help. *I'm so into this book, I can't stand it! I hear the garage door open and know that my husband is home. I don't have a reaction, really. I'm not happy, and I'm not excited to see him. I'm not cringing, though. I don't feel anything. I wonder if that's normal. It must be after 10 years of marriage, right?*

I hear him walking around downstairs for a few minutes and then he comes into the bedroom.

"Hi, honey," he says, leaning down and kissing my cheek as he unties his tie.

"Hey..." I say, "Are you hungry? Did you eat? I can heat up some chicken."

"Thanks, I had Subway earlier."

As we make polite conversation about our days, Paul undresses. He throws his suit pants in the dry cleaning hamper and then begins to unbutton his shirt. A dark pink blotch on it catches my eye. Is that lipstick? I wonder. As if he senses something's wrong, Paul quickly takes it off and throws it into the dry cleaning hamper.

The next morning, Paul is downstairs drinking coffee. I wake up and the first thing I do is go to the dry cleaning hamper to examine the white shirt. Really strange. The shirt isn't in there anymore.

I go downstairs and I'm about to ask Paul about the shirt, when he pours me a cup of coffee, smiles and says, "Good morning, beautiful. I made your favorite kind, vanilla hazelnut."

I look at him and decide it's not worth it. What is probably an innocent lipstick stain from a secretary bumping into him will probably turn into a huge, useless, unproductive fight.

"Thanks, honey," I say. I'm smiling, but I feel really sad and lonely.

Chapter 33

When I was pulling into my driveway, I noticed a car parked in front of my house. I pulled into my garage and when I got out of the car, I turned around and to my surprise, Parker was standing in my driveway.

"Hi, what are you doing here?" I asked.

He seemed a little angry when he answered, "It's 10:30 at night and I haven't heard from you. I was worried. Didn't you get my calls, my texts?"

"I'm sorry. I walked out the door and completely forgot my phone."

He walked up to me and gave me a huge hug. "Where have you been? I really was worried. Are you okay?"

I started to cry. "No," I said through tears, "I'm not okay."

Parker hugged me again and we stood there embraced for awhile.

"Shh..." he kept saying, "It's okay."

When I was finally able to compose myself, I stepped back and I said, "No, it's not okay. Come in the house and we'll talk." I took his hand and led him inside.

"If it's about last night," he began, "I'm over it. I'm not the kind of guy who holds grudges. I forget about stuff in two minutes, I swear. It's one of my best qualities."

"Thanks," I smiled. He was so endearing. "I'm really sorry about how I acted," I continued, "I was such a psycho."

"Don't worry about it. Really."

"Parker..."

He smiled. "What?"

"Sit down."

Parker took a seat on the couch.

I sat down next to him and blurted out, "Derek's dead."

"What?"

"Derek got into a car accident this morning and died."

"Oh my God! How? What happened?"

"A drunk driver hit him. I just came from Cassie's apartment. She called me. She found Derek's e-mail to me. She knows all about the ring."

"God, no wonder you're so upset." He pulled me close to him, "I'm here for you, Missy."

I pulled away. "There's more. Do you know where I have to go in the morning? I have to meet my attorney and give her my ring to hold in escrow until a judge decides who gets it in the settlement."

"Why don't you just offer to pay Paul for it?"

"I did. It's now come down to principle, according to his lawyer. In my opinion, it's a control thing at this point."

"Can I ask you something without you getting upset?"

"Yes."

"Why do you still want it so badly? I mean, now, with Derek and everything..."

"Because I do, Parker. I just do. Please understand that."

"Look, you're a really smart woman," he said, "I'm not sure I get your reasons for doing what you're doing, but I do support you."

"You do?"

"Yep."

"Why do you think?" I asked.

"Why do I support you?"

"Yeah."

He smiled and then he held my face. "Because you're my girl."

My reaction to Parker's charming comment was, "Priscilla's pregnant."

"Who?"

"Priscilla. Paul's fiancé."

Parker literally gasped, which was almost humorous to me. He cleared his throat, I think to compose his shock, and then said, "Things are going to get better. I promise."

I looked up at him, my eyes welling with tears, "Paul is having the life he wants. The best thing he ever did was leave me. Now he's got a young, perfect wife and he's going to have a baby. The baby I failed to give him. He's getting everything he wants."

"But your life is going to be what you want it to be, too."

A couple tears dropped down my cheeks. "What do I really have, Parker? What? I have all this money, but I'm totally alone. I'm 38. I have no baby, no family..." I giggled bitterly, "Ha! I barely even see my own sister."

Parker looked at me with a kind, gentle expression that only his eyes could offer. "You're not alone," he said softly, "You have me."

I was so sad at this moment. "Parker...I can't see you anymore."

He was shocked. "Why?!"

"Because this is so much bigger than you can imagine. I've got major issues I have to deal with and I can't do it hiding behind a new relationship."

"No, it doesn't have to be that way. I'll help you deal with your issues. I want to be here for you."

"Don't you understand, Parker?" I said sadly, "I have nothing to offer."

"That's not true."

"You don't get it," I said, sadly.

"Get what?"

I took a deep breath and then I looked right into his eyes. "I'm broken," I whispered, "I'm broken and you can't fix me."

The look of sadness on Parker's face made me almost physically nauseous. Here was this good, good man who wanted to help me. He wanted the damaged, divorced girl. He was in, and he was willing to take on all the baggage that came with me. And I had just told him no, and he looked sick about it.

He took my hand, gently kissed it, and then got up and headed for the door. For a brief second, I wanted to run after him and tell him to fight for me, yet I was glad he conceded because the breakup was what I wanted. For some unknown reason, I felt compelled to do what I'd just done: end a relationship that was making me really happy.

Was I punishing myself? Was I wallowing so much in self-pity that I couldn't see straight? Did I feel like I was undeserving of another man in my life because I treated my own husband so badly? I wasn't sure, but I needed to figure it out on my own.

So, the guy who had taken my breath away walking into Starbucks was now taking my breath away once again, while he was walking out of my house. And out of my life.

Chapter 34

The next morning, as promised, I delivered the ring to Denise. We were standing in the doorway of the restaurant when I handed her the ring box. I must have had a really sad look on my face because she made an attempt to lighten things up, "Okay, let's get a look at this!"

She opened the box and her expression made me laugh.

"Nice, huh?" I asked.

"Nice isn't how I'd describe this ring. Big is a better word."

"Yes, it is big," I replied. "But, a big ring doesn't guarantee a happy marriage."

"Whatever size it is, no ring guarantees a happy marriage," she said, "In fact, no piece of jewelry, no material item or anything else in the world guarantees anything."

"How about the promise of love?" I answered, "Shouldn't that be a guarantee?"

"Is that a question a divorced person can ask?"

"Maybe I was a divorced person who really wasn't in love."

She smiled, "Okay, that's a good argument. But, I still think you sound a little naïve."

"So, what's the plan? I mean, are you just going to hold the ring until the judge decides who gets it?"

"Yep," she said, "Then I'll either give it to you or your ex-husband. But, I promise I'll do my best, and then I hope I will be personally delivering it to your house."

I smiled. "Thank you." Denise was so pretty. I had a thought for a split second that I couldn't believe she was single.

"So, want to get a table and have something to eat?"

"Actually, I'm going home. I think I might have to go back to bed. I'm exhausted."

"Are you feeling okay?"

"Physically, yes. Emotionally I have a high fever and a bad case of 'everything gone wrong.'"

"When was the last time you did anything relaxing for yourself?"

"Never?"

"I have a great idea for you. There's a terrific spa up in Wisconsin. It's called Sun Lakes. It's tucked away in a private, secluded forest. I would recommend going there, having some spa treatments and decompressing for a couple of days. You owe it to yourself."

"That's not me. The last time I had a massage I had to get up four times to check my e-mail."

"That's not good."

"I don't know how to relax."

"At this place you can."

"How did you get to be so upbeat and positive?" I asked, "Divorced people are supposed to be bitter. They're not supposed to end their e-mails and texts with smiley faces."

"Newsflash," she said, "Bitter is for losers." She winked at me. Then she put the ring box into her purse.

"Bye, ring," I said with sadness.

"Only for a little while," she smiled, "Are you sure you won't join me? I'm going to sit down and have a three-cheese omelette and a side of pancakes. Come on, the firm's treating."

"No, thanks."

"Okay then. Go home and get some rest. And think about Sun Lakes." Then she kissed my cheek, turned around and headed to the hostess stand.

With my ring now in her bag, I stood there watching her walk away. She was so pretty on the outside, but there was so much more to her. Just like me, *her* husband had a new family and *she* was alone, but she seemed at peace with it. "Bitter is for losers," I kept saying to myself.

I drove home thinking about the spa she'd recommended, and by the time I pulled into my driveway, I decided to go. Maybe a few days in isolation, somewhere other than in my home would do me good.

I never traveled for work, and Paul and I had stopped taking vacations soon after our marriage, due to our demanding, time-consuming jobs. So, other than holidays and other visits to Gina and my mom (when she was still alive) and one visit to New York (that's right, ONE visit in the eight years Gina had lived in New York) I literally had not left town.

Plus, I'd never been to a spa before. I made more money than almost anyone I knew, and yet I'd never treated myself to a spa retreat or any kind of weekend getaway. I'd never treated myself to anything, come to think of it. Really. All my hard earned cash was sitting in the bank. And there was lots of it.

Two days later, after attending the most depressing wake of my entire life (Derek's), I headed north to Sun Lakes.

"Why would you go to a spa in the Wisconsin Dells when you could go anywhere else in the country? Or the world, for that matter! California, Arizona, Miami..." That's what J.J. had to say about my trip.

"Because I trust Denise. If she says this is a good place, I'm sure it is. Plus, I googled it and it was written up last year in the *Sun-Times* as the best Valentine's Day getaway in the Midwest."

"So it's a couples place."

"Please support me on this," I pleaded, "I need to get away. I need to think. I feel like I'm going crazy."

J.J. smiled, "Fine. I guess I'm just jealous. You get to heal your broken heart at a spa while I stay here holding down the fort and suffering."

"Thanks," I smiled, "Are you going to be okay?"

"Sure," she said with a shrug, "But if one more person we work with—including gossip queen, Kiley Davenport–brings me one more tabloid picture of Christian, I may get arrested for assault."

I hugged her and thanked her, and then I left the office, but not before making a stop into Kiley's office to tell her that under no circumstances was she to upset my assistant, which meant no pictures, no tabloid rumor talk and no questions.

"Do not even mention the name Christian when J.J.'s in an earshot. Are we clear?"

"Sure, Missy, no problem," she answered. There was a subtle tone of sarcasm in her response, and as I turned to leave, I could have sworn I saw her mouth the word "bitch." It made me giggle inside.

I drove home, packed a bag, and within a couple hours I was headed north for the three-hour drive to a quiet, romantic escape place for people in love. I thought about how nice it would be if Parker was in the car. I hadn't seen or talked to him in four days, and I missed him terribly. Yet, I still felt like breaking up with him was the right thing to do.

I was reflecting more and more, and realizing that I broke up with Parker because I wasn't healthy enough for romance. Don't get me wrong. I wanted it. It just wasn't the right time. I needed to work on my inner being. I needed to work on fixing what had been broken for a long, long time, perhaps even before I met Paul. So, getting involved with Parker right now would undoubtedly end in failure, and Parker meant too much to me for that.

All that said, it didn't help matters that when I was looking for radio reception in no man's land, the seek button stopped on an oldies station that just happened to be playing, "Me and Mrs. Jones." Was this a sign? Was God telling me I'd made a huge mistake by letting Parker go? Mrs. Jones was in a much worse dilemma than I was and *she* stuck it out. 'Mrs. Jones would have zero respect for me,' I thought to myself. Still, I managed to keep driving north solo, despite a few tears and the fact that my heart literally felt like it was hurting.

Once I got into the Dells and started to pass all the cheesy, obnoxious hotels, motels, water resorts and other gaudy tourist attractions, I began to wonder if J.J. was right. Why was I going to a spa in the Dells? I could be on a plane right now headed to Phoenix. Instead, I was in my car in Cheeseville, Wisconsin.

But things began to change once I turned onto the road leading to the resort. It was like entering a different state. No more showy, flashy, neon signs. No more noise and chaos. I began to see snow covered trees, untouched snow on the ground, and a frozen lake. By the time I saw the Sun Lakes sign with the arrow, I knew the place was going to be everything Denise had said: quiet, serene, and hopefully relaxing enough to de-stress me.

I checked in and was told by a lady with a soft, soothing voice to be in the lobby in an hour, dressed in the thick, plush white robe and thongs that were waiting for me in my suite. With some help from the concierge over the phone, I'd scheduled a signature massage, a "Care for your back" treatment, and a thermal mud wrap.

My room was beautiful. It was two stories and had a fireplace, a huge bathroom with a tub big enough for four people, a king size bed with a huge, fluffy down comforter and at least ten pillows, and a big basket of snacks and bottles of red wine, their version of a mini-bar.

I unpacked and then I put on the robe and thongs. I felt completely ridiculous. I was supposed to go downstairs like this? I had nothing on underneath! I was just about to throw on a pair of jeans and a t-shirt when I decided that for once in my life, I'd take a break from being type A, go with the flow, and just do what the nice lady had instructed me to do.

The second I got into the elevator, I almost burst out laughing because there were two people in robes just like mine, a very large man and a woman who I assumed was his wife. Once in the lobby, I noticed several people in the same robes. It was so bizarre to me, people comfortably walking around in bathrobes. But, it made sense. I was at a spa, wasn't I? J.J. was right, though. So far, the guests I'd spotted were all couples. I was the odd man out. Ugh.

I quickly forgot about feeling sorry for myself, however, when a cute guy named Rico started rubbing oil on me and massaging my body. It felt amazing. In the past, being touched by a stranger had always had the effect of making me uncomfortable. Plus, I had always been afraid that maybe I was missing something, that maybe someone was trying to reach me, that I should get back to the office.

For some reason, now, during perhaps the lowest point in life, being massaged felt unbelievably great. I had no husband to get home to, I wasn't worried about the office, thanks to J.J., and I absolutely loved the fact that no one on earth could reach me at this very moment. It was a feeling of freedom that I'd truly never experienced. I had a fleeting worry about Gina, but I had left her a voice mail telling her where I was going. I figured she'd be shocked, and would probably call the office, in which case J.J. would explain.

My relaxation continued during my back treatment, and as far as the mud wrap, it was quite an odd feeling. I liked the actual sensation of the mud on me, but there was some serious symbolism going on here.

Having my body covered with mud and then having it washed off was like washing away my past. Like the mud, my life was dark and dirty and ugly. And maybe when the esthetician rinsed it off, she was rinsing off more than just mud. Maybe I was being cleansed, given a chance for a fresh start. And maybe having the mud on me, as ugly and cold and uncomfortable as it was, would make my life (like my skin) prettier and healthier and more vibrant.

By the time I got back to my room, I felt more relaxed than I'd felt in ages. My body felt like jelly. I was too tranquil to be upset or angry or worried or stressed. At this moment, if someone would have walked into my room and said to me, "Missy, your husband dumped you and is really happy right now. He's so excited to be a dad. Also, your friend was buried yesterday, and your young, sweet assistant is suffering from a broken heart. Lastly, you're 38 years old and you've never had any fun in your life, you're childless, and you just blew it with a guy who really likes you," I'd have simply looked at the person, given him or her a pleasant smile and said, "Okay, thanks for letting me know." That's how truly relaxed I felt at this moment. It was kind of like being really drunk, minus the headache and room spins. All I wanted to do was lie down and sleep, so I did.

Chapter 35

Age 34…

"This is by far the best birthday I've ever had," exclaims my mom, just after she's blown out the candles on the amazing cake Gina baked. It's three layers and looks like three wrapped birthday gift boxes piled on top of each other, topped with a huge bow. All of the boxes are different shades of pink, my mom's favorite color, and all around the edges of each box are pastel-colored nonpareils, her favorite candy.

"Sixty and fabulous!" I say, leaning over and giving her a kiss on the cheek.

"And hot!" adds Gina.

My mother giggles and as I look at her aged but still beautiful face and say, "You really are beautiful." Tears have sprung to my eyes.

"Look who's talking," says my mom.

"Really," Gina adds.

"Oh, please," I say, patting my stomach that's still big and round from my recent pregnancy that resulted in nothing but leftover fat, "This is really attractive, huh?"

"Oh, stop it," says Mom, "That'll come off faster than you think."

"Not if I eat as much of this cake as I want to."

"Why do you care?" says Gina, "You've got a hot husband who loves you and you're just going to get pregnant again soon anyway. Worry about it after you have a baby. That's what I say."

I realize right then how naïve my little sister is, thinking one, that my marriage is so great and two, that it's going to be so easy to get pregnant again. Did she forget that it took me almost five years to get pregnant with this one?

Instead of saying what's really on my mind, I just respond with, "Thanks cutie." Then I look at my mom, who winks at me as if she's reading my mind.

"Well, let's cut this damn thing and go for it!" says Gina.

"At least take a picture of it," says Mom, "This must have taken you hours to make."

Gina smiles, "Yes, it did, but I loved doing it."

I take my camera out of my purse and take a picture of my mom and Gina with her cake. Then, Gina takes a picture of my mom and me next to her cake, and then my mom takes a picture of me and Gina with the cake.

"As always, three pictures," Gina says with a laugh.

I laugh too. I say to Mom, "I bet if someone saw your photo album, they'd see that for every special occasion, there are three pictures. One of you and Gina, one of you and me, and one of me and Gina."

My mom smiles, but there's sadness underneath it. It's obvious that even after all these years, the pain has never even been close to gone.

"I wouldn't have it any other way," she says with immense acceptance in her voice that I'm not sure is genuine.

"I would," says Gina, "I'd have dad here. He'd be in every picture."

"And then there would be another picture of just him and mom," I say.

"Right," says my sister, "so there would be four pictures for every special occasion."

My mom now has tears in her eyes. "I wonder what he'd think of me at 60."

In the house we grew up in, the three of us sit at our dining room table eating birthday cake, reminiscing, and laughing for hours.

"Thank you girls for coming home to see me on my birthday," says Mom, "You have no idea how much it means to me."

"Sure we do," says Gina with a smile. Then she shoots me a look as if to say, "See? Aren't you glad I stalked you to come home this weekend?"

"This worked out great," I say, "I'm so glad to be here with you guys."

"Hey, can I ask you something?" asks Gina.

"Anything," I say.

"Okay, this is really hard for me and I'm kind of scared to bring it up, but here goes. I'm thinking of quitting my job and starting my own bakery."

I sit there saying nothing. I'm so full I'm about to throw up, but Gina's cake is unbelievably amazing, so I take another fork full of cake and put it in my mouth. I chew it slowing, savoring the buttery, sugary, vanilla flavor. I let it melt in my mouth.

My mom is just sitting there waiting for me to respond.

"Will someone please say something?!" exclaims Gina, "Tell me I'm a complete idiot or that this is a totally ridiculous pipe dream that's crazy and stupid." She looks right at me. "Speak!" she says.

I give her a big grin. "Not only do I love the idea," I say, "I want to be an investor. I'm going to loan you the money to do it."

Gina screams so loudly that I drop my fork. It hits the plate so hard, it sounds like it just broke. She gets up and dives into me, hugging me really tight. I start to giggle.

"You're THE BEST sister ever!"

"Hey, I'm just looking for a good investment and I can see this is it."

"I have to go call Rick and tell him!" she shouts, running out of the room to find her cell phone.

I look at my mom and ask, "Do you like Rick?"

"I better," says Mom, "I think she's going to marry him."

"I'm not sure about him," I say.

"I know one thing I'm sure about," says Mom.

"What's that?"

"I'm proud of you."

"Why? Because of the money?"

"What you just did was amazing and giving, and now I see what kind of a daughter I raised."

"Oh, mom, it's just money. I have it. Plus, I think she's really talented. Why wouldn't I help her?"

My mom gets up from her chair, kneels down in front of my chair and puts her hands on my knees. "Oh, Miss, when did you stop liking yourself?"

I could tell her the exact date and time I stopped liking myself but I don't. "Please, mom, no therapy tonight."

"I look at you and I see such sadness. I feel like you're blaming yourself for losing the baby. This wasn't your fault. Miss, I promise you, you'll have your baby. It's only a matter of time."

I sit there looking at my mother, wondering if she'd be saying all this if she really knew what was going on. If she knew how bad my marriage really was, if she knew all my secrets, if she knew how much I hated what I did all those years ago, if she knew all the mistakes I made in life. If she knew everything, would she even want me to be her daughter, let alone say I was amazing and giving?

I lean over and give her a really tight hug. "I love you, Mom. You're the best mom in the world and I'm so lucky I have you."

She squeezes me back and says, "I'm the lucky one."

I don't know at the time that this is the last night I'll ever spend with my mom. She dies of a rare complication of pneumonia three months later.

Chapter 36

When I looked at the clock and saw it was 10:12 a.m, I was shocked. I hadn't slept past 7:00 in over ten years! Plus, I'd probably fallen asleep at 7:30 the night before. The fact that I'd gotten fifteen hours of sleep spoke volumes about how much I probably really needed it.

I got out of bed and put on my robe, still giddy inside, thinking about what a funny concept it was to me that people in a public place were wearing terry cloth robes with nothing underneath. Then, I made a beeline for the breakfast buffet, which was only open until 11:00. Coffee, scones, muffins, a huge fresh fruit platter, eggs, bacon, pancakes...they had it all and trust me, I *ate* it all. I wasn't counting calories, carbs or fat grams for the first time in years, and it felt good.

While reading the Lake Delton newspaper and sipping my second cup of coffee, a group of five women (in spa robes, of course), who looked about my age walked in. They were talking and laughing, and there was a certain comfort level I detected that made it obvious they were all close friends. I could also tell they'd known each other for a long time.

Couples at other tables seemed a bit annoyed that the very quiet, tranquil atmosphere had just changed, and that these women had emerged like a flock of squawking geese in response to a pile of breadcrumbs. I, on the other hand found myself pleased by their presence, one because I no longer felt like the only single person on the planet, but even more so because the girls seemed really close, like they had each others' backs. And keep in mind, I felt this way before I actually heard anything they were talking about.

One by one, the women sat down at the table next to me. Each was carrying a full plate of food, and coffee or orange juice. I looked down at my paper and pretended to be reading, but I was eavesdropping.

"What time's your first appointment, Katy?" one of the girls asked.

"12:30," she answered, "I have a peppermint pedissage and a bikini wax."

"Brazilian?" asked one of the girls.

"Is there any other option?" joked another one.

"I'm getting a berry chocolate delight facial with a luxurious lip service add-on treatment," said someone else.

"That sounds awesome," said Katy.

Right then, one of the girls' cell phones rang. The ring tone was the theme song of *Sex and the City.*

"Jenny, that's yours," said one of the girls.

I looked up and smiled, and Katy said to me, "She's obsessed with that show."

"Oh, I loved that show, too."

"Wasn't it the best?" another girl asked me, "I've seen every episode at least five times."

"Me, too," I smiled. I took another sip of my coffee and looked back down at my newspaper.

A couple minutes later, the mood at their table drastically changed. All I heard was, "Oh, honey, it'll be okay."

I looked up and saw a tear roll down Jenny's face. She had obviously just ended her phone call and was upset. All the girls were trying to comfort her.

"He's such a jerk," exclaimed Katy.

"I swear to God, Jenny, if I ever see that guy again, I am going to go off on him," said one of the other girls.

"Thanks, Beth," Jenny said through tears.

"Every time he calls, you end up crying. I can't stand it!" said another girl, "Why can't he just leave you alone?"

"Because he wants to torture her because he's an asshole!" someone said loudly.

"Mindy is right," said Katy.

"So, why'd he call?" asked Beth.

"To tell me he's inviting *her* to Max's birthday party," Jenny answered.

All the girls gasped.

"I mean, I have to see that bitch who stole my husband at my own son's fucking birthday party?!"

"That fucker!" a girl said.

"Susan!" Jenny said with a laugh.

"I'm sorry," she responded, "He's not a fucker?"

At this moment, Katy held up her glass of orange juice. "I'd like to make a toast."

Every girl held up either her juice or coffee.

"I'd like to wish Jeff and his new ho the best of luck."

"Katy, what are you doing?" asked Beth.

"Let me finish."

Jenny had a big grin on her face.

"I'd like to wish them and their sex and lust based relationship all the best. Because when the physical part and the newness wears off, they're in for a real treat."

"What's the treat?" asked Mindy.

"The realization that their whole relationship started with lies and deceit and cheating on both ends."

"Right. If Jeff marries her, this will be her third marriage, right?" asked Susan.

Jenny nodded and Katy put her arm around her friend. "It's going to be okay, sweetie. Your life is going to get better and his is going to turn to shit. You'll see."

"Cheers!" exclaimed Beth.

While the girls were all toasting, Mindy (who was sitting the closest to me) leaned over and whispered, "Her husband left her for some bitch."

I responded softly, "My husband left me too."

"Oh my God, can I tell them?" Mindy asked me.

"Uh..."

She announced to the table while pointing at me, "Divorced girl. Right here."

It was as if everything stopped. Everyone froze and just looked at me. I immediately scanned the room to see who else heard the loud declaration, but there was only one couple left, and they seemed to be in their own little world.

Normally, I'd have been horrified by a loud announcement that declared me the divorced girl, but strangely enough, I wasn't. Was I getting comfortable in my new role? Yeah, maybe so. It wasn't so new anymore. Like it or not, I was the divorced girl. And that was sort of beginning to feel okay.

Beth turned to me. "Don't mind her. She's got no tact."

Mindy laughed.

I turned to Jenny. "I'm really sorry about your divorce."

Jenny looked right into my eyes and there was this understanding between us that felt so good. Not that I was happy that her husband left her, but it was comforting to know there was someone sitting just three feet away from me who probably really got me.

"Thanks," she said with a slight grin, "Same to you."

"What time is it?" Susan asked to the table.

"11:04," answered Katy.

I stood up. "I have to go," I announced to the table, "I have a noon stone massage, and they want me to do the purifying bath ritual beforehand. Have any of you guys done that?"

"Actually, we'll see you down there," said Mindy, "We're doing it too."

"Sounds good," I smiled.

I turned to go and heard, "What's your name?"

I turned around and answered, "I'm Missy."

"I'm Mindy," said Mindy. Then she pointed to each girl and introduced me.

"Nice talking to you guys," I said with a smile.

"You too," they all said.

I got into the elevator and found myself suddenly really happy. I loved these girls. I loved how they stood up for their friend and cursed her soon-to-be ex-husband. I loved how they joked around with each other. I loved how they called Jenny's husband's girlfriend a ho. Jenny was lucky to have them.

I thought about *my* girlfriends. Then I thought about how I'd pretty much thrown them away.

Chapter 37

Age 36…

It's early morning and I'm getting out of the shower. I hear my cell phone ringing in the bedroom. I hope it's not J.J. calling to tell me that the Steinberg couple changed their mind about the home on Violet Street. They've reneged on two purchases already and I'm tired of doing paperwork and making phone calls on their behalf.

I towel off, wrap the towel around me and head to my nightstand to look at caller ID. Not J.J. It's a 4-1-2 area code, and instantly I know it's Nan, since she's the only person I know who lives in Pittsburgh. I love Nan dearly, but I don't have time to talk to her right now. I'm just too busy to chit-chat and catch up. That's what I tell myself anyhow.

The dirty truth is that I don't want to talk to anyone. I'm still mourning the loss of my mother, I have no baby, and I can't even fathom what has happened to my marriage.

It's like I'm living with a roommate. Paul and I are polite to each other, we don't really fight because we don't talk, so there's nothing to fight about. We basically just come and go our separate ways. It's a little creepy to think that he sleeps next to me every night, just because I feel like I'm sleeping alone. We never have sex. Ever. I can't remember the last time I saw him naked.

Here's what we do. We go to company parties together, we put on a good show for the world, we smile at each other in public, so people will think we're happy. We buy each other gifts on holidays, I make him dinner on the few nights he gets home before 10:00, and on the weekends, we both work.

If Nan or any of the other Cinnamon Girls knew what my marriage was like, and how sad I really am they'd be devastated. So, why do that to them? Why get them involved in my pitiful existence?

Sweet, kind, Nan seems like she's got a picture perfect life, and I'm very happy about that. I'm just not up for those painfully awkward moments of silence when she asks me how everything is. I'm in no mood to fake it, say everything's great, knowing full well she knows I'm full of shit.

I don't even listen to Nan's message until late that night while I'm lying in bed.

"Hey cutie," she says to the person who never even calls her back, "It's Nan. I hope all is well. I hate to do this, but I'm calling with some really bad news. Catherine is getting divorced."

At this moment, my heart sinks. My friend...

Nan continues, "I'm really worried about her. Call me. Or call her. She needs us now. Love you, Missy. Please call."

I text Nan. "Got your message. Thanks for letting me know. I'll call Catherine right now."

I dial Catherine. I get her voicemail. I leave a message. "Hey girlfriend...I heard some really shitty news about you. I'm so sorry. Call me if you want to talk. I'm thinking of you."

I hit end. I sit there in bed. I look over to Paul's side of the bed, thinking to myself how he's never there anymore. And that's why I know deep down that MY divorce is coming some day. I mean, where the fuck is my husband? How many nights does someone have to work late? Is he really working late? It's such a cliché. Then again, he's a high-powered attorney at one of the biggest, most prestigious and well-known firms in Chicago. Of course he's working late.

I go to bed. I wake up hours later to the sound of the garage door opening. I look at the clock next to my bed. 3:37.

Catherine calls me back the next morning, but I can't pick up because I'm in the middle of a meeting. I call her back later that day, but I get her voice mail. We continue to play phone tag for three days. When we finally talk, Catherine tells me that her husband is a really bad alcoholic and that he's been in and out of rehab for years, but she never wanted to tell anyone.

"I'm so sorry, sweetie," I say, "You should have told me."

"Well, we don't really talk that much, Missy," she says, and I feel like she's angry with me and has every right to be, since I truly am the reason "we don't really talk that much."

"I know, Catherine," I say, "I'm really sorry. What can I say?"

"Say you'll come to L.A. with us for the weekend!" she exclaims, her tone instantly brightened. "Nan, Anna and I are going there on the 5th for a girl's weekend. Please come. You've never taken one trip with us. And I need you. Please?"

"Gosh, I wish I could," I answer, "But I have a really big showing that weekend, both Saturday and Sunday. I have to be here."

"I figured," she says. She sounds almost defeated.

"I'm sorry, Catherine."

"You know, Missy, I've been trying to figure you out since we were 20. That night…"

"Please, you're not really going to go there, are you?"

"Okay, fine. We'll miss you on the trip," she says sadly, "Like we always do."

No more than an hour later, I get a call from Anna. I wouldn't have taken the call if I had caller ID at work.

"Are you seriously going to blow off this trip?" she asks.

"Look, I feel awful about Catherine's divorce and everything, but I really don't have time to sit here and get my ass chewed out by you because I have to work. I'm sorry, but my job is my life right now."

"Yeah, great life Missy," she says with a lot of sarcasm.

I'm speechless, pretty much because I know she's right.

"Listen. No matter how much you work, and no matter how much you try to hide behind your job, what happened when we were 20 isn't going to disappear."

"Did your law degree come with a free psychology education?"

"You don't have to be a psychologist to see how fucked up you still are over the whole thing."

My voice rises. "I'm doing just fine. I don't need this."

"Really, Miss? Just fine?"

"Yeah."

"Okay, whatever," she says, "If you change your mind about the trip and decide to put Catherine's feelings ahead of your own baggage, we're leaving on the 5th."

"Baggage?"

"Yeah, baggage. Set it down, Miss. We all love you and we miss you and we want to spend time with you. You're one of the Cinnamon Girls."

"You mean you haven't kicked me out yet?"

"Trust me, the thought has crossed my mind, but I say, 'Once a Cinnamon Girl, ALWAYS a Cinnamon Girl.'"

"Thanks, Anna. I'm sorry I'm so defensive."

"And I'm sorry to be such a bitch. That's just me when I don't get what I want."

I'm smiling when I hang up. Anna. Tough as nails on the outside, but on the inside, her heart is one of the biggest I've ever seen. She's anything but a bitch. I'm the bitch.

Chapter 38

I went upstairs, threw on my bathing suit, and then headed to the area where guests were supposed to engage in the "purifying bath ritual." It sounded a little bit gimmicky to me, but I'd promised myself before I got to the resort that I wasn't going to act like my normal, rigid, closed off self. For the next couple of days, I was going to try new things and go with the flow.

"Your Apple Cinnamon Healing Stone massage is at 1:00, followed by your warm oil scalp massage at 2:15, and then at 3:00, you'll go upstairs for your eye bright add-on treatment," said the lady working the appointment desk outside of the bath ritual area. She then educated me on the five steps of the ritual, and again, I had to grit my teeth and remind myself that today I wasn't going to roll my eyes and have a bad attitude. I was embracing new things.

"Hi Missy!" I heard Mindy shout when I walked in. She and three of the other girls I'd met at breakfast were sitting in a huge hot tub.

"Hi," I said with a wave and a smile.

"This is the fourth out of five steps in the ritual," said Katy, pointing her finger into the hot tub, "You have to shower and do the other stuff first before you come in here."

"I know. I got the whole shtick."

I then proceeded to take off my robe, get into a shower (in my bathing suit, of course) and scrub myself with this stuff called sandstone scrub that looked and felt exactly like sand. Next, I went into the steam room. Jenny was sitting in there.

"Hi," I said.

"Oh, hi," she answered.

You never know if people want to talk in places like a steam room or sauna, plus, it seemed like Jenny had had a tough morning, so I decided not to start up a conversation. We were probably sitting there in the hot steam for about 35 seconds before Jenny spoke.

"So, how long have you been divorced?" she asked me.

"Oh, I'm not divorced yet. But, we split up about five months ago. My husband's actually engaged already."

Jenny shook her head in disgust. She continued, "My gem of a guy ended our fifteen year marriage for this girl who lived across the street from us. She left her husband for mine, and he left me for *her.* Now they're living together in the next town over. They actually found a house they want to buy, and as soon as we sell the house, and her husband sells their house, they're planning on buying it. It's their dream house." She put her finger down her throat, mimicking making herself throw up, and finished sarcastically, "Dream house. I mean, are you really supposed to buy your dream house with the woman you left your wife and child for?"

"What about the woman's husband? What's he like?"

"He's really sweet, actually. I feel sorry for him. He's not taking it too well."

"Do they have kids?"

"Three. So now, my husband is going to be a father of four. Do you have kids?"

"No."

I felt like Jenny didn't know what to say.

"My husband's fiancé is pregnant," I continued.

"That's got to be hard."

"It is."

"Sometimes I feel like I'm never going to get over it. He's blissfully happy and starting a life with someone else, and I'm all alone."

"Yes, but his relationship started with cheating. Where can it really go that's good? I really believe in karma."

Jenny smiled. "Same with your husband then."

"I wish I could say it's the same, but it isn't," I said. "The thing is, I really think I drove him to cheat."

"You're blaming yourself for his cheating?"

"No, I'm just owning up to some of the blame. I didn't give him the love he really needed. I didn't give it to him because I didn't have it to give."

"Why do you think?"

I took my towel and slowly wiped off my face. Then, I looked up at Jenny and said, "Baggage."

I could tell Jenny didn't know how to respond, so I said, "Want to get out of here and continue to the next step?"

"Sure," she said with a big sigh of relief, "I believe the cooling rinse is next."

After the cool shower, Jenny and I joined her friends in the hot tub.

"So, where are you from?" asked one of the girls, who I was pretty sure was Susan.

"Chicago. The suburbs, actually. Wilmette."

"Oh my God!" she said, "I'm from Winnetka and so is Jenny!"

Katy added, "The rest of us live in Northfield, except for Beth. She lives in Lake Forest."

"Wow," I answered, "I've probably seen you guys around the area."

"I'm sure," said Mindy.

I turned to Jenny and said. "You know, I'm a realtor."

"Yes! I knew you looked familiar! I've seen your picture," exclaimed Susan, "You're like a famous realtor."

They were all smiling at me, so I smiled. "What house is it?" I asked Jenny, "The dream house."

"1775 Glen Oak Road in Winnetka."

"I know that house. I've had showings there."

"Is it nice inside?"

It was probably one of the most beautiful homes I'd ever seen. "No, nothing special."

At this moment, someone asked Jenny a question. She turned to answer it. I looked at Mindy and she winked at me, as if she was thanking me for lying to her wounded friend in order to spare her.

"Hey, what are you doing tonight?" Katy asked me.

"Um, relaxing in my room with a healthy dinner? Isn't that what you're supposed to do here?"

"No," she said firmly, "You're going into town with us."

"Yeah," replied Jenny, "We have reservations at this really fancy steakhouse. Want to join us?"

"It's her birthday," added Beth, pointing to Jenny.

"It's your birthday?" I asked Jenny.

She nodded sadly.

"I would, but I don't even have anything to wear. I mean, I only brought jeans and sweatshirts and t-shirts. I didn't think I'd be leaving the hotel."

"Girl, you're in the Wisconsin Dells," joked Mindy, "Do you really care what you look like?"

I laughed. "Actually, no."

"Come on," exclaimed Susan, practically jumping up and out of the hot tub. "Take the plunge!" she shouted. Then, she jumped into the freezing cold pool next to the hot tub (step number five.)

I decided to take the plunge and when my body hit the icy water, I felt unbelievably rejuvenated, both physically and emotionally. These girls were great. Each and every one of them was down to earth, so real. And though I barely knew them, these women had sort of adopted me for the day. And it felt great.

Chapter 39

The six of us met in the lobby at 6:45 and took the shuttle bus, which was a Lexus SUV, into town to the steakhouse. Katy had planned it that way so no one had to be the designated driver.

Just after we ordered our first cocktail, Susan turned to me. "Can I ask you something?"

"Sure."

"What's your deal? I mean, what are you doing here all alone?"

"Susan!" Jenny snapped.

"What? I'm just asking a question."

I smiled. Every single girl was fixated on me, waiting anxiously for my answer. I took a deep breath. "Well, I kind of needed to get away. Four days ago, my friend died in a car accident. He was about to be engaged."

All the women gasped and some put their hands over their mouths.

"I also just found out that my husband's fiancé is pregnant." I took another sip of Cab. "I've never been able to have kids."

Now the girls' looks went from shock to sorrow, and I felt unbelievably exposed, sharing my grief and disappointments so openly.

"Would you guys please not look at me like that?" I said, "It's not like I just told you I was dying of cancer."

The girls nervously laughed.

"I'm just the divorced girl," I smiled, "What's the big deal, right?"

"I'm the divorced girl, too," Jenny said.

"Cheers! To the divorced girls!" said Beth.

All the girls held up their glasses and we toasted, and at this moment I was really having fun, but I was also thinking of The Cinnamon Girls.

They were always taking trips together just like this group of women. For years, they had asked me to join them, and I never did. At this moment, how much I was missing on those trips was really hitting home. I felt really sad about it.

"I have another question for you," said Mindy. "Have you dated anyone since you got separated?"

At this moment, I started laughing. Really hard.

They all just looked at me, knowing there was story coming.

I kept laughing, and I know they thought I was a little crazy.

"Do you guys want to hear a story?" I said through giggles. And that's when I told them about selling my ring on *craigslist*.

To say the girls were flipping out, both with curiosity and enthusiasm for what I did is an understatement. They asked me a million questions about the whole thing, and it was so funny recalling all of the crazy nutcases who I interviewed in various Starbucks locations in and around Chicago.

I shared so many of the unbelievable stories, how someone's mother wrote the letter, how one guy was playing poker on his iPhone during the interview, and how another guy was afraid his girlfriend would "kill him" if he didn't get the ring.

The girls roared with laughter. "Tell us more!" they demanded.

I went on, sharing the story about the guy who had to check in with his parole officer, and the guy who had the germ phobia. One would have thought I was a comedian who was performing, judging by the way these girls were laughing.

But giddiness turned to warm sentiment when I told them about Tony Lionetti and Claudette.

"Aww…" they all said, and I agreed. I missed them. I missed their cute family. I'd been so focused on Derek and Cassie and Parker, plus all of my own problems, that I hadn't thought about this adorable couple who really did radiate true love.

The mood turned to complete and utter sadness when I brought up Derek and Cassie.

"Oh my God," whispered Katy, "That's the worst thing I've ever heard."

"Tragic," said Beth, shaking her head slowly.

Then, I told them about Parker. From start to finish, I pretty much shared everything, including the fact that I hadn't spoken to him in almost a week, since I'd ended our short-lived relationship.

Every girl told me I was crazy to give him up.

"I know you guys are right," I said, "But right now, I have to focus on my own problems. It's funny. My husband left me for someone else, and yes, that was wrong. But looking back, I'm starting to realize I contributed so much to the demise of our relationship. There are a million things I'd do differently if I could."

"Like?" asked Susan.

"Like be a better wife."

No one knew what to say. The table was silent, and for a moment it was awkward.

"Hey," I asked, "Does anyone work out at Lifetime?"

"I do," answered Mindy.

"Me too," said Jenny.

"Same here," said Susan.

With a giggle I asked, "Do you guys know a trainer there named Priscilla Sommerfield?"

"Yeah," said Susan.

"Sure we do. Blonde, huge boobs…" said Jenny.

"That's her," I said.

"Why?" asked Beth.

"She's my husband's new fiancé."

At this moment, they all looked at Mindy, who was sitting there in disbelief.

"What?" I asked them all.

Mindy cleared her throat and then declared, "She slept with my husband a couple of years ago."

My jaw hit the ground.

"Check please," I heard Susan say to the waitress. "Let's move this party," she continued.

"I agree," said Beth, "I think we all need to drink more."

So, not more than fifteen minutes later, our driver dropped us off in front of a bar that was suggested by our waiter at the steak place.

When I got out of the car and saw the stand-alone building, I started giggling. It was so old and dilapidated that it literally looked like it was going to fall over.

"Great place!" exclaimed Susan, strutting in, all of us following behind.

The inside of Three Brothers Bar and Grill was just as rundown as the outside. The place stunk like stale beer and cigarettes, and when I went to sit down on a stool at the bar, it was so old and wobbly, I was afraid it might break.

Katy ordered a round of beers and we all began scoping out the customers. It was undoubtedly a local crowd, a "biker bar," in the words of Jenny.

"If anyone here tells anyone we're staying at Sun Lakes, I will kill you!" joked Susan.

"Good point," Beth agreed, "We might get beaten up if someone finds out."

"Well, they might guess," added Mindy, "We don't exactly look like locals.

All of a sudden we heard a guy on a microphone. "Are you ready? It's time!"

The crowd cheered. I looked over to where the mic was coming from, and there stood a guy on a stage in back of the bar.

"Time for what?" asked Katy.

The guy on the mic answered her. "Who wants to be the first singer of the night?"

"Karaoke?" laughed Jenny.

"Oh my God!" shouted Susan, "I'm so psyched!"

"You're going to sing?" Mindy asked her.

"I sure as hell am, and so are all of you!" she declared.

"I don't think so," I said.

Susan responded by putting her hand up to the bartender and telling him I needed another beer.

A guy got up there and began singing Phillip Phillips's *Home* and I have to tell you, it was amazing! These people really took their karaoke seriously. I found myself smiling and enjoying the sound of this talented guy. But watching an amateur up there singing was bringing me back to my great night with Parker, or I should say, *one* of my great nights with Parker. All our dates had been so wonderful. I missed him terribly.

What happened in the next few hours is fuzzy, due to extreme alcohol intake. Here are the things, however, that I know for sure took place. I had a long conversation with Katy about her job. She explained that she worked for a non-profit organization that focused on helping children and their families with financial problems. Katy was in charge of placing homeless children temporarily in homes until their parents could get back on their feet financially. I found myself very intrigued and had such a deep respect for her.

I also recall that after a shot of tequila, I pulled Jenny aside and told her not to worry about her soon-to-be ex-husband and his new girlfriend getting their dream house.

"Why?" she asked.

"I'm a realtor," I slurred, "And I'm a good one. If you want, I'll have that that thing sold next month to a really nice family."

Jenny was so elated, she actually kissed me on the lips.

I also had a long conversation with Mindy about Priscilla. Think about it. Both our husbands had been unfaithful, but there was a bond that existed because of the fact that it was the same woman. I think the commonality factor gave us both a little bit of comfort in knowing that Priscilla was a husband stealer. She'd unsuccessfully tried to steal Mindy's husband, but succeeded in stealing mine.

"If you can work it out with your husband, you really should try," I told her.

"We are," she smiled.

"And now that Priscilla is happily married and pregnant, she's no longer a threat anymore!" I joked.

Mindy hugged me and told me how sorry she was.

I then proceeded to do the craziest thing all night: I sang. Yes, I got up on stage and I sang at the top of my lungs. I sang with as much heart and soul as I could. I sang *Me and Mrs. Jones.*

All of my new friends were howling with laughter, and the rest of the crowd was cheering. That's how I knew I was doing a good job. True, I was singing an old love song about another woman, but no one seemed to care, and neither did I.

I was singing it for Parker. I felt like if he saw me up here belting out our favorite song, he'd be proud of me. Even more so, though, I was singing it for myself. It was very liberating, letting go of fear and embarrassment and shyness.

Around 1:00 a.m., I crawled into my luxurious bed, covered myself with the thick down comforter, and put my head down on one of the soft, airy pillows. Then I called Parker.

"Hello?" he answered, sounding half asleep.

Softly, I asked, "Will you tell me a story?"

"Hmm..." he said. There was a long pause, and I could tell he was smiling. After a few moments, I heard, "Okay, I've got a good one. Ready?"

"Yes."

"Once upon a time, there was a princess who had a closet full of dresses. Each dress was very different and when she wore them, each gave her a different personality..."

The next thing I heard was, "Are you listening? Or are you sleeping?"

I realized I'd fallen asleep. "I'm sorry, Parker. I dozed off."

"You're missing a good one," he joked.

"I miss *you,*" I said.

"Are you okay?" he asked me.

"I think so," I responded, "Good night, Parker."

"Don't you want to hear the rest of the story?"

With a tired smile and my eyes half mast, I replied, "I just wanted to hear your voice."

Chapter 40

The next morning, my new gang and I were all checking out of the spa at the same time.

Mindy hugged me really tight. "I have your number."

I hugged her back and then I hugged each of the other girls.

"Thanks for letting me hang out with you," I said to them, "I had such a great time. You guys are great."

When I pulled out of Sun Lakes, I felt happy. Giddy, almost. I was gleaming that a group of really nice, successful women liked me. They wanted to be friends with me.

Friends. Did I really have friends? My husband was never my friend. My mom was my friend, but she was my mom. Plus, she was gone. I had J.J., who for years had been a true friend to me, but she also worked for me. She *had* to like me. Then there was Gina, who had grown up without a father, now had no mother, and who idolized me, her big sister. What kind of a friend was I to her?

And of course, the Cinnamon Girls: the best friends I could ever have asked for. I wondered, at what point was I careless enough to throw away those precious friendships? Deep down, I knew exactly what point, or what night, I should say. But now I was trying to figure out why. Why did I let my own personal issues stand in the way of friends who really, truly thought of me as a sister?

It finally occurred to me that it took a divorce, a ring contest, a friend dying and a trip to a high-end spa in the middle of nowhere to make me realize that the bad decisions I'd made came solely from really bad baggage, and that instead of putting the baggage down, I chose to alienate some of the people in my life that meant the most. Did I really hate myself that much?

Every single one of those girls I'd just spent the weekend with was special and important. Katy, friendly, smart, and someone whom I respected immensely; Jenny, whose husband, like mine, had unexpectedly left her for another woman; Mindy, a woman with rock solid courage who was fighting to make her marriage work after infidelity (with my soon-to-be ex's fiancé); and Beth and Susan, two feisty, funny, full-of-life women who had included me, accepted me, and not judged me, not for anything, not even for my ring contest.

Because I was so grateful for their warmth and kindness, I decided to help the ones who needed help, starting with Jenny.

The first thing I did once I got on the highway was call J.J. and tell her to set up showings at 1775 Glen Oak Road in Winnetka with every single one of our clients in the million plus price range.

"Why?" she asked, "Did you get the listing?"

"No," I answered, "I just want that house to sell quickly."

"Because?"

I didn't want to tell her that I was doing it to spite Jenny's soon-to-be ex-husband and his new girlfriend because I knew deep down it was childish and immature. It didn't matter, though. I felt Jenny's pain and I felt like I wanted to do something to soothe the sting of her humiliation.

"Please don't ask," I said gently, "Just make the calls and set up the showings."

"Okay, boss," she answered, "You got it."

"Thanks," I replied, "How are you feeling?"

"Not as good as you. You sound really good," she said, "I'm glad about that. It sounds like getting away was the right thing for you."

"Well, I wanted to talk to you about that. See, I'm not really done traveling yet," I said.

"What do you mean?"

I took a deep breath. "I'm going to take some time off."

"What? How long?"

"A few weeks. Maybe a month. Can you manage without me?"

"What?! Are you crazy? No!"

"Here's your chance to step up, J.J. And don't worry because I'm going to pay you for it."

"But why? You never take time off. What are you going to do for a month?"

"A lot," I said with a grin, "I'm doing the whole *Eat, Pray, Love* thing."

"You're going to Italy?!"

I laughed, "No, I'm not leaving the country. I'm just going to do a few things I've been too busy...or I should say too stupid to getting around to. I'm going to fix some things in my life that need to be fixed."

"Like what?"

"When I have the specifics of what and where and when, I'll e-mail you my itinerary. In the meantime, go get 'em Miss Realtor-in-charge!"

"Fine," she said with a pout.

"Are you okay?" I asked her.

"Actually, yeah. Your putting me in charge comes at a great time. I don't want to think about you-know-who, so I'll just work."

"Things will get better. I promise."

Three hours later, I pulled into my driveway. I unpacked, and then I spent the rest of the day making reservations and plans and arrangements and phone calls. By that evening I had a schedule and a "to do" list for the next few weeks that almost felt like a business trip. The purpose? Like I told J.J., I was fixing some things in my life that needed to be fixed. In other words, I was fixing me.

Chapter 41

High-school…

We walk into the house, just home from the cemetery. There are lots of people at our house and I hate it. I just want to go up to my room and go to bed. I don't want to talk to people any more. I'm tired. I'm tired of hearing my parents' friends say, "I'm so sorry about your dad," or "Your dad was a great guy," or "Things will get better, you'll see."

I want to say, "No, they won't."

My mom's talking to some lady and she's smiling, but I can tell she feels the same way as I do. Thank God for my three best friends. They haven't really left me since my dad died four days ago. Nan spent the night the day of the accident. Anna keeps bringing over all this food her mother has made for us. Catherine came over yesterday with a jar full of Hot Tamales (my favorite candy) and a really nice card. All three have been living at my house, they came to the funeral, and now they're here again, mingling with all my parents' friends and hanging out with me and Gina.

Gina loves Catherine. She's always sitting on her lap and asking Catherine to brush her hair. It has always embarrassed me, but it doesn't bother me anymore. The thing that's bothering me now, really, really getting to me, almost killing me in fact, is that my dad's dead. He's gone. He's never, ever, ever coming home again. Ever.

I keep looking at the clock and hoping time will pass so I can go to sleep.

"I love you girlfriend," says Nan as she's leaving. She kisses my cheek, says something in Korean, and then tells me it means "May God bless you and watch over you."

"Call me the second you get up," says Catherine.

"Why?"

"I don't know," she says defensively, "I just want to make sure you're all right."

I smile sadly and hug her.

"Feel free to melt down in front of me anytime you need to," Anna says, "You can sob or scream or do whatever it takes to feel better. You can even hit me if you need to."

"Why would she want to hit you?" Nan asks.

"I'm not saying she wants to, I'm just saying if she needs to hit me to get some of her anger out, I'm cool with it."

We all laugh.

"What? Any therapist will tell you to hit something to help release your anger," Anna says.

Everyone ends up leaving by about 9:00 and Gina is already upstairs sleeping. My mom and I clean up the rest of the dishes. There aren't too many because her friends have been in the kitchen for the past few hours loading and unloading the dishwasher, hand washing bowls and platters, putting food away and wiping the counters.

"I'm hitting it," says Mom, "You ready?"

"Yeah."

"Mrs. Bennett couldn't stop saying how beautiful you're getting."

"Was I ugly before?"

"No, I'm just saying, she's right."

I smile sadly, "When I look in the mirror sometimes, I think I look like dad."

Mom gives me a hug and I burst out crying. She holds me for a long time.

Once in bed, I fall asleep in about three seconds. Gina wakes me up in the middle of the night and asks if she can sleep in my bed.

"Sure," I say.

My second grade sister who now has no father climbs in my bed and says, "Miss, will you scratch my back?"

"Okay," I whisper.

I begin scratching her cute, little back and she whispers, "Are you going to die, Miss?"

"What? No. I'm not going to die, sweetie."

"Please don't die."

"I won't."

"Are you sure?"

"Yes."

"Okay, good," she whispers.

"Go to sleep, okay?"

"Are you sure you're staying alive?"

"Yes."

"Okay, great," she whispers.

"Good night, Gina," I whisper.

"Is mommy staying alive?"

"Yes."

"And you are, too?"

"Yes."

A tear runs down my cheek, but I don't want my sister to see. I'm relieved when I hear her soft breathing, confirming she's asleep.

Chapter 42

"Hi honey," I exclaimed.

"Why do you talk to me like I'm five?" answered my sister.

"What are you talking about? I don't."

"Whatever," she said, "To what do I owe this *very rare* phone call?"

"I just wanted to say hi."

There was a long pause. I think my thirty year old sister was speechless.

"What?" I said, "Am I doing something wrong?"

"Actually, you're doing something right. You're calling your own flesh and blood just to say hello. I swear to God, Missy, I thought you were going to tell me someone died."

"I'm not that bad, am I?"

"Do you know how many unanswered texts I've sent in the past month? Do you realize how many times I've called you since you and the jerk split up? I was toying with the idea of jumping on a plane and coming to see you but I figured you submerged yourself in work and you probably wouldn't give me the time of day, not that you gave me the time of day when you were married...or even before you were married, for that matter."

"Ouch."

"You know it's true."

"I know. Look, the thing is...I called to see if you had any vacation time coming up."

"Umm...why?"

"I want to go somewhere. Just us."

There was another really long pause.

"Hello? Are you still there?"

"Since when do you take vacations?"

"Since now."

"Okay, that's pretty cool, I guess."

"So, can we go somewhere together? It's my treat. I was thinking Mexico or Aruba, somewhere where there's a beach."

"When do you want to go?" she asked.

"Yesterday."

"Seriously?"

"Yeah, can you get away?"

"Sure, but I need time. I can't just leave. I have customers and orders and things." I could hear my sister flipping through a book, which I figured was a calendar or planner. "There's the Saperstein Bar Mitzvah this weekend..." she went on, "And the Brinkman wedding..."

"I'm sure your staff can handle the events, don't you think?"

"My staff is me and one other person."

"Well, she can handle it, right?"

"It's a *he* and I'm not sure. We have to make and decorate two hundred cupcakes, a wedding cake and a bar mitzvah cake, and that doesn't even include the bakery. Can you give me a couple weeks to figure this out?"

"Listen to me, Gina. If I don't do this now, I never will. Please? I'm begging you. Take a trip with me."

"You're unbelievable."

"Please?"

"If it were anybody else..."

"But, it's me.

"Yes, it's you. My sister, the workaholic who never calls me. Never mind the fact that for the past three years I've pretty much given my life to my bakery, and that you've never even come to see it, or to see *me.*"

"I'm sorry."

"Yeah, yeah, yeah."

"Gina, we have a lot to talk about. Please let's go on a trip. I'll pay for the whole thing."

Gina laughed. "Well, that's a given."

"Pick the place and I'll take care of everything."

"Anywhere I want?"

"Anywhere."

"Vail."

"What?"

"Vail. That's cool, right?"

"No way. I'm not going to a cold place in the middle of winter. It's out of the question."

"Okay, then, forget it," she said, "It's been great chatting with you sis. Gotta run!"

"Wait!"

"Yes?" she said with a giggle.

"Fine. I'll go on a stupid ski vacation, even though I'm a horrible skier and I hate cold weather."

"Miss?"

"Yeah?"

"Thanks for calling. I mean it."

At this moment, I was bursting with happiness.

"Oh my God! I've got to go!" she exclaimed, "Sarah's calling me!"

"Who's Sarah?"

"Sarah Freakin' Jessica Parker!"

My mouth was hanging wide open. My sister was a cupcake baker to the stars!

Chapter 43

Sitting in first class at 35,000 feet, staring out the window, I was truly enjoying the bright sun shining on my face and the puffy white clouds below me. It felt very calm and at peace. No one I knew in the entire world could reach me at this moment. People could text me or call me or e-mail me, but I wouldn't be responding right now. So uncharacteristic of my personality, I loved the feeling that there was nothing to do except read a book or watch a movie or what I had chosen: look at the beauty outside my tiny window.

"So, are you from Chicago?" I heard. The older guy seated next to me had been sleeping almost the entire flight, and now he had just woken up.

"Yes, you?"

"Yup."

"So, what brings you to Vail?" he asked me.

"My sister and I are meeting there for a vacation. She lives in New York City."

"That's really nice," he said.

"How about you?"

"Business trip. I work for the Callahan Corporation. You know, the big restaurant chain and catering company?"

"Yes, I've heard of it."

"We're having a sales meeting. No skiing for me."

"Oh."

We sat there in silence for a few moments.

"So...my wife left me," the guy blurted out.

"I'm sorry, what?"

"My wife...she left me. It's been about a month."

"I'm so sorry," I exclaimed. And thanks for sharing...

"It's okay. There's a huge list of things she hated about me. After twenty-five years of marriage, she finally decided she didn't want to put up with them anymore, I guess."

"Twenty-five years... Wow. Are you okay?"

"Sure," he said. There was sadness in his voice and I could really empathize.

"You know, my husband left me almost six months ago for another woman."

"Seriously?"

"Yeah. The thing is, the more time that goes by, I'm realizing, I wasn't exactly the perfect wife."

"Well, congratulations," he said with a grin.

"For what?"

"You're healing. When you start to see your faults and come to grips with the fact that what happened may have had something to do with *you,* you're getting to a healthy place. I bet you've already met someone."

I must have had a look on my face like I was going to start crying, because the guy said, "I knew it."

"Yeah, but I think it's over."

"Already?"

"I'm just not sure a relationship is a good idea for me right now. I've done a lot of things to screw up my life and I think before I get involved with someone, I need to work on myself."

"Smart girl."

"Getting smarter and smarter all the time."

"That's what happens to divorced people."

"I think you're right," I said.

"You know what else I've learned since I've been single?" he said, "I've learned how to enjoy myself. I've learned to have fun. I do things. Fun things. Seems like you do, too. Meeting your sister in Vail. That's doing something fun and meaningful. It's something both of you will remember as being special for the rest of your lives."

"I wasn't always like this. I should have been taking vacations with my sister a long time ago."

"Well, you're starting now," he smiled. "That's all that matters."

We spent the rest of the time talking, and when we landed, we exchanged business cards, and he told me his name was Tom Mitchell.

"I've never talked to someone for so long without even knowing their name," I smiled.

"Me neither," he said, "I really enjoyed it."

"Same here."

"Remember, have fun," he said, "Will you do that?"

"Yes, I will."

He turned toward the exit and started to walk away.

"Hey, Tom?" I called out.

He turned around.

"You know those guys who sell the beer in the stands of Wrigley field?"

"Yeah."

"Are those guys employed by Callahan?"

"They're contracted out, but yes. We pay them. Why?"

"That's something I've always wanted to do."

Tom laughed. "Really?"

"Yeah. I've never told anyone that."

"Well…uh…I could connect you with someone…"

"That's okay," I laughed. "It just seems like a really fun job. The real estate business is really working for me. I think I'm good."

With a smile and a wave, Tom walked out to the cabstand.

Chapter 44

There she was, standing in the baggage claim area where we planned on meeting. My little sister, all grown up was so truly beautiful. She looked just like my mom had looked when I was very young. Seeing the strong resemblance made me happy and sad at the same time.

Gina had always been tall and slender like my mom, whereas I was built more like my dad's side of the family; "curvy" my mom would say, to which I would respond, "You mean, chunky." As an adult, however, I'd obsessively watched my weight, so I was slim, as well, but not like my sister, who ironically baked cakes and cookies and cupcakes all day, and never had to watch her weight in her life.

My sis had beautiful long, dark black hair, high cheekbones and big, full lips, so full that a few people in her life had asked her if they were fake.

It was funny to think that someone as beautiful and successful as Gina still idolized me. She had all her life. As a child, she'd play with my makeup, she'd try on my shoes, she'd snoop through my desk drawers. Unlike most big sisters, I didn't mind that much. It was cute. But Gina also needed me to be kind to her, especially after my dad died. So, I never minded when she listened in on my phone conversations, cozied up to me on the couch when my boyfriend was over, or tried on my dresses when I wasn't home.

When we got older, she had always wanted to be closer than we actually were, and it was my fault that we weren't. I was always too busy. Too busy working, too busy trying to have a baby, and too busy being self-centered, not realizing the importance of a sister.

Gina had done great in college, had made some really good friends, and had moved to New York City. She'd fallen madly in love, and had gotten her heart trampled on by this guy named Rick, (who I met once and hated), but she'd managed to get back up and was truly a success with a great business, lots of friends, and a fast paced, celebrity like lifestyle. My sister reminded me a little bit of J.J., but she was lot more organized and responsible.

When Gina looked up and saw me, she let out a shriek that was so loud it made lots of heads turn. I giggled and walked toward her. She was jogging to me, and when she reached me, she threw her arms around me and hugged me just like she did every time she saw me, so tight it was almost comical.

She stepped back and declared, "Look at you!"

"Shut up," I said, "Look at *you!* You got bangs!"

"You've always been cuter than me, bitch!" she joked.

"Gina, really, you're so so pretty," I smiled.

Gina hugged me really tight and we stood there embraced for a long time.

When she let go of me, she said softly, "It's going to be okay, I promise."

I grinned. "I know it is."

We went to get the bags, and once in the shuttle on our way to our hotel, we never stopped talking, not even for two minutes. It was non-stop, as if we hadn't seen each other in twenty years.

Gina told me all about her love life and about all the guys she'd dated since her broken engagement. And there were lots.

"Are you sure dating a million guys is the answer to heal your broken heart?" I asked her.

"Absolutely," she laughed, "You should try it."

I felt like telling her I wasn't dating tons of guys. Instead, I was meeting them at Starbucks and teasing them with my thirty-six thousand dollar ring. Later.

We talked about her bakery. Gina was doing quite well, her business growing at a tremendously high rate. She'd paid me back the money I'd loaned her and was now earning enough to live comfortably in a one-bedroom apartment on Manhattan's Upper East side. She gleamed while showing me an article that had just been written about her in *New York* magazine.

I was so impressed. But along with being immensely proud of her came overwhelming feelings of guilt and shame. My sister was thirty and here I was at a ski resort with her in the Rockies, on our first vacation together since childhood. Why had I let all these years go by without spending time with the person I loved most in this world, not to mention my only living immediate family member?

"I'm thinking we get some dinner tonight and then hit the slopes bright and early in the morning," she said, "The weather report says it's going to be gorgeous!"

"Sounds perfect," I said with a grin.

We unpacked and then headed to a popular bar right in Vail Village called The Tap Room, and it wasn't until we were seated at the bar that my sister demanded with authority, "Look around."

"Yeah?"

"Are you looking?"

"At what?"

"What do you see?"

"People?"

"No, not people," she said, "Guys. Did you notice that this whole place is filled with men?"

Gina was right. There were countless men (and good looking ones, I might add) and no women.

"Where are all the women?" I asked.

"Girls don't take ski trips unless it's with their boyfriends. Do you realize now why I chose to come here?"

"The last thing I need is a guy," I said, "I just wanted to spend some time with *you.*"

"I feel the same way, but what's wrong with flirting while we bond?"

"Nothing," I said with a smile. Then I held up my beer to make a toast.

"What are we toasting to?" she asked.

"Cheers to my little sister who turned out so amazingly well with no help from her big sister."

Gina put down her glass. "No help? What about the money you loaned me to start my business? What's that?"

"So I gave you money. Big deal. What you really needed was a sister who returned your phone calls."

"Sort of true, but you know what you were to me? You were my role model."

I looked at her, my eyes begging to make sure she was telling the truth. "Really?"

"Yes," she said emphatically, "I would never have had the guts to start my own business had I not seen how successful you had made yours."

"That means a lot to me," I said.

Gina clanged her beer mug on mine, took a big gulp and said, "Hey, do you think that guy over there looks like Jake Gyllenhall?" Subtly, she motioned to a table of guys a few feet away. "He keeps looking at us."

"How can we even be related?" I asked her.

Chapter 45

"You know, I could be putting sunscreen all over my body right now instead of this," I complained, as I snapped on my ski boots. I stood up and was now 100% ready to hit the slopes. Physically, that is. Mentally, I was tired, feeling chilled, and a little nervous since I hadn't been on skis in several years.

"Shut up," said Gina, "Just go with it. You were so much fun last night. Let's keep that up, huh?"

All I could do was laugh. Gina did have a point. From the second we saw each other, we'd been having a great time. The previous night we'd had a nice dinner, and had stayed up talking in our beds half the night. There was no need to ruin it with whining.

Halfway up the mountain on the chair lift for our first run, my attitude completely changed. The snow covered mountains and the bright sun shining on me were breathtakingly beautiful. The scenery was calming and peaceful.

I thought about how I'd never appreciated this kind of beauty in the past. I'd been too close-minded to realize how big the world was and how insignificant all the little, unimportant things in life really were. Petty little details that were so meaningless. Things like Paul's bosses and closing statements and house showings. Not that work didn't mean anything to me. Helping people buy and sell homes was important and I did feel self-worth in this regard.

But, I'd been so focused on my bad marriage, my inability to have a baby, and ultimately my cheating soon-to-be ex-husband and his blissful relationship that I failed to realize the big picture. I neglected to see that if I was willing to go outside my little box, I would learn how vast and full of opportunities the world was.

"Earth to Missy…hello…" said Gina, giving me a nudge with the top end of her ski pole and making a funny face, "What are you thinking about?"

I looked at my sister, who was adorable but goofy at the same time with her bright pink wool headband and ski goggles. "I feel happy," I smiled. "I just feel really happy right now."

She gave me a wide grin. "You have no idea how great that makes me feel."

We skied all day, stopping only once at the top of the mountain for lunch. Two guys, who seemed like they were in their mid-thirties befriended us, and the four of us ate chili on the outside patio, the hot sun beaming down on our faces, so warm that we were able to take off our jackets.

"So, what are you guys doing after this?" one of them asked Gina.

"We'll be at The Red Lion as soon as the slopes close," she flirted.

"Is that an invitation?" he asked her.

"We will?" I asked, but no one seemed to hear me.

She answered, "Yes, but you need to R.S.V.P."

I turned to the guy's friend and replied, "I hope you like CHEESE with your chili."

Everyone laughed except for Gina, who told me to remember that I was in Vail, and that it was completely acceptable to act ultra friendly and flirtatious.

So, at around 4:15, Gina and I were sitting at a table at The Red Lion with our lunch buddies, having a beer and listening to this adorable guitar player singing James Taylor's *Sweet Baby James.*

"I love this song!" exclaimed Gina as she swayed to the music, putting her arm around the guy she was flirting with so blatantly it was nauseating.

The guys asked if they could take us to dinner, but Gina declined. "Sorry, we have plans. Otherwise, we would for sure!"

Walking back to the hotel, I asked her who we had plans with.

"No one," she replied, "I just don't want to spend the whole trip with those guys."

"When did you get so boy crazy?"

"I'm fun, right?"

I realized right then how much pain she was still in over her ex-fiancé, Rick, who had called off their wedding about a year earlier.

I stopped walking and said, "Listen to me. You can date a thousand more men and that's not going to get you over Rick any quicker."

Now Gina got a little bit angry. "You don't know what you're talking about."

"Yes, I do. You think that by dating all these guys, it's going to help you forget him. That's not how it works."

"Oh, I see," she said, "My sister, who just had this revelation that she needs to be a part of my life is now offering me free therapy." With more anger in her voice, she went on, "You know what, Missy? I've handled life pretty fucking good without you. I'm doing just fine. You know when I needed you? Last year, when Rick fucking bailed on me. But you weren't around. So, please don't start trying to psychoanalyze me now. Because I'm fine now. No thanks to you."

I put my head down in shame, because I knew she was right. When I looked up, she was just staring at me, her eyes burning with tears.

"You're right," I said to her, "I'm so sorry. Please forgive me. I've been really selfish and self absorbed. I should have been there for you and I wasn't. Can you ever forgive me?"

My sister didn't say anything for a few moments. She just looked into my eyes. Tears were spilling down her cheeks. Then, she gave me a smile that made my heart explode. "I do love that Prada bag you sent me. I wear it all the time."

Both of us burst out laughing, and now I was crying, too. I was relieved that the very necessary conversation that had to occur between my sister and I had just taken place. After all, how could Gina not have harbored some resentment about the fact that her only sibling wasn't there for her during one of the worst times of her life? Especially since she had no parents and no other really close family? Gina needed to tell me what a crappy sister I had been and even though I already knew it, I needed to hear it from her. Perhaps now we could move on.

"No more advice," I said, "I promise."

"Look, Miss, I know I have issues about Rick and relationships and moving on, but I have to handle them my own way. And if that means dating three quarters of New York, then so be it."

"I understand. I certainly have my own coping mechanisms."

"Yeah, like distancing yourself from your sister and your best friends?"

I nodded.

"What made you realize?" she asked, "I mean, why now? Because of the divorce?"

I stood there speechless. I wanted so badly to share some secrets that would make her understand me more, and that would help explain my behavior all these years, but the words just wouldn't come out. If I could only find the guts to start talking, the hardest part would be out of the way. I couldn't, though.

"Just tell me, Miss," Gina whispered, "Whatever it is, it's okay."

I took a deep breath and then I blurted out, "You know what? I'm in the mood for pizza. Are you?"

Gina smiled. "Sure." I could tell she was disappointed.

Chapter 46

Age 20

"Ten...nine...eight...seven..." the crowd shouts, "Six...five..." It's New Year's Eve of my senior year in college. The other Cinnamon Girls and I are at Catherine's brother's party. He lives in an apartment in downtown Cleveland. He's 24. He's gorgeous, and all of us have been in love with him for years. "Four...three..." I'm staring at him and wishing he would kiss me when the clock strikes midnight.

"Two...one...HAPPY NEW YEAR!" the crowd shouts. I look around at everyone kissing each other, and suddenly I'm swarmed with my three best friends hugging me. The four of us have spent New Year's together for at least the past six years and every year at midnight, we hug like it's the last time we're ever going to see each other.

I'm giggling and laughing, when all of a sudden Catherine's brother appears. He's standing about an inch away from me.

"Happy New Year, Missy," he says with a smile.

My heart pounds.

"You too," I say with a nervous smile.

"Can I have a kiss?"

"Uh..." Before I can answer, John is kissing me, and I mean REALLY kissing me. Wow. Not only is he totally gorgeous, athletic and gainfully employed, he's kissing me like I've never been kissed before. He really seems like he knows what he's doing.

"Oh my God!" I hear Nan say.

I hear a few more gasps and giggles and I assume it's the Cinnamon Girls, but I keep on kissing John. We kiss for what seems like a really long time, and when I finally pull away, he says, "What a great start to the New Year."

I smile. I'm so in love with him I'm bursting. And he actually likes me!

Throughout the rest of the night, my friends tease me. In a loving way, though. "Done with those college boys, huh?" jokes Anna.

"He's so hot," gushes Nan, "I say go for it."

"Plus, he's got a real job," Anna adds.

"Oh my God, what if you guys get married?" asks Nan.

"I would love that!" Catherine replies, hugging me, "Then we'll be sisters."

"Just be careful," Anna cautions, "I love you Catherine and I love your brother, but he's a major player."

Deep down I know Anna's right, but I really like this guy and I'm thinking he likes ME. That kiss…

I try to act normal for the rest of the night, hoping John will come over and talk to me, but he doesn't. A few times, I look over and catch him glancing at me. At one point, he smiles. And literally, I'm melting. A gorgeous man (not a college kid) likes me!

The crowd starts to fizzle out around 1:30 a.m. and we're the only people left. "Should we go, girls?" asks Catherine, jingling her car keys. She's the designated driver.

Everyone agrees and we all start heading to John's bedroom to get our coats. John stops me and whispers, "Hey, why don't you stay here and hang out with me."

I'm shocked. "Uh…I didn't drive. I…uh…"

"No problem, I'll drive you home later."

"No, I can't. I'm supposed to be sleeping at Nan's house tonight."

He gently kisses my neck. "Sleep here. Sleep with me."

I'm having a hard time breathing. "I can't."

"Hey, what's going on in here?" asks Nan.

"Nothing," I say defensively.

"Ready, Miss?" Anna asks me.

I look at John. He's so hot. I've loved him for years. I want him to kiss me again. It's freezing outside. I don't want to go out there. I want to sleep here in his warm bed with his arms wrapped around me.

"Actually...I think I'm going to stay here."

"What?!" asks Catherine.

"It's fine, right?" her brother asks her. Catherine looks like she has no idea what to say.

"Are you sure?" Anna asks me.

I nod emphatically and smile. I'm sure but I'm not sure.

"Excuse me," Anna says to John. She pulls me into another room and says, "Look, are you sure you want to have sex with him? He'll never call you again after tonight."

"I think he will," I respond.

"Listen to me," she says, "He won't. If you realize that, then you should stay. But it will kill me if you get hurt by him. He's never had a girlfriend in his life."

"Thank you for being so concerned, but I'm good. Really. I can handle this."

Anna kisses my forehead and we walk out.

"How'd the meeting go?" John asks with a chuckle. Then he looks at me and says, "Missy, I'd really like you to stay, but only if you feel comfortable. I'm pretty loveable. I promise I won't do anything you don't want me to do."

"Are you seriously having this conversation in front of us?" asks Catherine.

"Sorry," he replies. Then he looks at me. "Please stay," he says with his puppy dog eyes.

"Oh God!" says Nan, "How can you say no to that?"

I laugh. "Good-bye, girls. If my mom calls your house, Nan, can you tell her I'm sleeping and just call me here?"

"No problem," she says.

They all hug us good-bye and when the door shuts, John and I start to laugh. We laugh really hard for a long time, and then John slowly walks over to me. I stop laughing.

"I'm scared," I whisper.

"Of me?"

"A little bit."

John gives me a gentle smile, takes my face in his hands and kisses me. And at this moment, I'm sure I'm going to end up being his wife.

Chapter 47

"Isn't this fun?" said Gina, "But you better start answering some questions or I'm going to have to carry you out of here!"

We were sitting in a booth at Blue Moose Pizza–"By far the best pizza place on the mountain," according to the guy who worked at the front desk of our hotel–and playing a drinking game Gina made up, which was kind of like "Truth or Dare" without the dare. We were taking turns asking each other really personal questions, and we had the choice of answering the question or taking a huge swig of beer.

Gina had just told me the name of the first guy she'd ever kissed, the first time she had sex, and the weirdest place she'd ever had sex, which was on a balcony on the 46th floor of a high-rise apartment building overlooking Manhattan's Upper East side. I, on the other hand was drunk, since I kept choosing beer over answering her questions.

"Okay, I'll answer one," I said, "But take it easy on me."

"What fun is that?" she joked.

"Fine, ask me anything."

"Hmm..." said my sister, pondering her next inquiry.

"Ask me about the first guy who ever went up my shirt," I chuckled, "Or ask me about my senior prom. Oh my God, that was a funny night."

What came out of Gina's mouth at that moment sent chills up my spine. "I want to hear about John."

"John?"

"Yeah, Catherine's brother, John. You loved him. Remember? Whatever happened to him? Did you ever go out with him?"

"Ask me anything else."

"Why? Is there a story here? You have to tell me!"

"Gina, I can't talk about him. Please."

"I knew it! I'm dying," she exclaimed, "You have to tell me!"

"Gina!" I shouted, "Enough! I'm not talking about him!"

My sister now looked scared, and I immediately apologized. "I'm sorry, sweetie, I just can't discuss him. Ever."

Gina nodded sadly, "Okay, I won't ever bring his name up again. Just tell me one thing. Is he the reason you barely talk to Catherine?"

"Yeah," I said with sadness.

We each took a sip of our beers in an effort to fill the awkward silence. Then, Gina declared, "Okay, I have another question for you. An easier one."

"Shoot," I said with a smile of pure relief that we were moving on.

"The best sex you ever had. Who was it?"

"This one I will answer," I said with a proud smile, "Brad Harrison."

"Wow! No hesitation there. When was this?"

"He was the guy I was seeing when I met Paul."

"What was so great?"

"Where do I begin? If Brad even looked at me a certain way,

I could barely breathe. If he touched my arm, I'd start hyperventilating, I swear to God. He was a musician, and maybe that was the attraction. I don't know, but he had a really sexy way about him. He was so uninhibited, so free, so expressive."

"Like how?" Gina asked.

"This sounds a little crazy, but he was sort of violent. He'd push me up against walls and grab my hair. But then, he'd be really gentle and sweet. It was so weird, but so exciting and fun. Everything he did to me felt great. One time, he poured honey on my body and licked it off. Sex to him was like a game. It was *Fifty Shades of Grey* without the pain and sex toys."

"Sounds like you liked it."

"Is that bad? Do you think I'm sick?"

"No."

"It's like it was acceptable to do certain things with him that weren't acceptable with any other man, including Paul."

"So, why did it end? I mean, what happened?"

"I met Paul."

"You dumped the best sex you ever had for Paul?"

"Yup. The thing is, looking back, I think I felt guilty for the way things were with Brad, like it was wrong to have that kind of a sex life. And now, I realize how stupid that was. I'm not saying that Brad Harrison was my soul mate. Trust me, he wasn't the guy I wanted to spend the rest of my life with. But, I should have let myself enjoy the relationship for what it was instead of focusing on the fact that things with Brad were never going to be long term. I don't know why that mattered to me so much. And then I met Paul, and he looked so good on paper: a gorgeous attorney and a nice guy who wanted a wife and a family. He was a little boring, but I overlooked that. And the sex...it was never really amazing or anything, because I felt like it was inappropriate to have crazy sex with my husband. And ironically, I think that's why Paul left me. I think he got bored. I think he wanted the kind of sex that I wouldn't give him, the kind that I gave my boyfriend before him." I looked at my wide-eyed sister and finished, "I'm mad at myself for that. If I'd have loved my husband with half the passion I loved Brad Harrison with, we might still be together."

Gina nodded and then asked, "Why don't you find him?"

"Who?"

"Brad. You should Facebook him or something."

I smiled, "Maybe I will. How about you? Who's your best sex?"

"Rick. Rick was my best sex," she said sadly, "Rick, who dumped me after our wedding invitations were already out."

"You know, I never liked that guy."

"I know. I could tell. I don't think mom did, either."

"I'm really sorry I didn't say something. I just felt like I didn't have the right to butt in when I was so far away and had only met him one time."

"No, you did the right thing," she answered, "I wouldn't have listened to you, anyhow. What didn't you like about him?"

"He wasn't that nice to you. Just the way he acted around you, it was... not respectful, and he didn't seem like he worshipped the ground you walked on. Know what I mean?"

"Yup. I do. I loved him way more than he loved me. It was like I was always trying to get him to love me more."

"Do you ever hear from him?"

"I'm choosing to not answer and drink." She took a big swig of beer.

"Why?"

"Nope. No more questions about Rick." Gina held up her beer mug and then took another swig.

"Please tell me, Gina."

"Fine. I slept with him last week."

At this exact moment, a semi-nice looking guy walked by our table and said, "Hey girls!" I was still in shock by what Gina had just told me, but I managed to smile and say hello back.

"Hi," Gina flirted.

"My friends and I are headed to The Club. Meet us there?" he asked.

"Absolutely!" said Gina.

He walked off and I asked her, "Did you just wink?"

"I'm in Vail. Winking is acceptable here."

"Are you okay? I mean, about Rick."

"Here's what happened. He called and told me he was in town for the weekend, and we met for a drink that turned into four drinks. He told me he was sorry and that he still loved me, but he panicked. I started crying and he hugged me. And then we started kissing and we ended up back at my place. Before I knew it we were having sex."

"Does he want to get back together?"

"I don't think so, but it doesn't matter. I don't. He decided he didn't want to marry me and called off our wedding. I don't think a couple can ever come back from something like that. If he really loved me, he would never have called it off."

"You know something? You really turned out well."

"I had amazing parents and you."

"I miss them," I said sadly.

"Me, too," Gina answered. My sister took my hand across the table and we sat there until our new friend passed by our table again, shouting, "See you there?"

"You got it!" Gina shouted back.

Fifteen minutes later, we found ourselves standing in the middle of a huge crowd at The Club, listening to live music. With beers in our hands that kept spilling over the sides because of people bumping into us trying to get by, we danced to the music. We were having a great time and there was something very familiar about all of this.

Maybe it was because I was with my sister, my own flesh and blood, but there was something else that seemed oddly recognizable. When I heard John Mayer's "Your Body Is A Wonderland," I figured it out. I gasped.

"What's wrong?" shouted Gina.

"Oh my God!" I shouted.

"What? Tell me!"

I started making my way closer to the stage. Gina followed me. It was hard to get through the packed crowd, but utter determination was my powerful, driving force. After a minute or so of weeding my way through the mob of beer drinking skiers, I was able to get a glimpse of the band, and of the singer who was belting out John Mayer. When I saw him, I was literally unable to move.

"What is it?" asked my sister.

"Brad," I simply said, staring up at my ex-lover, who I'd been talking about minutes earlier.

"Brad Harrison?!" she asked.

"Yes!" I laughed.

My obnoxious sister then started screaming to him, "Brad! Brad!" and before I could stop her, he looked down and saw us. I smiled and waved and could not have felt like more of a complete idiot.

Brad continued singing, but when he registered who was waving at him, he broke into a huge grin. Now my grin got even bigger, and our two sets of eyes never left each other for the entire song.

Chapter 48

Age 26…

"This is so not me," I say to Brad, who's lying on his back with his fingers laced behind his head, softly singing Maroon 5's "She Will Be Loved." We've just been having sex for the past few hours and it's hard to believe I met him less than a week ago. Yet, something about how I feel is far outweighing any feelings I have that sleeping with someone I barely know is wrong.

Brad stops singing. He turns to me and puts my hair behind my ear. "You're cute, you know that?"

Now I feel like Brad thinks I'm a little girl, naïve and clueless when it comes to anything in the bedroom, which is pretty much true since he's only one of three guys I've ever been with.

"Cute?" I ask in a flirty tone, desperately fishing for a compliment, "Is that what I am in bed? Cute?"

Brad slowly climbs back on top of me and says, "Cute AND very, very sexy."

I'm hungry for him. These feelings of desire are overwhelming. It feels so very right, but wrong at the same time. I decide I'm going with right.

I start kissing my hot musician again and he whispers, "Missy, you're getting really, really good at this."

"I have a good teacher," I whisper in between kisses, "I like my teacher."

Now Brad starts kissing my collar bone. He goes lower and lower and whispers, "Is it time for another lesson?"

My heart is ready to explode with passion and I am so conflicted at this moment I can barely stand it. Is this guy in love with me or is he using me? Does Brad do this with a lot of girls? I wonder. I hope not. I hope I'm special. I hope I'm different. Something tells me I'm foolish to think that this musician, who can go home with any girl any night of the week, wants only to be with me.

As if he's reading my mind, Brad whispers, "Don't think too much, Missy. Just enjoy yourself. I'm crazy about you, and I plan on seeing you a lot more. If you want to, that is."

It is with those words that I dive into this crazy, heart-pounding, extraordinary, powerful and mostly physical relationship that ends up lasting for almost a year.

Chapter 49

"We're going to take a short break," Brad said into the microphone, "See you in a few." Then, he put the mic down, literally jumped off the stage and threw his arms around me. As I laughed, I got a sense that everyone around us was watching with fascination.

"What the hell are you doing here?" he asked.

"Skiing?" I giggled.

Brad held me in a tight hug for what seemed like a really long time. When he finally pulled away, he said, "You're still freakin' hot!"

I laughed and then I introduced him to Gina. "I'm going to get another beer," she said. All three of us looked down at her full beer.

"What?" she asked. Then she walked off.

"I can't believe you're here!" I said to Brad.

"This is wild," he replied, "How long's it been?"

"Twelve years."

"How do you know the exact number?"

"Because I met my husband twelve years ago and we were married a year later."

"Married," he said with a frown.

"Separated."

Enthusiastically and with a smile, he replied, "Oh, I'm so sorry! I'm devastated, actually. You must be really upset."

I burst out laughing and right then I felt like I was young again, hanging out at some bar, waiting for my hot musician to finish working so he could take me home and make mad passionate love to me for hours.

We talked and flirted until it was time for Brad to go back on stage. "Will you wait for me until after the show?"

"Seriously?"

Brad got really close to me and looked right into my eyes. "I bet you never knew how upset I was when you broke up with me."

"Brad, we never really broke up, since we were never really committed to each other."

"Who says?"

"Come on," I said, "Are you changing history? Pretending what we had was more than just sex?"

"You know, just because you have amazing sex, it doesn't mean you can't actually care about the person, too." He took my hands. "What I gave you in the relationship was as much as I could give. To anyone. For me, it was a lot."

"What time does the show end?" I said, barely able to breathe.

Chapter 50

Gina took a cab back to the hotel around 1:30 a.m., and it was past 2:00 when Brad and I left The Club and headed back to his apartment. In his Jeep, we rode up the mountain on snow covered roads. The outside air was extremely cold and crisp, but that had nothing to do with why I couldn't stop shivering. I was excited, nervous, and fearful all at the same time. I was on my way to Brad's place to do what we'd done so so many times before. But now, twelve years had passed. Everything was different. I had been married, I had established myself in my business, I had been pregnant, I had lost my baby, and now, I was getting divorced.

I knew absolutely nothing about Brad's life since he'd been my boyfriend. Had he been in love? Had HE had a child with someone? Was he still trying to become the next John Mayer?

Brad and I were both very different people now, both older, and with more life experience. But, sitting here next to him, watching him grip the steering wheel and drive up the curvy mountain, part of me felt like I'd just seen him last week. After all, how much could both of us have really changed? In our cores, weren't we most likely the same people we were twelve years earlier? That's what made me thrilled to be here with him. To have the chance to relive this breathtaking, over-the-top physical relationship (even if it was just for one night) was a gift. Most people would only have memories. I got to have the real thing again. And I couldn't wait.

Then, something awful happened. I began to think about Parker. Sweet, adorable, Parker, who I cared for and missed deeply. It was as if I'd forced myself not to think about him on this trip, to the point that I didn't even tell my own sister about him. And now, on the brink of having sex with someone else, he had crept his way into my heart.

How could I do this to him? I asked myself. Yes, we were broken up, but still, I felt like I was cheating on him. How would I feel if he slept with someone else right now? Sick with jealousy.

"Hey, you okay?" Brad asked, "Want me to turn up the heat?"

"No, I'm fine."

"What are you thinking about?" he said with his cute grin.

"Parker!" I wanted to shout. Instead, I answered, "You must have lots of girlfriends."

"It's not about women for me. Never has been. It about my music. Always."

"Except for me," I joked.

"Actually, that's true."

"And you're not saying that because I'm in your car, headed back to your place?"

"Nope."

He just kept driving and my heart pounded with thoughts of this electrifying relationship that needed me to open its door for tonight, explore why I had the love affair, and decide if the door could stay open or if it would have to close for forever after tonight. And nothing else, not even Parker had anything to do with any of this.

"Why are you slowing down?" I asked Brad, "Are we here?"

Brad came to a stop and put the Jeep in park. "No."

"Oh..." I gave him a nervous smile, but he didn't react. He just continued staring at me. He had this look in his eyes that was literally taking my breath away. All I wanted was for him to kiss me, and it was like he was teasing me, torturing me, making me wait.

"Brad, what are you doing?" I finally asked.

"This," he said softly. Then he leaned over and began kissing me passionately and hungrily to the point where it almost felt like it does when you haven't eaten all day and you get somewhere and you start eating food that's been put in front of you. Only much worse. I was kissing Brad as if I'd been starving myself for two weeks. And ironically, I realized that in a way, I'd been starving myself from any real passion for years.

"Please get me home," I whispered in between kisses.

Brad put the car in drive and continued to his place. "This is going to be fun," he said with a soft smile.

Just before we pulled into his driveway, I heard a bling and realized I had a text. I pulled my iPhone out of my purse and checked it. It was from Gina.

"Check inside pocket of purse," it read.

It was dark, so I had to search around. When I felt what my sister had stuck in the side pocket of my purse, I burst out laughing.

"What is it?" asked Brad.

"This!" I exclaimed, pulling out a handful of condoms.

"Wow," he said.

"She really looks out for me," I said, thinking about how funny it was that I was just now realizing my baby sister was a grown up. She wasn't the little six year old who would climb on my lap and beg me to read *Cloudland* to her. I wasn't putting Band-Aids on her little boo-boos and I wasn't making her mac and cheese on the stove anymore. Gina would always be my baby sister, but now she was my very best friend, too.

"I'm a little disturbed that my sister carries condoms in her purse, but I guess that's reality, right?"

"It's smart," said Brad.

It was at this moment that I wanted to throw up. Gina used condoms, Brad believed in them, in fact, he and I had always used condoms when we were together. But I was thinking of a time in my life when I didn't use a condom, and just like every time I thought about it, it made me physically nauseous.

"You okay?" Brad asked.

"Yes," I smiled.

We were barely in the door of his apartment when we began tearing off each other's clothes. Jackets and hats and scarves and gloves and shirts and jeans and socks were scattered all over his foyer, his kitchen and his living room. No more than two minutes later, I was lying on Brad Harrison's living room rug making love with him in front of the fireplace. And it felt the exact same way it did every single time we'd been together. It was as if not a week went by since the last time we'd had sex.

Did I love this guy? Was *he* the one I was supposed to marry? Maybe I could have changed him. Maybe I could have made Brad into a good husband, a family man. Yeah, right.

"Oh my God, Missy, I forgot how amazing this was," he whispered.

"I never forgot," I said, "Never."

"Then why'd you dump me?"

"Do you really want to have this conversation while we're having sex?"

Brad laughed. "No."

Brad and I made love and then we cuddled naked under a blanket and made love again. All night we kissed and hugged and touched each other, and then we talked.

"Hey, Brad?" I whispered.

"Yeah, gorgeous?"

"Have you ever been in love?"

"Once," he smiled.

Now I panicked, "Who was it? Was it before me or after?"

"During."

"During?!"

"Yeah."

"Well, who was she?!"

With a soft laugh, he answered, "It was you."

I was speechless. Was he joking around? Was he trying to be nice?

"I told you last night," he continued, "I gave you all I could give. And for you, that wasn't enough. But for me, I never told you how I really felt because that's not what I do. I didn't want a wife. I didn't want a family. I still don't. I want to sing. I want to perform. And in my opinion, there's no room in that life for a woman in any real way. So, I kept it to myself. I felt lucky that it lasted for as long as it did with you, and that you were willing to stay with me for almost a year."

"I missed you a lot for a really long time."

Brad kissed my forehead. "Thanks. That makes me feel good."

"I'm sorry I ended things the way I did. I never even broke up with you in person."

"I know. You just stopped coming to see me. That made me realize you wanted more. You wanted something real."

"But this *was* real. It was more real than my marriage."

"What was he like? Your husband?"

"Perfect," I said, "Handsome, smart, an attorney, polite, pretty much a parent's dream for their little girl."

"What happened?"

"I screwed it up. I was closed off, distant, and cold."

"That doesn't sound like you."

"That's because you and I never got close enough for you to really get to know me. And I think that was the attraction. What we had was really, really easy. Sex is easy, isn't it? And then, when I wanted more, I thought *you* were the problem. And now I realize what the problem really was. The problem was me."

Chapter 51

It was mid-morning when Brad and I finally pulled up to my hotel. He put the car in park and then just looked at me and said with a sad smile, "Now what? When do you leave town?"

"Tomorrow."

"I'm playing tonight. Come see me?"

I gave him a sad smile and replied, "It's my last night here. I think I'm just going to hang out with my sister. Otherwise, you know I would."

"I understand. Text me if you change your mind?"

"Sure."

Brad put his head down and said in a shy voice, "I'll miss you."

"Same here, but we both know what we are, right? It's all about the music. Those were your exact words."

"Yes, that's true."

"That's a good thing!"

Brad nodded in agreement. Then he asked, "Are you going to be okay?"

"Sure. I'm on this whole self-improvement program. Think I can stick to it?"

"I'd never doubt it."

I kissed his lips and said, "I'm really glad I ran into you."

"Me too. Think we'll ever see each other again?"

In my heart I knew the answer was no, but I couldn't say it. "Are you on Facebook?"

Brad laughed. "Is that what we're going to be? Facebook friends?"

"We're more than Facebook friends," I said with a grin.

Brad kissed me good-bye and as I got out of the car he said the weirdest thing. "Hey...whoever the guy is that you're seeing...give him a chance. I have a good feeling about it."

"How did you know?"

"I don't know. I just did. Am I right?"

I was smiling so wide, my cheeks were starting to hurt. I gave him one last wave, closed his car door and went into the hotel.

When I walked into the room, I saw that Gina was still asleep, so I tiptoed around, took off my clothes and took a shower. When I came out of the bathroom, I heard her groggy voice. "How was it?"

"Fun," I smiled.

"You're so lucky. That guy is so cute!"

"Yeah."

"Are you okay?" she asked.

"Gina, I have to tell you something."

She sat up in bed and something was telling me she had been expecting this. "Okay, say it," she said softly.

I sat down on the edge of her bed, one towel wrapped around my body, one wrapped around my head, and said, "Well, I don't really know how to."

"Just say it. Whatever it is."

I took a deep breath. "Catherine's brother, John... It was over the holidays during my senior year in college. We went to a party at his apartment."

"He was living downtown, right?"

Tears filled my eyes instantly. I nodded. "I thought I was in love with him and I slept with him."

Now I was having a hard time continuing, and I was trying not to break down. With another deep breath, I continued, "When I got back to school, I waited for John to call me. Every day, I'd come home from class and pray there was a message. But there never was. I was so depressed. I felt used and dirty. And then..." I took another deep breath. "I found out I was pregnant."

Gina gasped and that's when I lost it. I started to cry so hard that I was hyperventilating. I had never told the story to a single soul, and hearing the words out loud brought it all back.

Gina grabbed me and hugged me really tight. We stayed that way for a long time, and when I finally pulled back and was able to speak, I said, "I have to finish."

Gina nodded emphatically, handing me a little packet of Kleenex from the nightstand.

I took one, wiped some tears and continued, "So, I called John and told him."

"What'd he say?"

I finished the story through tears. "He said he'd pay for the abortion. That I should tell him how much it was and he'd send me a check."

"What a jerk," Gina said, her eyes now brimming with tears.

I stopped crying, looked right into my sister's eyes and said very unemotionally, "Gina, I went to a clinic and I had an abortion. I killed my baby. That's why God would never give me another one."

"What?! No! That's not true!"

"Yes, it is."

"Missy, stop it! I would have done the same thing. You were too young to have a baby and in this country, the law says you have the right to make that decision. You did what you thought was the right thing to do."

"No. I killed my baby. And because of that, I never deserved to have another one. That's why my baby with my husband died in my belly after five months."

"Missy, this is crazy! Is this what you've been thinking all these years? Is that why you never talk to those girls anymore? Is that why you became a workaholic? Oh my God, it all makes sense now! Do the Cinnamon Girls know? Catherine? Anna? Nan? Did you ever tell them?"

"John told Catherine, and Catherine told the other girls. They all tried to call me and comfort me. None of them were judgmental. Anna even flew to Chicago and stayed with me for a weekend shortly after. And Catherine was so angry with her brother that they apparently didn't speak for awhile because of it."

"I don't understand why you would cut your best friends out of your life because of this."

"I know, it was a terrible thing to do. I was guilt-ridden and ashamed. I hated myself. So, I didn't want anyone around me. I felt like I didn't deserve their friendships."

"Oh, Miss, your heart is so fragile and so incredibly tender, and you didn't know how to handle the sadness."

"You're the first person I've ever actually come out and told. I never even told Paul. I mean, I couldn't be honest with my own husband. What kind of chance did that really give our marriage?"

"You didn't tell Mom either?"

"No, and I'm so glad I never did. I can't even imagine what she would have thought of me."

"She wouldn't have judged you. She would have understood. I'm sure of it. Stop judging yourself. Okay? Please? The guilt stops right now. You didn't do anything wrong, and you certainly didn't have a miscarriage because you're a bad person. And if that's what you think, that's really sick."

"I think you're right," I said. I wept in my baby sister's arms for a little bit longer. The relief was incredibly overwhelming.

Chapter 52

Gina and I skied all afternoon, and then spent our last night in Vail at a Mexican restaurant, munching on chips and salsa, and once again, chatting nonstop. That's when I told my sister about the *craigslist* ad and about Parker. I'm not sure I've ever seen Gina so captivated and entertained as she was while I told her the stories.

"I think my favorite one is the poker player," she laughed.

"A lot of the guys were really funny characters like him," I reflected, "But I did meet some very genuine guys, as well, with some really nice stories. It was an interesting experience."

"I don't understand why Paul would care so much about the contest. He left *you.* You should be able to do whatever you want with the ring. It's *your* ring."

"Not according to the law. We'll see what happens. Now that Derek is gone..."

"Who's Derek?" Gina asked.

I then told my sister all about Derek and Cassie, and about the amazing Lionetti family, and as she listened, completely wide-eyed and captivated, I realized I was really, really proud of myself for having the ring contest. It was genuinely an extraordinary experience that I felt would forever enrich my life.

Meeting Derek and Cassie gave me so much excitement and joy, and in a way, seeing their vivacious chemistry and the electricity between them brought me back to life.

The Lionettis gave me a sense of what it was like to be part of a large, very ethnic family with a powerful closeness and strong bonds made of steel. Growing up with my small family, I'd never gotten to experience anything like that.

I leaned across the booth and said, "Me, the divorced girl was looking for the perfect husband, but not for myself. I just wanted to believe true love was out there. What I ended up with was so much more than I could ever have imagined. Aside from all of the nut cases, I experienced family, friendship, trust, intense physical attraction, loyalty, death, and the biggest surprise of all."

Gina was waiting for my next word with baited breath.

I took a deep breath and whispered, "Love."

"What?"

It was right then I realized I was in love with Parker.

"You waited the whole trip to tell me you're in love?! Who is it?"

"His name is Parker Missoni."

"Do you really think you love him?"

"Yes," I smiled, "I'm sure of it."

I told Gina all about Parker, and I found myself missing him more than ever.

"Let's text him!" she said.

"No. We aren't texting anybody. Let's just have a nice night together."

We spent the rest of the night talking and laughing and reminiscing. We also talked to lots of men. Gina ended up giving her number to a seemingly nice, normal guy, who coincidentally lived three blocks from her in New York.

The next morning, we said goodbye in the Vail airport. It wasn't as hard as I thought it would be, the reason being I knew I was going to start getting together with my sister a lot more often. Gina had already committed to coming to Chicago for my birthday, which was in a couple months, and I told her I'd book a trip to New York the following month so that I could finally see her cupcake bakery.

"I love you," she said, hugging me as tight as she always did.

"Me too." I let go of her, looked her right in the eyes and said, "Thank you, Gina."

"For what?"

"For being my sister."

Chapter 53

The day I got home from Vail, I wrote the following e-mail:

To my three dearest friends, Anna, Nan, and Catherine,

I owe each of you a huge apology. I've been a horrible friend, and that's the last thing any of you deserve. All three of you gave me nothing but love, encouragement and your true friendship. And stupidly, I let my problems and my own self-hatred ruin the valuable bond I had with each of you.

I'm not proud of what I did all those years ago, but I can't go back and change that. It's done. What's very much not done for me is my relationship with all of you. I'm not sure if you're willing to forgive me and let me back into your hearts, so I'm begging you. I am so sorry that I hurt you.

I would love to plan a weekend to get together. My treat. Please let me know if either of the first two weekends in May will work for you to go to Las Vegas. I want to pay for everything. I would like to arrange flights and hotel rooms at the Bellagio if that's okay with you. It would be just the start to so much that I owe you for the horrible way I've neglected our friendships.

I love you all and I hope to hear from you.

Your Cinnamon Girlfriend forever,
Missy

I hit send. I had no idea what type of reaction I'd get from each of my friends. Knowing Nan, she'd welcome me back with open arms and accept my apology with no questions asked. Catherine would probably do the same thing. In fact, she might even apologize again about her brother, as I knew she always felt somewhat responsible for what had happened, which was ridiculous.

It was Anna who I suspected wouldn't be so easily forgiving. It would take time with her. Maybe she wouldn't even accept my invitation. Maybe she wouldn't want to take a trip with me. She'd begged me countless times to travel with them. I'd never even gone once. Did I expect everyone to drop everything and come with me on a trip I planned in a whim?

I wasn't sure how each girl would react, but what I was certain about was that I had to try to fix what I'd so badly broken: friendships that I'd promised to uphold forever.

Chapter 54

Age 28…

I'm giggling while Paul is trying to take off my wedding dress.

"There must be a hundred buttons on this thing," he laughs, "By the time I get this dress off, I'm going to be too tired to have sex."

I'm actually happy to hear him say that because I'm exhausted and the last thing I feel like doing is having sex right now. I suddenly wonder if it's normal to feel this way on your wedding night. Shouldn't I want to have sex with my brand new husband?

I turn around and face Paul.

"What?" he says.

He looks really gorgeous. He's pretty drunk and it's kind of funny to see him this way, because he rarely drinks. "Can I ask you something?"

"Anything."

"Why'd you marry me?"

"Because you're hot," he jokes.

"No, seriously."

"Why'd you marry ME?" he asks.

"Even though I asked you first, I'll answer. First of all, you're a gorgeous attorney who's on the fast track to make partner at one of the best law firms in the city, but it's more than that. I think you're a good person, a really, really good person with good values and a kind heart."

Paul smiles and it's really strange, but he seems disappointed by my answer.

"Your turn," I say.

Paul takes a deep breath and says, "Did you know that I knew I was going to marry you the first time I met you?"

I smile, "I think so."

"Will you always love me, Miss?"

"Of course. I just signed a piece of paper that says I'm required by law to do that."

"Well, maybe you should be putting up your end of the bargain right now," he says softly. Then he starts kissing my neck. I really do care for Paul, and wish I wanted to have sex, but I really don't. Do I have to? I wonder.

"Turn around," he says. I oblige and he starts unbuttoning the buttons again, this time quicker.

"Hey, Paul?"

"Yeah?"

"There are dozens of envelopes sitting on the nightstand, all for us. Don't you want to see how much money we got?"

"After..." he says. Now he's kissing the back of my neck and unbuttoning the buttons even quicker, which I didn't think was possible. He must be getting the hang of it, I think to myself.

The entire time we're having sex, I think about the envelopes and I decide to try to add up in my head the total dollar amount of what we just got as wedding gifts tonight. I'm doing this not because I'm greedy, or that I even care so much about the money. I'm doing this because I'm bored. It is on this night I begin to hate myself more than I ever have in my life.

Chapter 55

When I got off the elevator and looked at the familiar name, *Concerto, Fane and Manus* on the glass door, I cringed. No matter how much time went by, the thought of Paul's bosses never failed to make me squeamish.

Even though I had a polite smile on my face, the receptionist gasped when she saw me, to the point where I had to say, "Hi, Amy, don't worry. I'm not here to go on a shooting spree. I just need a word with my ex-husband."

"Uh...sure..." she said nervously, "Let me give his secretary a ring and see if she's available." Ring. Nice choice of words.

Just as Amy was making the call, her voice sounding like a gun was being pointed at her head, I heard a familiar voice that made me shudder.

"Well, well, well..." he said.

I turned and not surprisingly, there stood Michael Fane, the phony baloney.

"Hi, Michael," I said with a sugary smile.

"Missy, darling, you look wonderful," he faked, "Divorce truly does become you."

"But I'm not divorced yet."

"Right... How's the ring contest?" he asked.

"It's not a contest. It's..."

"Whatever it is, if it makes you happy then I'm glad."

What a faker! He was actually pretending to support the sale of my ring? Unbelievable! I was dying to ask him how his brother-in-law's loser friend, Chris Middleton was. (He was the guy whose mother wrote his letter for him, and he was the reason Paul found out about the ring contest.) I didn't, though. Instead, I decided to play his game and act as fake as he always did.

"Thank you so much for standing behind me on this, Michael," I said, feeling like I deserved an Academy Award for my performance.

"It's my pleasure," he said. And then, the slime did something that made my skin crawl. He got really close to me and whispered in my ear, "Have a great time with it."

He walked off and I shouted after him, "I will! Thanks!"

"Missy?!" I heard next. I turned and there stood Stuart Manus. Great...

"Hi, Stuart, how nice to see you," I continued faking.

"And you as well." He kissed my cheek and I wanted to throw up. "You're looking fit, as usual."

My insides burned with rage because I knew this was his dig to try to upset me by rubbing in the fact that I wasn't pregnant and that Priscilla was. "Thank you," I said, gritting my teeth.

"You've always had such a nice figure. My wife actually never lost the baby weight, and what's funny is, our baby is going to Northwestern in the fall!"

He started laughing heartily and at that moment, I decided I'd had enough of his cruel jabs to last a lifetime. This was it for me. I had no husband to protect any longer, and no reason to put up with any more of his crap.

"Yes, not having a baby does have its perks. I'm thin, no stretch marks, no varicose veins, my boobs don't sag, no cellulite..."

At this point, Stuart was just standing there waiting to hear what I was going with this, and Amy looked scared.

"Those of us who just couldn't ever have babies do have really nice bodies. I mean, look at this ass!"

I turned to him and slapped my own butt.

"Let's be honest, you can't have a tight ass like this after you have a kid. Am I right? I'm just so so so glad I never had kids!"

I looked at Amy. "Know what I mean, Amy?"

Stuart cleared his throat. "Um...my two o'clock is waiting for my call," he said. He then hurriedly walked down the hall, almost tripping he was so nervous. The transformation was hilarious. The man who loved to abuse me for not having children was now a clumsy wreck who didn't know how to handle my weird way of letting him know he couldn't mess with me anymore.

I was no longer the wife of one of his best attorneys. I was the divorced girl who had no reason to put up with any bad behavior, from him or anyone else.

"Nice..." I heard.

I looked at Amy and she had a huge grin on her face. I smiled back.

"I went through six rounds of in-vitro," she said softly, "I just found out I'm pregnant."

"Congratulations," I whispered, "That's wonderful!"

"Thanks," she smiled, "Your ex-husband will see you now. You can go on back."

I headed back to Paul's office. On my way there, I got one last surprise. "Well, well..." I heard.

I looked up and walking toward me was John Concerto, looking very Hugh Hefner-ish. I thought I'd be more disgusted by the sight of him, but I wasn't. I found myself genuinely smiling. Yes, he was a dirty old man, but he wasn't a bad person. I actually had respect for him professionally, and I could tell he genuinely liked me, which was more then I could say about the other two partners who both went out of their way to make me feel badly about myself. John was just a playboy who couldn't help his perverted urges.

"I'm going to hug you right now," I said with a giggle, "So keep your hands to yourself."

We hugged and for the first time ever there was no funny stuff. I felt like this was a good sign.

A second later, I heard Paul clear his throat. I pulled away from John, looked up, and saw the soon-to-be dad standing a few feet away in the doorway of his office. I'd forgotten how good looking he was, or maybe he just looked especially handsome because he was happy? Surprisingly, the sting of that thought wasn't unbearable.

"Hi," I said.

In his loud, commanding voice, John said, "It's always a pleasure to see you, Missy."

"Same with you."

He laughed, "Tell your assistant I said hello."

"Sure thing," I replied.

John turned and walked away. I looked at Paul, who motioned for me to walk into his office. At this moment, it was clear to me how angry he was, how resentful, and how at war with me he really felt. It was sad.

Paul sat behind his desk and I sat in a chair across from him. "How can I help you?" he asked in a cold, unemotional voice.

"How are you?" I asked softly.

"How am I?" he replied, his voice rising, "How *am* I?!"

With a deep breath, I answered, "Forget it."

Now Paul seemed annoyed. "Why are you here?"

I stood up, walked around the desk and stood before my ex-husband. "Paul," I began softly, "I came here to tell you that I'm sorry."

Paul's face transformed so fast it was comical. He went from having a pissed off, bitter look to the appearance of utter confusion. I knelt down and took his hand, and my eyes welled with tears.

"For a really long time, maybe for our whole marriage, I was cold and distant and really, really hard to live with, I'm sure. It was probably like living with a stranger." I took a deep breath and continued, "The cheating…it wasn't all your fault. I think you just wanted to be loved, and I couldn't give that to you because I couldn't give love to anyone. So, you went elsewhere."

"Missy…"

I wiped a tear off my cheek and finished, "That hurt me a lot, but I think I get it now. I really do. And I'm happy for you. I know you always wanted kids."

"Thank you," he said softly.

I stood up, walked to the chair across from his desk and sat down.

"Are you okay?" Paul asked.

Through tears, I smiled. "For sure."

Now Paul had a little smile on his face.

"Hey, Paul?"

"Yeah?"

"I want to move forward and finalize the divorce as soon as possible."

"Really?"

"Yes. And about the ring, I've arranged for it to be delivered here to you today. I want you to have it back."

"What? No."

"Yes, absolutely."

"Are you sure?"

"Yes."

"Should we just sell it and split the money then?"

"No, you gave it to me and now you can have it back and sell it yourself."

I could tell Paul didn't know what to say. I stood up, walked back over to him and hugged him.

"Missy," he said softly, "I'm really sorry too…for everything."

"Thanks." I pulled away from him and said, "And congratulations. I hope the baby gets your good looks."

He laughed.

"Take care of yourself," I said. And then I walked out of his office.

"Missy?" I heard, just as I stepped into the hallway.

I turned around.

"I really did try for a long, long time."

With a sad smile, I said, "I know you did."

At that moment, a stab of panic set in. Was I ever going to see Paul again? I'd see him in court for the final divorce hearing, but other than that, I wasn't sure. Was I okay with that? Yes, because this was what divorce was, and Paul had a new fiancé and a baby on the way. He'd moved on. But there was something heart breaking about never seeing a person you shared a bed with for almost a decade, and for a second, I wanted to run back into his arms and cry in them for awhile. But what would that do besides make me look like a crazy, dysfunctional, emotionally wrecked nutcase?

With tears now brimming in the corners of my eyes, I quickly walked out to the lobby, and realized I was walking out of this office for the last time. I would never be here, ever again. I glanced up and looked at the sign, *Concerto, Fane and Manus* for the last time, and I didn't feel squeamish or bitter anymore. I felt a strong sense of finality.

I'd never go to another *Concerto, Fane and Manus* Christmas party that entailed petty comments and ass-grabbing. In fact, I'd probably never see any of Paul's partners ever again. *Conceited, Fake and Manipulative* were most likely out of my life forever. I giggled while I pressed the elevator down button, but tears were running down my cheeks.

Chapter 56

When I returned home and got online, here are some of the e-mails that were waiting for me:

1. *"I've been with my girlfriend for eight years and I think I'm finally ready to get hitched..."*
2. *"I'm getting older and I figure, 'Who's going to want me when I hit 50?' So, I'm biting the bullet and marrying my longtime, girlfriend, Gayle..."*
3. *"I just got fired and I need the benefits of my girlfriend's insurance plan. I'm sure you can understand that..."*
4. *"Suzy's hot. I'm not. Suzy's sweet. I'm no treat. Suzy's great. I'm always late. So save my life. Help make Suzy my wife!"*

It had been like this the whole time since I'd placed the ad. I was always swarmed with responses, e-mails that ranged from bizarre to heartfelt to disgusting to entertaining. But no matter how many comical or witty or boring or sexually graphic e-mails I read, the fact that I'd actually put my engagement ring up for sale for $.99 still seemed surreal.

And now, the contest was over and the ring was going back to Paul. He'd sell it for half of what it was worth and eventually a nice, young couple would walk into a jewelry store and buy it, or buy a version of it (if the jeweler decided to reset it.) And the couple would never know the history of Paul and Missy Benson, and how we managed to screw up the commitment we made to each other in front of God.

They'd never know the joy I felt when Paul put the ring on my finger and asked me to marry him. They'd never know about the times Paul complained because I wasn't wearing the ring.

"I don't like to shower with it on," I'd tell my husband, "And then I forget to put it back on. What's the big deal?"

They'd never know about the day he left me, when I took the ring off my finger and put it into my jewelry box, and they'd never know about the night I watched *An Officer and a Gentleman*, put the ring back on and held it to my chest while I sobbed. And I was at peace with that. A whole new story would begin with the ring.

One by one I deleted each e-mail, knowing this was the last batch of responses I'd be reading. After I read the last e-mail, which was actually kind of cute because the guy had fallen in love with his girlfriend when he went into the hospital for triple bypass surgery and she was one of the nurses, I hit delete, and then I took my ad off *craigslist.*

Then I headed to Tony's Shoe Repair. When I walked into the shop, Tony was nowhere in sight. Tony's dad was busy sanding something. He looked up at me and smiled, "Hello, Young Lady!"

"Hi Mr. Lionetti, it's nice to see you," I exclaimed.

"Same to you," he said, his thick Italian accent warming my heart instantly.

"Is Tony here?" I asked.

"He be right back. He went to Starbucks."

"Okay, I'll just wait for him."

"We have coffee maker in back. Why he need to pay four bucks for coffee? I don't get it!"

I laughed.

"Such a waste," he mumbled.

Right then, I heard the bells on the store door jingle and then I heard, "Hi there!" I turned around and there was Tony, walking in with a Starbucks cup in one hand, a little brown pastry bag in the other.

"Hi Tony," I smiled.

Tony walked over to me and hugged me. "Hang on a second," he said, turning and walking behind the counter. "Here, Paps, I brought you a donut."

Mr. Lionetti laughed, "How much this was?"

"Who cares?" Tony chuckled.

"Such a waste," he said, shaking his head.

Tony was smiling when he looked at me. "So, how are you?"

"I'm good," I replied, "Sorry that you haven't heard from me. I've been out of town."

"No problem."

"Tony, can we talk for a minute?" I asked softly.

"Sure," he said, "Want to go for a walk?" Before I even answered, he said loudly, "Paps, I'm going to walk outside with Missy. I'll be back in a little while."

"Okay," he responded.

"Bye, Mr. Lionetti! Take care!"

"Same to you!," he replied.

Out we walked, heading for a little side street right by the store. "So, how's your family?" I asked, "Your mom?"

"Good, really good."

"And Claudette?"

Tony's face instantly lit up. "She's good."

"I'm glad," I grinned.

"Look, if I'm not getting the ring, it's okay. Really."

"Well, the thing is…" I said. I stopped walking, took my purse off my shoulder, unzipped it and took out a check I'd written earlier in the day. It was for ten thousand dollars. I handed him the check.

"Wait a minute!" he gasped, "What are you doing? Why are you giving me money?"

"Because I want you to have it. I want you to go out and buy Claudette a beautiful ring."

"I don't understand."

"My ring isn't for sale anymore. It's…unavailable."

"Why?"

"Actually, I gave it back to my ex-husband."

"Really?"

"I put my ring up for sale on *craigslist* because I wanted to prove something to myself. I wanted solid evidence that there were good guys out there who would make great husbands, who would treat their women like gold, who would make a commitment to a marriage and stick to it. And I realized, partly because of you, that yes, there are some great guys out there. You *will* make an incredible husband and you will make Claudette very happy. I'm sure of it. But as far as the test of time, there are no guarantees. Not only because of infidelity or because two people might grow apart, but because of fate and what's meant to be."

"I believe that," he said.

"A very close friend of mine was about to get engaged and he died suddenly."

"Oh my God, that's horrible." Tony said softly.

"Do I think he would have made a great husband? Absolutely. But we'll never really know."

"Were you planning on giving the ring to *him?* If you were, please tell me. It's okay."

"Honestly, I loved you both. But in the end, I realized that the ring doesn't belong to anyone who read my ad on *craigslist.* The ring belongs only to one person: my ex-husband, the guy who gave it to me. And guess what? He *was* a good husband for a long time. Was I a good wife? At the beginning, maybe. But we both killed our marriage."

"Can I ask you a question?"

"Sure."

"Think you'll ever get married again?"

I responded, "Well, I have to say, I kind of like this single thing. It's kind of cool. I'm learning how to get comfortable in my own shoes, no pun intended."

"That's great."

"But there is a part of me who thinks there's another diamond ring out there with my name on it."

"I wish that for you."

"You're a great guy with a beautiful family, and a woman who loves you dearly. I hope it stays like that for you forever."

"Are you sure about this?" he asked me, holding up the check, "I feel weird about taking it."

"Please, Tony, I really want you to have it. I wouldn't have given it to you if I didn't."

"Will you come to the wedding?"

"I wouldn't miss it!"

Chapter 57

"Cheers!" I said, holding up my thin mint martini.

"What are we celebrating?" asked J.J.

"A lot of good stuff, especially to the fantastic job you did while I was away."

"I'll drink to that!" she said, clinking her martini glass on mine.

"Thank you so much. I could never have taken all this time off if I didn't know I could depend on you."

"To tell you the truth, it saved me," she said, "Being a workaholic helped me to not think about Christian."

"Have you talked to him?"

"No, but it's okay. I feel good. I feel strong and independent. It's... empowering, I guess."

"I was kind of thinking, if you're ready, you should get in touch with Jake. I really liked him."

"Him and his ass grabbing grandfather?" she joked.

"I even like his ass grabbing grandfather. But seriously, now that you're single, text him or something."

"I heard he has a girlfriend."

"It could be over."

"Could be," she said with a smile.

She ended up texting Jake, who texted back within thirty seconds, asking where were we and did we want to meet up with him.

"Go for it," I said with a smile.

She texted him back and then said, "Your turn. Text Parker."

"Hmm... I don't really know what I would say."

"How about, 'Hi?' He'd love anything you texted."

"I miss him."

"Then do it!"

"I'm not ready. Things are going really well. It's nice to just get to know myself for right now, the new self, the self I really want to be."

"But what if Parker's the one?"

"He can't be the one. He's the first guy I dated after getting separated. I do adore him, though. He sent me a card while I was away."

"What did it say?"

I grinned. "I miss you, Mrs. Jones."

"Who's Mrs. Jones?"

"Me. It's a long story."

"He's a good guy, Miss."

"I know."

"And thoughtful, too."

"You think?"

"He just got this big award for all this free physical therapy he did on special needs kids. He organized this whole project..."

"How do you know?"

"Uh...well...he's called the office a couple times and you know, we got to talking..."

"Really?"

"Yeah, that's okay right?"

It was now very obvious that Parker was calling J.J. to get information about me. It was a little stalker-ish, but I was happy about it. Plus, I loved hearing about his philanthropic activities. He was a giver, and if I remotely thought I was in love with him before, knowing he gave his time for special needs kids was sealing the deal.

"Sure." I gave J.J. a wink. "Put on a little more lipstick before Jake gets here. I'm going home."

I got up and gave her a kiss on the cheek, and just as I turned around to leave, she called out my name.

"Yeah?" I said.

"I can't believe I forgot to tell you this. Our client...the Sachs are going to make an offer on that house tomorrow. You know, the one you told me to show to everyone. 1775 Glen Oak."

"Jenny's husband's dream house?!"

"Who's Jenny?" J.J. asked.

I laughed. "Never mind. That's wonderful!"

The cab driver dropped me off where I'd parked my car, and I headed home, happy for J.J., and happy to drive back to the burbs, go home, get into bed and go to sleep. Once under the covers, though, I broke down and texted Parker. "Tell me a story?" I typed.

A few minutes later, as I was dozing off, a text came back that read, "Once upon a time, there was a guy...just your basic, ordinary guy..."

"Tell me more," I texted back.

"A guy who just wanted his girl back."

"Then come and get me," I texted with urgency. But, then, just as I was about to hit send, I couldn't bring myself to do it. I wasn't ready for passion and commitment and let's be honest, love. So, I deleted the draft.

Then, I tried to think of something casual to text back. I couldn't, though. How could I type, "Call me sometime" or "Let's get together this weekend"? We were so far beyond that. It seemed there was only one text appropriate. And that was "Then come and get me." And I was too scared to send it. So, I took the coward's way out.

"Hope you are well. Good night," I texted.

Then I pretended my pillow was Parker, hugged it really tight and fell asleep.

Chapter 58

Age 38…

I'm in the children's clothing department of Bloomingdale's, browsing.

"May I help you?" asks a kind, older, heavyset woman.

"I'm looking for a gift for a newborn."

"Girl or boy?" she asks. At this moment, I'm absolutely sure this woman is a grandmother.

"Girl."

"Come this way, honey," she says.

I follow her to an area where there are racks of little outfits for newborn babies.

"About how much were you thinking of spending?"

"Um…I'm not sure yet," I say, looking at all the outfits, each one more adorable than the next.

"Well," she says, "I'll just let you look. I'll be at the register if you need my help."

"Thank you," I smile.

She walks away and I now I find myself smiling from ear to ear. These tiny little outfits are taking my breath away. The gift is for Stuart Manus's grand daughter, so I've had a bad attitude about running this errand from the start, and I'm only doing it because Paul keeps nagging me to get it done. However, now that I'm here, actually looking at the stuff, I realize it's making me feel warm and happy. It's causing me to remember the innocent people in this world and forget about all the jerks, like Stuart, who has to address the fact that I don't have babies every time I see him.

I'm feeling like my problems in life are so little, because the tiny people who wear these clothes, their biggest problem is that they're overtired, or that their little bellies are having a hard time digesting formula or breast milk, or that they're teething and it hurts.

I hold up a pink leopard outfit, size 3m (three months.) The long sleeve top has pink fur trim around the bottom, and the leggings have the same trim around the bottom of each leg. There's a matching leopard headband attached to the hanger. I giggle. Why does a three month old need a headband? I wonder. Is there a possibility that her hair is going to get in her eyes?

Intense sadness comes on suddenly, and now I find myself fighting back tears. Why am I here shopping for Stuart Manus? Why am I not shopping for MY baby? Where IS my baby? Why have I been cheated like this?

It gets even worse when I answer my own question. 'Your baby is dead. You went to a hospital and you had someone kill it,' I say to myself, 'You don't deserve to get pregnant with another baby. You're a murderer.'

"Are you okay?" I hear the saleswoman say to me.

I realize I have tears running down my cheeks. I wipe them away and answer, "Oh, yeah. I'm fine. I'll take this." Then I hand her the outfit.

"Aww, this is so cute, isn't it?"

"Yes, it is," I answer.

The lady rings me up and just after she hands me the bag and the gift receipt she says, "Don't lose faith, okay?"

I'm alarmed. How does she know what I'm thinking?!

In response to the look of surprise I have on my face, she says, "It took my daughter four years to have a baby, four in-vitros, and then she had twins. Miracles do happen."

"Thank you," I answer with a smile. What I want to tell her is that the difference between me and her daughter is, her daughter had the guts to keep trying. I want to tell her that I, the coward, have stopped having sex with my husband, which makes it impossible to procreate. I want to add that I've decided to live a life of self-pity and self-hatred, instead of trying for another baby, and that not only am I hurting myself, but I'm ruining my husband's life, too.

"Take care," I say. It is then that I head to the boutique next door to Bloomingdale's to find a dress for Paul's company Christmas party.

Chapter 59

I was dreaming. In my dream, I was at my church in Cleveland and I was the only person in the sanctuary. I was kneeling in front of a pew, and I was praying.

"Dear God," I said softly, "I am so sorry for having an abortion. I was young and really scared and at the time, and I thought it was the right thing to do. But now, since I'm 38 and I've never been able to have a child, I'm thinking that my unexpected pregnancy with Catherine's brother was supposed to be my baby." I began to cry, and I continued through tears, "I'm asking for your forgiveness, God. I'm so sorry..."

Suddenly, I heard my mother's voice. "Stop it! Stop it right now!"

I turned around and there was my mom, standing behind me.

"What are you doing here?"

"I'm here to tell you to stop punishing yourself. You didn't do anything wrong! You are a goodhearted, wonderful soul and I don't understand why you're torturing yourself."

I heard a male voice next. "She's right." I turned my head a few feet away from where my mom was, and there stood my father. The first thing I noticed was that he looked young. I don't know why I was surprised, but he looked just like he did when I was in high school. It was at that moment I realized something: my dad died when he was 38. My age. I always knew the number, but now that I was this age, it made me realize just how very young he was when his life was cut so short.

I got up, ran to him, threw my arms around him and burst into tears. "I missed you," I cried.

My dad and I hugged for a long time and then my mom joined in and the three of us were embraced.

"I miss you," I said softly, "Both of you."

"We're so proud of you, Missy," said my dad.

"We want you to be proud of *yourself,*" my mom added.

"For what?" I asked.

"What do you mean, 'for what?'" said Mom, "You are incredibly successful professionally. You find people homes. A home and a family is everything, and you are part of that for so many people. Don't you understand how valuable your life is in this regard?"

"You were a wonderful daughter to me," said Dad, "I couldn't have asked for better. You were wonderful to your mother and your sister, too. Do you remember when she was four and she broke her arm on the Kleins' trampoline?"

"Yes," I smiled sadly.

"I saw you," he said.

"What do you mean?"

"The night it happened, after we got home from the emergency room. I saw you. It was around midnight. I got up to check on her and there you were, sitting on the edge of her bed, playing with her hair while she slept."

I smiled as I recalled the scene, remembering how worried I was about Gina's arm. Meanwhile, I could never have known that two years later, my dad would die.

"That's when I saw your character, your warmth, and your gentle heart. You were only twelve years old, but I knew the kind of person you were. I was so happy, so proud."

I was sobbing now.

"We want to tell you one more thing," said Mom, "About your ring contest..."

"You did the right thing when you gave Paul back the ring," said my dad, "You don't need your ring anymore to help people. And, the best thing about that ring contest was that you helped yourself. You truly helped yourself. It caused you to look at things and reflect on your life. You now have acceptance, accountability for your mistakes, and your anger is gone. There's nothing left to do except start your new life. And it's going to be a great one. I can tell."

I woke up to the alarm on my phone. When I went to shut it off, I noticed the date. It was my dad's birthday.

Chapter 60

During the twenty years I'd lived in Chicago, I'd been to dozens of Bulls games, some with Paul and some with clients. Tonight by far was the most I'd ever enjoyed a game. I was able to get seats just one row behind the floor seats, courtesy of an old client of mine who started a ticket broker business a few years back.

The guy would do anything for me because several years earlier, we had been involved in a bidding war for a completely overpriced mansion in Glencoe and I won out for him. How'd I do it? I basically worked my butt off to find another house for the other contender, while wining and dining the seller's broker, to the point where I took the couple to Charlie Trotter's for dinner!

Even more unbelievable, the other buyer decided to buy the house that *I* found, and I let his broker have the commission. That's how badly I knew my guy wanted the Glencoe place. So, ever since I'd gotten my client the house he wanted so badly, I was one of his favorite people.

So, why was I having such a good time at the game? Because here I sat with two dear friends of mine: Cassie and her nine year old son, Kenneth.

Seated between his mother and me, Kenneth was having a blast eating popcorn and jumping out of his seat, cheering wildly every time his favorite player, Joakim Noah made a shot. And although his demeanor was making me happy, I couldn't help but constantly think that this poor little boy, whose parents split up when he was a baby was now dealing with loss once again, this time with the death of a man who was not just his mother's boyfriend, but a person he admired and loved, and who he probably thought was going to move in with them and be there for him for the rest of his life.

Kenneth's wide-eyed gaze and huge grin was melting me, and regardless of what had happened, I had a sense that he was a very special child, and that he would turn out just fine, especially since he had Cassie for a mother. Watching her with her son, it was so obvious to me that she was an exceptional caregiver, role model and mom. And it made me very happy and very envious at the same time.

I hadn't seen Cassie since Derek's wake, and when I'd called to ask her to the game, I wasn't sure she'd be up for going out with me. I felt maybe the sight of me would be too painful. Maybe every time she looked at my face, she'd be thinking about the engagement ring she'd never get to wear on her finger.

I was wrong. Cassie was very happy to hear from me, and in her true nature, she seemed to be putting on a happy face and going through the motions of life, trying to get enjoyment out of it for herself, while truly looking out for her son.

During halftime, Cassie switched seats with Kenneth so we could talk. While her boy watched the *Luvabulls* dance, followed by a million dollar free throw contest, Cassie opened up to me.

"What a strange time this is," she said, "I wake up every morning and I still can't believe he's gone. Seriously, sometimes when my phone rings, I feel like I'm going to answer it and Derek's going to be on the other end." She imitated Derek, "Hey, baby, whatcha wearin'?" and then laughed.

"I'm so sorry," was all I could say.

"I miss him," she said, tears forming in her eyes.

I nodded.

"This is so difficult, almost unbearable at times," she continued, "The only thing keeping me going is Kenneth. I think without him, my broken heart would kill me." She looked over at her son, who was completely oblivious to our conversation, since he was so engrossed in watching the slingshots that were shooting t-shirts into the crowd.

"It seems my only purpose now is to make sure this boy gets a good life. He needs me."

"Yes, he does. He's really lucky to have you."

"Thank you," she said softly.

"I know it seems like things aren't going to get better, but they will. You'll see. I'm by no means comparing my divorce to a death. I've actually had my share of deaths, too. Both my parents are deceased, and I know that feeling, like you're not sure you'll ever be able to smile genuinely ever again, or that the aching pain in your gut seems like it will never stop. It gets easier. I promise."

"Thanks," she smiled sadly.

Both of us began looking up to see where in the crowd the t-shirts were landing. I looked at Kenneth's face, filled with hope every time a t-shirt came even remotely close to us. Then I looked at his mother, smiling at her son's expression.

"Cassie..."

She turned to me. I zipped opened my purse, took out an envelope and handed it to her.

"What's this?" she asked.

"It's for Kenneth. For college."

Cassie looked shocked.

"Go ahead," I smiled, "Open it."

When she saw the ten thousand dollar check, she gasped.

"If you invest it in a 529 college plan, it will be worth a lot more by the time Kenneth starts applying to schools."

Still dazed, she asked, "Why?"

"Why?!" I exclaimed with a giggle.

"Yes, why?"

"Because you didn't get the ring."

"I don't understand the connection."

"Don't try to figure it out. I just wanted to do this. It felt right. Please, let me."

Cassie hugged me so tight, it was humorous. "Thank you," she said through tears, "Thank you."

All of a sudden, we heard Kenneth scream. Cassie pulled away from me and when we turned to him, we watched his arms reach really far out in front of him to catch one of the rolled up t-shirts.

"Yes!" he shouted.

Cassie and I started laughing. "What are the odds of that happening?" she asked.

"Pretty slim," I answered, "But anything's possible, right?"

Cassie gave me a big grin, and for the first time all night, I saw hope in her expression. "Yup," she answered, "anything's possible."

Chapter 61

A few days later, on a cold, dark, damp day with rain slightly falling, I attended one of the first Chicago Cubs games of the season. Not as a spectator, though. As a beer vendor! Tom Mitchell, (the guy who was on my flight to Vail) recruited me as part of a promotion that the Callahan Corporation was having, getting regular people to do jobs in their company.

"The second I heard about it, I remembered what you said to me and I knew you were the perfect person for this," he'd told me on the phone a couple weeks earlier.

"Really?"

"You told me you always wanted to do this, remember? Now's your chance! Plus, you only have to do it for a couple hours and then you'll be interviewed and a photographer will snap a few shots. What do you think?"

"It's funny. Ordinarily, I'd never consider it," I replied, "But now...what the heck? I'm in!"

So, here I was, walking up and down the aisles soliciting, wearing a big harness with twelve sixteen-ounce cups of cold *Old Style* attached to it.

My first impression of the job was that I'd never given these poor beer vendors half the credit they deserved. This was hard work! The load I was toting was heavy, to the point it was really straining my back muscles. In addition, it was rainy and cold, and walking up and down the steps, shouting out, "Cold beer! Get your cold beer!" was tiring, not to mention a tad bit annoying at times, due to several drunken Cub fans shouting out comments and opinions.

"Over here," I heard one guy yell to me. "I'll take one," he said, "And then I'll take *you!*"

He laughed in this creepy, obnoxious way and the guy sitting next to him said, "Hey! Watch yourself punk!"

I mouthed "thank you" to the guy and handed the obnoxious guy his beer.

"Over here!" I heard a lot, which didn't bother me. But hearing "Hey, Beer Chick!" kind of did.

I would estimate that the people interested in *Old Style* were 70% male. I did have this one woman, who looked my age shout out, "Hey, girlfriend! How about a couple cold ones?"

Next, a cute, young guy said, "I've never seen a beer vendor as beautiful as you."

His friend sitting next to him replied, "Dude, you really need to get laid."

While I was cracking up, I heard, "Excuse me, can I get one?"

I turned to the patron and instantly my heart stopped. There sat a Cub fan I'd never expected to see: Parker.

"How much?" he flirted.

I stood there frozen for a moment, unable to move, unable to speak.

"How much is it?" asked the guy sitting next to him, who I could tell was Parker's friend.

Finally, I answered, "It's free." I handed Parker a beer and then I gave one to his buddy.

"Free beer?!" shouted the guy sitting a few seats down. A couple other buzzed guys started inquiring. "What?! Free *Old Style*? No way!"

"Where?" asked a guy.

"That girl right there's giving away free beer!" shouted another guy.

"Hey, can I get one?" some other girl asked.

I wasn't panicked by the frenzy of what people thought was free beer. I was still in shock that Parker was right here.

He and I didn't look away from each other for a long, long time, until he got up from his seat, which was about five seats in, and made his way to the aisle and to me.

"Quite the job change," he said with a big grin, "Real estate didn't work out for you?"

"Oh, it's just for today. I'm still a realtor."

"You look so hot," he said.

I giggled.

"Come here," he said softly, taking my face in his hands. Then he kissed me. Hard. The two of us started making out, and it looked kind of funny because Parker had to adjust his head away from the beers I was carrying that took up a big space in front of me. Nonetheless, kissing Parker in the middle of Wrigley Field, wearing a harness that was practically killing me felt amazing. I had missed him so much, and I wanted his lips on mine more than ever.

A couple seconds later, I heard cheering and clapping. It got louder and louder, and I figured the Cubs must have gotten a hit. I was wrong. The applause and the cheers were for me and my make out partner. Right then, I heard a couple cameras click. People were taking pictures of us on their cameras and their phones. We both looked up.

"Look!" a guy shouted, "You're on TV!"

We looked at a nearby television set and sure enough, I saw the replay of the beer girl and the Cub fan's long smooch.

"Oh my God!" I laughed.

"Hilarious," said Parker.

"I think you should go back to your seat, sir," I joked.

"Okay, and you should get back to work, young lady," he said with a chuckle.

I smiled and continued selling beer, which only lasted for about two minutes before I was whisked away by a security guard to a group of reporters who started asking me questions.

"Who was that guy?" one of them asked me.

"Umm...a close friend?" I responded, unsure of the real answer at this point.

"Have you ever seen him before?" someone else asked, "I mean, is he a stranger?"

"No, he's not a stranger."

"Why did he get out of his seat and start kissing you?"

"I think he missed me," I said with a chuckle.

"Tell us about him," another reporter asked, "Who is he?"

I paused to think about what I wanted to say, print reporters standing there with their recorders, a couple cameras practically in my face.

Then, I gave the reporters the sound bite they were all looking for. "He's a gifted physical therapist, a great cook, and a talented singer." Tears welled in my eyes. "He's the man I love."

When I got in my car to head home, I looked at my iPhone. I had 24 missed calls. My voice mailbox was full. When I walked into my house, my home phone was ringing. This was crazy! People must have seen what happened during the game and were calling me. The callers included J.J., Gina, who informed me on voice mail that the video was now number one on *You Tube,* every Cinnamon Girl, Cassie, Tony Lionetti, and Katy and Jenny from Sun Lakes.

Parker called, too. "Did you mean it?" was his entire message.

I called him back. When he answered the phone, he said it again. "So, did you mean it?"

"Yes."

"I have to ask you a question," said Parker. "Do you think it was a coincidence that I saw you today?"

Right then it hit me. I couldn't believe I had thought running into Parker was a fluke. I realized right then that he had found out I'd be there.

"Been talking to J.J. again?" I asked.

"Yup. She's been keeping me informed of your whereabouts," he flirted, "She was a good hire."

I laughed.

"Guess where I am right now?" he asked.

It was at that moment my doorbell rang.

I threw my phone down on the couch, ran to the door, opened it, and practically dove into Parker.

We kissed passionately until Parker pulled away, put his hands on my shoulders and pushed me back. His warm, kind brown eyes were looking right into mine.

"I love you," he said, "I have loved you since the minute I met you. Nothing has ever been more clear to me."

"Me, too," I said with a big grin, "It just took some time for the divorced girl to figure it out."

Chapter 62

When I say my clothes and Parker's clothes were off in less than a minute and a half, I'm not joking. We had both just said the L word, and I think we really needed to fully express how we felt naked.

Parker and I made our way upstairs to my bed, and then we made love for hours. We kissed, and giggled and talked and scratched each other's backs. We hugged a lot, but mostly, we held each other. Being in his arms was safe and comfortable, but the feelings were sexy and exciting, too.

I realized that I'd never experienced both of these feelings together. The two most significant men in my life before Parker, Paul and Brad, had offered extremes at both ends of the spectrum.

Paul had given me security and comfort, but the relationship had always suffered when it came to sex. On the other hand, Brad, who took my breath away when he so much as touched my arm, was someone I never saw myself with long term. Now, with Parker, I felt as if I was sleeping with two men: my best friend and a guy who I physically hungered for immensely.

"Want me to tell you a story?" he asked in the middle of the night.

"No," I said, "I want you to touch me more."

"I can do that," he joked.

He made love to me again so intensely, it was like entering a new place I'd never gone before. It was strange. And wonderful. I couldn't believe this kind of love existed. I seriously had never experienced it until this very moment, and in a way it made me sad because this was the kind of closeness I should have with my husband. In a sense, Paul wasn't the only cheater in our marriage. I had cheated him out of having this kind of bond, either because he wasn't the right man, or because my issues had blocked any capability of giving this kind of love to him. Either way, it didn't matter anymore. Being with Parker felt like such a gift, and I wanted more and more of it. More and more of him.

When the sun began to come up, I was still lying naked in Parker's arms.

"I have some things I want to tell you," I said softly.

"You can tell me anything, Miss."

"I hope so."

I knew I had to tell Parker everything. When it came to love, this time I wasn't going to keep any ghosts in the closet. Real, true love meant honesty and openness. How Parker would react to my abortion was out of my control. But I had to tell him, because that was part of who I was. And if love was going to work out for me this time, it was going to be because there were no secrets, no hidden baggage and nothing held back. It was scary, but I had to trust it.

I took a deep breath and I began talking honestly and openly to the man I loved.

Chapter 63

What's it like to be in a room with six girls who used to be your best friends, whom you have seen less than five times in two decades, and whom you know are disappointed and angry with you, and rightfully so? Very awkward and uncomfortable. For the first three minutes, that is.

We were all just sitting at the bar, drink in hand, not really saying much, as if there was an elephant in the room and no one wanted to bring any attention to it. Nan was the first to point out the large animal.

"Okay, is this how the whole weekend's going to be? Because if that's the case I'll jump on a plane and go home right now. Come on, girls! We're in Vegas! Let's clear the air already so we can have some fun!"

"Look," said Anna, looking directly at me, "Thank you for organizing and paying for this trip and everything. It was really nice. But, I'm having a hard time looking at you and not feeling really mad that you sort of took your friendship away from us for something we had nothing to do with."

"I know," I replied, "I'm so sorry."

"Why all of a sudden do you want to be friends with us again?" she asked.

Nan and Catherine were both looking at me and waiting for a response.

I took a deep breath and spoke to all of them. "When Paul left me, it changed my whole life. At first, it was shocking and devastating. I didn't see it coming. But in hindsight, I realize I shouldn't have been so surprised.

As my bitterness and anger started to subside, I began to look within myself. I started to recognize *my* part in the demise of the marriage, and I began to see things I never allowed myself to see. And in time, I realized some horrible mistakes I made. Not just the abortion, but even worse, the decisions I made and the person I became after that: a close-minded, workaholic who wanted to forget a mistake by throwing myself into work and marrying the wrong man.

I pushed away the people in my life who loved me the most. I guess I didn't think I deserved to have friends. It was really messed up. Then I hosted this crazy contest–I'll tell you more about that later–but it changed things. Everything is different. It's like I woke up. I can't explain it.

What's sad is all that time I lost that I'll never be able to get back. All the vacations you took, all the get-togethers. But, what I *can* do is start from right now. And if you are willing to let me back in to your lives, back into your hearts, I'd be so grateful. And I promise I'll be the friend I was to you all in high school. Even better."

I was surprised at how calm I was, and how I was able to keep my composure so well. My friends, on the other hand were in tears. Except for Anna. No tears, but I could tell she was touched.

She gave me a wink and then declared to Nan and Catherine, "Look at you emotional women! You're a wreck! Both of you!"

We all started laughing and that was it. It was like we were back in Anna's mom's living room, putting on our Cinnamon necklaces. It was bittersweet for me. I loved these women and yes, they were my friends again, but all of them had stayed in touch this whole time. They were closer than ever. And me, I'd missed out on twenty years of their lives, twenty years of reunions, twenty years of phone calls and laughter and good times, as well as their sorrows and heart breaks.

For the entire weekend while lounging at the pool, going out for nice dinners, shopping, gambling, going to bars, and even when we were getting ready in our rooms, we played catch up.

Nan had married a world-renowned cardiovascular surgeon. She was loaded! Even better, she was genuinely happy. She'd pleased her parents immensely, marrying a Korean guy (the first one she'd ever dated) and she'd ended up falling head over heals for him.

Anna was a highly successful attorney in Cleveland with two teenage daughters, not blissfully married, but contented in life, especially since she'd just signed a publishing deal with Harper Collins for two legal thrillers she'd written.

As for Catherine, she had gotten divorced a few years earlier, and although she was still trying to adjust to life as both a single parent to her nine year old twin girls, and a busy, working mother, she seemed happy. She'd just started dating a firefighter, who according to Catherine was completely enamored with her, not to mention gorgeous in that tough, heroic firefighter way.

One night at dinner, after two or three glasses of cabernet, I asked Catherine, "So, how's your brother?"

"My brother?" she responded nervously.

"Yeah."

"Fine?" she answered. I realized her voice was shaking.

"Is he still married?" I asked.

"No."

Nan chimed in, "Three kids."

I wasn't surprised that John ended up divorced. What was shocking to me was when I'd heard several years earlier that he was getting married. At the time, I couldn't believe he was able to commit to marriage. I was subsequently shocked every time I'd heard his wife had another child. It made me a little sick to think about the fact that he was a father of three, when sadly enough, he would have had four, had I not done what I'd done. I had to remind myself that he didn't want four. Or, I should say, he didn't want *my* baby.

As if she knew what I was thinking, Catherine put her arm around me. "I love you. I'm really sorry I didn't stop you from staying there that night."

"It wasn't your fault," I answered, "The only person to blame was me, for being stupid and not using a condom. I don't even blame John. I blame myself."

"You're not too old to have kids," said Anna, "You know that right?"

"Well, she needs to get married again first," said Nan.

"Actually, I have something to tell you guys," I said.

"What?" all three asked in unison.

I rolled my shoulders back, took a deep breath and announced, "I'm applying to become a foster parent."

Chapter 64

A couple days after I got back from my trip, I met Katy (Sun Lakes Katy) for breakfast at a little diner by my house.

"So, how are the other girls?" I asked her.

"Everyone's good. Except for Jenny," she said sadly, "She's really having a hard time."

"I'm so sorry. I know what that's like."

"I know you do," she said with a gentle smile.

"So, do you know why I asked you to meet me here?"

"I think so, but I hope I'm right," she answered.

"Yes, you are," I said with a big grin.

"You'll make a wonderful foster parent," she gleamed.

"I've always wanted children. And it took me a long time to realize that the reason I don't have them is not because God's punishing me. It's because it wasn't meant to be yet. And now, I feel like this is a chance for me to do something really good and experience parenthood, in a way.

I have so much money saved, and it's a shame that I don't have anyone to share it with. I want to share my home, and food and other material things, but I also have all this love to give, and I want to give that to a child who needs it."

Katy and I sat there and talked for almost two hours. She explained the process and all the training classes I'd have to take, and I told her I was more than willing to put in the time. I explained that I was definitely interested in a girl. Not that I didn't care for both genders, but I just felt like it fit me more, as a single mother, and as someone who had a much younger sister. We also discussed age, and Katy suggested that based on my job and my busy lifestyle, that in her opinion, a child between the ages of five and ten would be the best fit for me.

I was so excited I wanted to burst. I was actually going to have a child living with me! What a beautiful, wonderful thing I'd be doing, and what an amazing experience I was going to have.

I felt a tremendous sense of pride and self-worth I'd never really felt before. Missy Benson, shitty ex-wife and former brick wall was going to share the love I now had the guts to give.

"I don't know you that well, but I'm so proud of you," said Katy, "I think this experience is going to make you very happy."

"Me too," I glowed.

We sat there for a moment, both of us just smiling. I was thrilled. As for Katy, I could tell she was really psyched, not only for me, but for one of her children.

All of a sudden, Katy blurted out, "Sara."

"Pardon me?"

"She's going to be your foster daughter. I'm sure of it. I'm not supposed to be saying anything about any particular child until you've completed the training and gone through the interview process, but I can't help it. I just feel it.

Sara is seven years old. She's got this blond hair with big ringlets, and she loves wearing headbands to hold it all back. She's a great student. Her teachers love her. She's so kind. If a kid falls down, she's the first one to rush to his side and make sure he's okay. She wants to be a nurse when she grows up."

My heart was pounding. "Where are her parents?"

"Her father's never been in the picture and her mother's been on and off drugs for years. She's homeless. *They're* homeless."

I felt my eyes brim with tears. Then, I nodded emphatically. "Sara..."

Chapter 65

3 months later...

The table was set perfectly, and decorated with fresh flowers in a vase. Dinner was cooking in the oven, wine was chilling in the fridge, and several lit candles placed all over the first floor provided the only light in the room.

The mood was reminiscent of the night I'd tried to save my marriage, the night I'd tried to seduce my now ex-husband, who was too far gone and already in love with someone else. Only this time, the purpose of the romantic setting wasn't to salvage a relationship out of desperation. Tonight, I was celebrating.

I had invited Parker, my now boyfriend over for dinner to tell him about Sara, to whom I'd been awarded legal foster parent, and who was moving in with me in seven days. Sara was truly a reason to make a huge production out of an evening.

I wasn't telling Parker the news about Sara to see if he wanted to be involved. Choosing to become a foster parent was something I was doing purely independently. If Parker wanted to be part of her life, I welcomed that. However, there was no pressure. Parker lived downtown. He worked long hours. Maybe he didn't have time for Sara. Or maybe he did. That was entirely up to him. He would undoubtedly be thrilled for me. That much I knew. How much he wanted to be included was entirely up to him.

When the timer went off, I took the salmon out of the oven. I smiled happily, loving the store I once thought was discriminatory for packaging its fish for two. I realized that if any salmon lover opened his or her heart, eventually he or she would find someone with whom to share their fish. *My* person was on his way over, and I loved knowing that.

Just as I was uncorking the wine, Parker appeared in the kitchen doorway.

"What a total sweetie," he grinned, "This looks great! I'm starving!"

My heart pounded, like it always did now when I saw him. I realized I probably had that puppy dog demeanor like Tony Lionetti had.

I threw my arms around him and we kissed passionately.

"I missed you," I gushed.

"You just saw me last night."

"I know. I still missed you."

As I stood there wrapped in Parker's arms, I realized that I was giving him the love I'd never had the guts to give any man in my life. I felt vulnerable, and it was a little scary, but I liked it. A lot.

I waited until we sat down to eat, and while I handed Parker the serving platter of fish, that's when I told him about Sara.

"So, what do you think?" I asked nervously.

Parker gave me a huge grin. "I love the idea. I'm really excited to meet her."

"Why am I getting the feeling you knew about this?"

His grin got wider.

"My lovely assistant has been filling you in again, hasn't she?"

"Of course. Do you really think J.J. can keep anything to herself?"

"No," I giggled.

"Hey!" he said, "I just thought of something. Have you seen today's paper?"

"No, why?"

"Do you have it?"

"Yeah, I think so."

"Get it."

I got up and went into the living room, where the *Chicago Sun-Times* was lying on the coffee table, unread. I brought it back to Parker, who opened it up to the gossip section and pointed to:

BUSTED!!! Actor and comedian Christian Maverick Arrested for drug possession and solicitation of a prostitute.

Below the caption was Christian's mug shot.

"Wow!" was all I could say. It seemed karma certainly had a way of working itself out.

I sat there and read the rest of the article until I heard Parker say my name softly. I looked up. He was just smiling at me.

"What?" I grinned.

"Come sit on the couch."

I followed him into my living room and onto the couch.

"Are you okay?" I asked him.

He held my hands. "I think what you are doing is wonderful, and it just shows what a special, giving, person you really are."

"Thank you," I smiled, kissing his lips.

"You know, I was thinking...the day you announced to the general public that you loved me... I think that day was the best day of my life."

"Really?"

"Yeah," he answered. Then he knelt down on one knee in front of me and pulled something out from his jeans pocket.

"Oh my God, what are you doing?!"

He was about to hold up what I knew was a ring. Was he going to propose?! I was anticipating what he was about to say next, but when I saw the ring I gasped and put my hand over my mouth. Parker wasn't just giving me a ring, he was giving me MY big diamond ring!

"This is what brought us together. I bought it, Missy. I bought it from Paul. I went to see him, and I told him our story and asked if he'd sell it to me. He said congratulations, by the way."

I just sat there frozen and unable to speak.

Parker went on, "Because of this diamond ring, I met the love of my life. It's *your* ring and belongs on *your* finger. Only this time, you're with the right person."

I began to cry.

"I'm not sure where you stand on being married. Your divorce was just finalized, for God's sake. But, I wanted you to have the ring for when the time is right. Because I know at some point you'll tell me you're ready, and we'll get married. For right now, though, I just want to know you more and more, and I want to build a life with you and Sara. How does that sound?"

"That sounds perfect," I said through tears.

"It's a really nice ring, by the way," Parker joked, still on his knees below me. He placed my ring on my left ring finger, where it had sat for almost a decade.

I put my hands on the sides of his face, slowly pulled him toward me and kissed him passionately.

I honestly could not believe what was happening. I had won my own contest. I had read hundreds of e-mails and I'd interviewed dozens of men, all because of my obsession to give my big diamond ring to someone who deserved it.

Ironically, I never dreamed it would be me who ended up with the ring. How unbelievably unpredictable life could be. I had started the contest as an insecure, angry, bitter, messed up, baggage-ridden, almost broken divorced girl. The contest had been a journey, taking me to places that taught me valuable lessons, and that gave me precious gifts. Now, in the arms of the man I truly loved, at peace with my past, and hopeful for a future filled with love, family and friends, the contest winner wasn't the divorced girl any longer. I was the semi engaged girl, but it was so much more than that. I was really happy. I was the divorced girl smiling, and it was the best feeling in the world.

The End

Epilogue

That night in bed, Parker whispered, "Good night."

"Hey Parker?"

"Yeah?"

"Will you tell me a story?"

"Not this again!"

"Please? It will help me fall asleep."

"Am I going to have to do this for the rest of our lives?"

"Yup," I giggled.

A moment later, I heard, "Once upon a time…"

I waited. After a few moments, I said, "Well?"

Parker was half asleep when he whispered, "They lived happily ever after."

I smiled and closed my eyes, and instantly, I was asleep.

Acknowledgments

Writing the acknowledgment page could be the hardest part of writing a novel. There's so much pressure to remember every single person who contributed to this process, and in my mind, that number is countless.

I am constantly in awe of what people are willing to do for me, how they are willing to help by offering advice, knowledge, their connections, emotional support, and anything else I might ask of them (and many times, I don't even have to ask!

First and foremost, I'd like to thank all my DIVORCED GIRL SMILING readers. Your comments and emails are what motivate me to keep going on my mission to help men and women as they navigate their way through divorce. When I hear from readers, it reinforces the importance and meaning of the blog.

Next, I want to thank my advertisers, who had faith in me from the beginning, many of whom signed up before I had any real viewing numbers. I am beyond touched by the support.

I also want to thank Marla Levie and Michael Craven, not only for your support as my first advertisers, but for recommending Bruce Jones. I'd also like to thank Matt Balson and Lizy Bloom who are both amazing website designers, and graphic designer, Eileen Noren, who designed the book cover, as well as my new website graphics. You are a gem, Eileen!"

Next, I want to mention Loryn Kogan, a wonderful editor who found every single typo (I hope.) She found a lot! And Laurie Levitt from Soben Studios for my author photo.

To Susan Freund, Bonnie Schoenberg, Kathy McCarthy, and Debbie Glickman, thanks for reading first drafts of the book. Your feedback was so so helpful!

I also want to thank my dad, Zack Pilossoph for coming up with the idea for the blog, DIVORCED GIRL SMILING. At 85 years old, he knew it was a topic that people wanted to hear more about.

I also want to mention my editors, Rich Bird, Marah Altenberg, Charles Berman, Beth Mistretta, Rob Elder, Sara Burrows and Jennifer Thomas from Sun-Times Media, and Dayna Fields and Alex Mayster from 22nd Century Media. Thank you for the opportunities you have given me and all you have taught me. And the staff at Huffington Post, thank you for the opportunity to be a regular divorce blogger.

I want to thank my wonderful family, the Pilossoph's, as well as my sweetheart, Mark. And of course, to Isaac and Anna, who are the loves of my life, and who make me proud every single day.

Lastly, I want to say that I wrote DIVORCED GIRL SMILING, the novel, not only for entertainment, and to offer a fun, romantic, heartfelt book to readers, but to inspire divorced people.

Divorce involves a long healing process that can include doing some pretty crazy things (and stupid things), and at times it can seem unbearably painful. It's heartbreaking and gut-wrenchingly sad, but by having the guts to reflect and admit your faults, and by learning acceptance, believing in yourself and your abilities, and having self-love, I believe all divorced people can end up happy, and have the life they want. It just takes time and the power to make good decisions moving forward. In other words, even if things seem hopeless at times, with the right attitude, you too can be a DIVORCED GIRL SMILING!

29774769R00165

Made in the USA
Lexington, KY
06 February 2014